Jane Austen

SENSE & SENSIBILITY

CLASSICS

Reprint 2020

FiNGERPRINT! CLASSiCS

An imprint of Prakash Books India Pvt. Ltd.

113/A, Darya Ganj,
New Delhi-110 002
Tel: (011) 2324 7062 – 65, Fax: (011) 2324 6975
Email: info@prakashbooks.com/sales@prakashbooks.com

facebook www.facebook.com/fingerprintpublishing
twitter www.twitter.com/FingerprintP
www.fingerprintpublishing.com

ISBN: 978 81 7234 451 1

Processed & printed in India

Jane Austen is one of the most well-known and widely-read English novelists of all times. Born on December 16, 1775, at the rectory in the village of Steventon, in Hampshire, England, she was the seventh child and second daughter of Reverend George Austen and his wife Cassandra Austen. Jane Austen was mainly educated at home by her father and her brothers, Henry and James. She read extensively from her father's library and that not only compensated for the absence of formal education, but also gave her much inspiration for the short satirical sketches that she wrote as a young girl.

Jane had a happy childhood with her siblings and was almost inseparable from her elder sister, Casssandra. The Austen children were encouraged to pursue literary and other creative pastimes. They often wrote and performed plays and charades and engaged in discussions about a variety of topics. In the words of Park Honan, a biographer of Austen, the Austen household had 'an open, amused, easy intellectual atmosphere'.

Jane's fascination with words and with the world of stories, therefore, began quite early. In the 1790s, during her adolescence, she started writing her own novels, the first one being *Love and Freindship* [sic]—a parody of romantic fiction organized as a series of love letters. The second one, *The History of England*, was a thirty-four page parody of historical writing about England, with about thirteen watercolour miniatures done by her elder sister, Cassandra. Later, Austen, herself, made 'fair copies' of her early works in three bound notebooks. These notebooks, containing novels, short stories, poems, as well as plays, are now referred to as *Jane's Juvenilia*.

As a young woman, still living with parents, Austen engaged in such social and domestic activities as were normal for women of her age and social standing. She played the fortepiano, assisted her sister and mother in running the Austen household, attended church regularly, and socialized frequently with friends and neighbours. Socializing often meant dancing, sometimes impromptu and sometimes in the frequently held balls in the town hall. As her brother Henry later commented, 'Jane was fond of dancing and excelled in it'. Austen also read novels—often of her own composition—aloud to her family in the evenings.

Somewhere around 1789, Austen decided to become a professional writer and 'write for profit . . . to make stories her central effort'. And beginning in about 1793, she began to write longer, more sophisticated works. The next two years saw Austen writing *Lady Susan*, a short epistolary novel about a woman who uses her intelligence and charm to manipulate, betray, and abuse her victims. *Lady Susan* was published as *Northanger Abbey* by Jane's brother, Henry, following her death.

From 1796 to 1797, Jane was occupied with the writing of a second novel, *First Impressions*. She would read it aloud to her family in the evenings, as she did with other novels, and soon it became an 'established favourite' with the Austen household. The first draft of *First Impressions* was completed sometime in the summer of 1797. Jane was just twenty-one-years old at that time. This work was to be later published as *Pride and Prejudice*.

Sense and Sensibility, Jane's second most-famous work, began as yet another epistolary story with the working title *Elinor and Marianne*. Though she started work on it much before 1796, it was only in mid-1798 that she picked it up again and finished revising it.

In 1801, Austen's father decided to retire and move to Bath with his wife and two daughters. Four years later however, he died after a short illness. As a result, the three Austen women found themselves in a strained financial situation and were forced to move from place to place, alternating between the homes of various family members and rented flats. It was only in 1809 that they were finally able to settle into a stable situation at Jane's brother Edward's cottage in Chawton.

Between 1811 to 1816, Jane started to anonymously publish her works. *Sense and Sensibility*, *Pride and Prejudice*, *Mansfield Park*, and *Emma* were all published during this time.

In 1816, at the age of forty-one, Asuten became ill with Addison's disease. However, she continued working—editing older works and even starting a new novel called *The Brothers* (which would be published after her death as *Sandition*). Austen's condition, however, deteriorated to such an extent that she was forced to completely stop writing. She died on July 18, 1817.

It was only after Austen's death that her identity was revealed to the public. Though her work had achieved a fair amount of fame and financial success while she was still alive, Austen's transformation into one of the greatest writers in English history began only after her death. Her works started attracting scholarly attention in the 1920s and came to be recognized as brilliant masterpieces and revealing commentaries on the social conditions of Austen's time. Today, Austen's works have become an important part of popular culture. They are not only a part of the English curriculum in schools and colleges, but there are also many film and television adaptations of *Emma*, *Mansfield Park*, *Pride and Prejudice*, and *Sense and Sensibility*.

Chapter 1

The family of Dashwood had long been settled in Sussex. Their residence was at Norland Park, in the centre of their property, where, for many generations, they had lived in so respectable a manner as to engage the general good opinion of their surrounding acquaintance. The late owner of this estate was a single man, and who for many years of his life, had a constant companion and housekeeper in his sister. But her death, produced a great alteration in his home; for to supply her loss, he invited and received into his home; the family of his nephew Mr. Henry Dashwood, the legal inheritor of the Norland estate, and the person to whom he intended to bequeath it. In the society of his nephew and niece, and their children, the old Gentleman's days were comfortably spent. His attachment to them all increased. The constant attention of Mr. and Mrs. Henry Dashwood to his wishes, which proceeded not merely from interest, but from goodness of heart, gave him every degree of solid comfort which his age could receive; and the cheerfulness of the children added a relish to his existence.

By a former marriage, Mr. Henry Dashwood had one son: by his present lady, three daughters. The son, a steady respectable young man, was amply provided for by the fortune of his mother, which had been large, and half of which devolved on him on his coming of age. By his own marriage, likewise, he added to his wealth. To him therefore the succession to the Norland estate was not so really important as to his sisters; for their fortune, could be but small. Their mother had nothing, and their father only seven thousand pounds in his own disposal.

The old gentleman died. He was neither so unjust, nor so ungrateful, as to leave his estate from his nephew; but he left it to him on such terms as destroyed half the value of the bequest. Mr. Dashwood had wished for it more for the sake of his wife and daughters than for himself or his son; but to his son, and his son's son, a child of four years old, it was secured, in such a way, as to leave to himself no power of providing for those who were most dear to him. The whole was tied up for the benefit of this child, who had so far gained on the affections of his uncle, by such attractions as are by no means unusual in children of two or three years old; as to outweigh all the value of all the attention which, he had received from his niece and her daughters. He meant not to be unkind, however, and, as a mark of his affection for the three girls, he left them a thousand pounds a-piece.

Mr. Dashwood's disappointment was, at first, severe; but his temper was cheerful and sanguine; and he might reasonably hope to live many years, and by living economically, lay by a considerable sum from the produce of an estate already large, and capable of almost immediate improvement. But the fortune, which had been so tardy in coming, was his only one twelvemonth. He survived his uncle no longer; and ten thousand pounds, including the late legacies, was all that remained for his widow and daughters.

His son was sent for as soon as his danger was known, and to him Mr. Dashwood recommended, with all the strength and urgency which illness could command, the interest of his mother-in-law and sisters.

Mr. John Dashwood was affected by a recommendation of such a nature at such a time, and he promised to do everything in his power to make them comfortable.

He was not an ill-disposed young man, but he was, in general, well-respected. Had he married a more amiable woman, he might have been made still more respectable than he was. But Mrs. John Dashwood was a strong caricature of himself; more narrow-minded and selfish.

When he gave his promise to his father, he meditated within himself to increase the fortunes of his sisters by the present of a thousand pounds a-piece. The prospect of four thousand a year, in addition to his present income, besides the remaining half of his own mother's fortune, warmed his heart, and made him feel capable of generosity. He could spare so considerable a sum with little inconvenience.

No sooner was his father's funeral over, than Mrs. John Dashwood, arrived with her child and their attendants. No one could dispute her right to come; the house was her husband's from the moment of his father's decease; but the indelicacy of her conduct was so much the greater, and to a woman in Mrs. Dashwood's situation must have been highly unpleasing. Mrs. John Dashwood had never been a favourite with any of her husband's family; but she had had no opportunity, till the present, of showing them with how little attention to the comfort of other people she could act when occasion required it.

So acutely did Mrs. Dashwood feel this ungracious behaviour, and so earnestly did she despise her daughter-in-law for it, that, on the arrival of the latter, she would have quitted the house for ever, had not the entreaty of her eldest girl induced her first to reflect on the propriety of going, and her own tender love for all her three children determined her afterwards to stay, and for their sakes avoid a breach with their brother.

Elinor, this eldest daughter, possessed a strength of understanding, and coolness of judgment, which qualified her, though only nineteen, to be the counsellor of her mother. Her disposition was affectionate, and her feelings were strong; but she knew how to govern them: it was a knowledge which her mother had yet to learn; and which one of her sisters had resolved never to be taught.

Marianne was sensible and clever; but eager in everything; her sorrows, her joys, could have no moderation. She was generous, amiable, interesting: she was everything but prudent.

Elinor saw, with concern, the excess of her sister's sensibility; but by Mrs. Dashwood it was valued and cherished. They encouraged each other now in the violence of their affliction. They gave themselves up wholly to their sorrow, seeking increase of wretchedness in every reflection that could afford it, and resolved against ever admitting consolation in future. Elinor, too, was deeply afflicted; but still she could struggle, she could exert herself. She could receive her sister-in-law on her arrival, and treat her with proper attention; and could strive to rouse her mother to similar exertion, and encourage her to similar forbearance.

Margaret, the other sister, was a good-humored, well-disposed girl; but as she had already imbibed a good deal of Marianne's romance, without having much of her sense, she did not, at thirteen, bid fair to equal her sisters at a more advanced period of life.

Chapter 2

Mrs. John Dashwood now installed herself mistress of Norland; and her mother-and- sisters-in-law were degraded to the condition of visitors. As such, however, they were treated by her with quiet civility; and by her husband with as much kindness as he could feel towards anybody beyond himself, his wife, and their child. He really pressed them, with some earnestness, to consider Norland as their home; and, as no plan appeared so eligible to Mrs. Dashwood as remaining there till she could accommodate herself with a house in the neighbourhood, his invitation was accepted.

Mrs. John Dashwood did not at all approve of what her husband intended to do for his sisters. To take three thousand pounds from the fortune of their dear little boy would be impoverishing him to the most dreadful degree. And what possible claim could the Miss Dashwoods, who were related to him only by half blood, have on his generosity to so large an amount?

"It was my father's last request to me," replied her husband, "that I should assist his widow and daughters."

"He did not know what he was talking of, I dare say. Had he been in his right senses, he could not have thought of such a thing as begging you to give away half your fortune from your own child."

"He did not stipulate for any particular sum, my dear Fanny; he only requested me, in general terms, to assist them. Perhaps it would have been as well if he had left it wholly to myself. He could hardly suppose I should neglect them. But as he required the promise, I could not do less than give it. Something must be done for them whenever they leave Norland and settle in a new home."

"Well, then, *let* something be done for them; but *that* something need not be three thousand pounds. Consider," she added, "that when the money is once parted with, it never can return. Your sisters will marry, and it will be gone for ever. If, indeed, it could be restored to our poor little boy—"

"Why, to be sure," said her husband, very gravely, "that would make great difference. The time may come when Harry will regret that so large a sum was parted with. If he should have a numerous family, for instance, it would be a very convenient addition."

"To be sure it would."

"Perhaps, then, it would be better for all parties, if the sum were diminished one half — Five hundred pounds would be a prodigious increase to their fortunes!"

"Oh! beyond anything great! What brother on earth would do half so much for his sisters, even if *really* his sisters!"

"I would not wish to do anything mean," he replied. "No one, at least, can think I have not done enough for them: even themselves, they can hardly expect more."

"There is no knowing what *they* may expect," said the lady. "The question is, what you can afford to do."

"Certainly—and I think I may afford to give them five hundred pounds a-piece. As it is, without any addition of mine, they will each have about three thousand pounds on their mother's death;a very comfortable fortune for any young woman."

"To be sure it is; and, indeed, it strikes me that they can want no addition at all. They will have ten thousand pounds divided amongst them. They may all live very comfortably together on the interest of ten thousand pounds."

"That is very true, and, therefore, I do not know whether, upon the whole, it would not be more advisable to do something for their mother while she lives, rather than for them. A hundred a year would make them all perfectly comfortable."

His wife hesitated a little.

"To be sure," said she, "it is better than parting with fifteen hundred pounds at once. But, then, if Mrs. Dashwood should live fifteen years we shall be completely taken in."

"Fifteen years! my dear Fanny; her life cannot be worth half that purchase."

"Certainly not; but if you observe, people always live forever when there is an annuity to be paid them; and she is very stout and healthy, and hardly forty. I have known a great deal of the trouble of annuities; for my mother was clogged with the payment of three to old superannuated servants by my father's will, and it is amazing how disagreeable she found it. Twice every year these annuities were to be paid; my mother was quite sick of it. Her income was not her own, she said, with such perpetual claims on it."

"It is certainly an unpleasant thing," replied Mr. Dashwood, "to have those kind of yearly drains on one's income: it takes away one's independence."

"Undoubtedly; and after all you have no thanks for it."

"I believe you are right, my love; it will be better that there should be no annuity in the case; whatever I may give them occasionally will be of far greater assistance than a yearly allowance. A present of fifty pounds, now and then, will prevent their ever being distressed for money, and will, I think, be amply discharging my promise to my father."

"To be sure it will. Indeed, to say the truth, I am convinced within myself that your father had no idea of your giving them any money at all. The assistance he thought of, I dare say, was only such as might be reasonably expected of you; for instance, such as looking out for a comfortable small house for them, helping them to move their things, and sending them presents of fish and game, and so forth, whenever they are in season. Do but consider, my dear Mr. Dashwood, how excessively comfortable your mother-in-law and her daughters may live on the interest of seven thousand pounds, besides the thousand pounds belonging to each of the girls, which brings them in fifty pounds a year a-piece. Altogether, they will have five hundred a year amongst them. Only conceive how comfortable they will be! Five hundred a year! I am sure I cannot imagine how they will spend half of it; and as to your giving them more, it is quite absurd to think of it."

"Upon my word," said Mr. Dashwood, "I believe you are perfectly right. My father certainly could mean nothing more by his request to me than what you say. When my mother removes into another house my services shall be readily given to accommodate her as far as I can. Some little present of furniture too may be acceptable then."

"Certainly," returned Mrs. John Dashwood. "But, however, *one* thing must be considered. When your father and mother moved to Norland, though the furniture of Stanhill was sold, all the china, plate, and linen was saved, and is now left to your mother. Her house will therefore be almost completely fitted up as soon as she takes it."

"That is a material consideration undoubtedly. And yet some of the plate would have been a very pleasant addition to our own stock here."

"Yes; and the set of breakfast china is twice as handsome as what belongs to this house. But, however, so it is. Your father thought only of *them*. And I must say this: that you owe no particular gratitude to him, for we very well know that if he could, he would have left almost everything in the world to *them*."

This argument was irresistible. It gave to his intentions whatever of decision was wanting before; and he finally resolved, that it would be absolutely unnecessary, if not highly indecorous, to do more for the widow and children of his father, than such kind of neighbourly acts as his own wife pointed out.

Chapter 3

Mrs. Dashwood remained at Norland several months; not from any disinclination to move when the sight of every well known spot ceased to raise the violent emotion which it produced for a while; for when her spirits began to revive, she was impatient to be gone. But she could hear of no situation that at once answered her notions of comfort and ease, and suited the prudence of her eldest daughter, whose steadier judgment rejected several houses as too large for their income, which her mother would have approved.

Mrs. Dashwood had been informed by her husband of the solemn promise on the part of his son in their favour. She doubted the sincerity of this assurance no more than he had doubted it himself, and she thought of it for her daughters' sake with satisfaction. His attentive behaviour to herself and his sisters convinced her that their welfare was dear to him, and, for a long time, she firmly relied on the liberality of his intentions.

The contempt which she had, very early in their acquaintance, felt for her daughter-in-law, was very much increased by the farther knowledge of her character, which half a year's residence in her family afforded. The two ladies might have found it impossible to have lived together so long, had not a particular circumstance occurred to give still greater eligibility, according to the opinions of Mrs. Dashwood, to her daughters' continuance at Norland.

This circumstance was a growing attachment between her eldest girl and the brother of Mrs. John Dashwood, a gentleman-like and pleasing young man, who was introduced to their acquaintance soon after his sister's establishment at Norland.

Some mothers might have encouraged the intimacy from motives of interest, for Edward Ferrars was the eldest son of a man who had died very rich. But it was enough for Mrs. Dashwood that he appeared to be amiable, that he loved her daughter, and that Elinor returned the partiality.

Edward Ferrars was not handsome, and he was too diffident to do justice to himself; but when his natural shyness was overcome, his behaviour gave every indication of an open, affectionate heart. But he was neither fitted by abilities nor disposition to answer the wishes of his mother and sister, who longed to see him distinguished—as—they hardly knew what. His mother wished to get him into parliament, or to see him connected with some of the great men of the day. Mrs. John Dashwood wished it likewise; but in the mean while, till one of these superior blessings could be attained, it would have quieted her ambition to see him driving a barouche. But Edward had no turn for great men or barouches. All his wishes centered in domestic comfort and the quiet of private life.

Edward had been staying several weeks in the house before he engaged much of Mrs. Dashwood's attention; for she was, at that time, in such affliction as rendered her careless of surrounding objects. She saw only that he was quiet and unobtrusive, and she liked him for it. She was first called to observe and approve him further, by a reflection which Elinor chanced one day to make on the difference between him and his sister. It was a contrast which recommended him most forcibly to her mother.

"It is enough," said she; "to say that he is unlike Fanny is enough. It implies everything amiable. I love him already."

"I think you will like him," said Elinor, "when you know more of him."

Mrs. Dashwood now took pains to get acquainted with him. She speedily comprehended all his merits; the persuasion of his regard for Elinor perhaps assisted her penetration; but she really felt assured of his worth: and even that quietness of manner was no longer uninteresting when she knew his heart to be warm and his temper affectionate.

No sooner did she perceive any symptom of love in his behaviour to Elinor, than she considered their serious attachment as certain, and looked forward to their marriage as rapidly approaching.

"In a few months, my dear Marianne," said she, "Elinor will, in all probability be settled for life."

"Oh! Mama, how shall we do without her?"

"My love, it will be scarcely a separation. We shall live within a few miles of each other.. You will gain a brother, a real, affectionate brother. But you look grave, Marianne; do you disapprove your sister's choice?"

"Perhaps," said Marianne, "I may consider it with some surprise. Edward is very amiable, and I love him tenderly. But yet there is something wanting—his figure is not striking; it has none of that grace which I should expect in the man who could seriously attach my sister. And besides all this, I am afraid, Mama, he has no real taste. Music seems scarcely to attract him, and though he admires Elinor's drawings very much, it is not the admiration of a person who can understand their worth. He admires as a lover, not as a connoisseur. Oh, mama! How spiritless, how tame was Edward's manner in reading to us last night! I could hardly keep my seat. To hear those beautiful lines which have frequently almost driven me wild, pronounced with such impenetrable calmness, such dreadful indifference!"

"He would certainly have done more justice to simple and

elegant prose. I thought so at the time; but you *would* give him Cowper."

"Nay, Mama, if he is not to be animated by Cowper! But we must allow for difference of taste. It would have broke *my* heart, had I loved him, to hear him read with so little sensibility. Mama, the more I know of the world, the more am I convinced that I shall never see a man whom I can really love. I require so much! He must have all Edward's virtues, and his person and manners must ornament his goodness with every possible charm."

"Remember, my love, that you are not seventeen. It is yet too early in life to despair of such a happiness!"

Chapter 4

"What a pity it is, Elinor," said Marianne, "that Edward should have no taste for drawing."

"No taste for drawing!" replied Elinor, "why should you think so? He does not draw himself, indeed, but he has great pleasure in seeing the performances of other people. He distrusts his own judgment in such matters so much, that he is always unwilling to give his opinion on any picture; but he has an innate propriety and simplicity of taste, which in general direct him perfectly right."

Marianne was afraid of offending, and said no more on the subject; but the kind of approbation which Elinor described as excited in him by the drawings of other people, was very far from that rapturous delight, which, in her opinion, could alone be called taste.

"I hope, Marianne," continued Elinor, "you do not consider him as deficient in general taste."

Marianne hardly knew what to say. She would not wound the feelings of her sister on any account, and yet to say what she did not believe was impossible.

At length she replied: "Do not be offended, Elinor, if my praise of him is not in everything equal to your sense of his merits. I have not had so many opportunities of estimating the minuter propensities of his mind, his inclinations and tastes, as you have;

but I have the highest opinion in the world of his goodness and sense. I think him every thing that is worthy and amiable."

"I am sure," replied Elinor, with a smile, "that his dearest friends could not be dissatisfied with such commendation as that."

Marianne was rejoiced to find her sister so easily pleased.

"Of his sense and his goodness," continued Elinor, "no one can, I think, be in doubt, who has seen him often enough to engage him in unreserved conversation. He and I have been at times thrown a good deal together, while you have been wholly engrossed on the most affectionate principle by my mother. I have seen a great deal of him, have studied his sentiments and heard his opinion on subjects of literature and taste; and, upon the whole, I venture to pronounce that his mind is well-informed, enjoyment of books exceedingly great, his imagination lively, his observation just and correct, and his taste delicate and pure. At first sight, his address is certainly not striking; and his person can hardly be called handsome, till the expression of his eyes, and the general sweetness of his countenance, is perceived. At present, I know him so well, that I think him really handsome. What say you, Marianne?"

"I shall very soon think him handsome, Elinor, if I do not now. When you tell me to love him as a brother, I shall no more see imperfection in his face, than I now do in his heart."

Elinor started at this declaration, and was sorry for the warmth she had been betrayed into, in speaking of him. She felt that Edward stood very high in her opinion. She believed the regard to be mutual; but she required greater certainty of it to make Marianne's conviction of their attachment agreeable to her.

"I do not attempt to deny," said she, "that I think very highly of him—that I greatly esteem, that I like him."

Marianne here burst forth with indignation—

"Esteem him! Like him! Cold-hearted Elinor! Use those words again, and I will leave the room this moment."

Elinor could not help laughing. "Excuse me," said she, "and be assured that I meant no offence to you, by speaking, in so quiet a way, of my own feelings. Believe them to be stronger than I have declared. But further than this you must not believe. I am by no means assured of his regard for me. There are moments when the extent of it seems doubtful. In my heart I feel little—scarcely any doubt of his preference. But there are other points to be considered besides his inclination. He is very far from being independent. What his mother really is we cannot know; but, from Fanny's occasional mention of her conduct and opinions, we have never been disposed to think her amiable; and I am very much mistaken if Edward is not himself aware that there would be many difficulties in his way, if he were to wish to marry a woman who had not either a great fortune or high rank."

"And you really are not engaged to him!" said Marriane. "Yet it certainly soon will happen. But two advantages will proceed from this delay. *I* shall not lose you so soon, and Edward will have greater opportunity of improving that natural taste for drawing, your favourite pursuit, which must be so indispensably necessary to your future felicity."

Elinor had given her real opinion to her sister. There was, at times, a want of spirits about him which, if it did not denote indifference, spoke of something almost as unpromising. A doubt of her regard, supposing him to feel it, need not give him more than inquietude. It would not be likely to produce that dejection of mind which frequently attended him. A more reasonable cause might be found in the dependent situation which forbade the indulgence of his affection. She knew that his mother neither behaved to him so as to make his home comfortable at present, nor to give him any assurance that he might form a home for himself, without strictly attending to her views for his aggrandizement. Elinor was far from depending on that result of his preference of her, which her mother and sister still considered as certain.

But, whatever might really be its limits, it was enough, when perceived by his sister, to make her uneasy; and at the same time, to make her uncivil. She took the first opportunity of affronting her mother-in-law on the occasion, talking to her so expressively of her brother's great expectations, of Mrs. Ferrars's resolution that both her sons should marry well, that Mrs. Dashwood could neither pretend to be unconscious, nor endeavor to be calm. She gave her an answer which marked her contempt, and instantly left the room, resolving that her beloved Elinor should not be exposed another week to such insinuations.

In this state of her spirits, a letter was delivered to her from the post, which contained an offer of a small house, on very easy terms, belonging to a relation of her own, a gentleman of consequence and property in Devonshire. He understood that she was in need of a dwelling; and though the house he now offered her was merely a cottage, he assured her that everything should be done to it which she might think necessary, if the situation pleased her. He earnestly pressed her to come with her daughters to Barton Park, the place of his own residence, from whence she might judge, herself, whether Barton Cottage, for the houses were in the same parish, could, by any alteration, be made comfortable to her. The whole of his letter was written in so friendly a style as could not fail of giving pleasure to his cousin; more especially at a moment when she was suffering under the cold and unfeeling behaviour of her nearer connections. Her resolution was formed as she read. To quit the neighbourhood of Norland was no longer an evil; it was a blessing, in comparison of the misery of continuing her daughter-in-law's guest. She instantly wrote Sir John Middleton her acknowledgment of his kindness, and her acceptance of his proposal; and then hastened to show both letters to her daughters, that she might be secure of their approbation before her answer were sent.

Elinor had always thought it would be more prudent for them to settle at some distance from Norland, than immediately amongst their present acquaintance. The house, too, as described by Sir John, was on so simple a scale, and the rent so uncommonly moderate, as to leave her no right of objection. Therefore, though it was not a plan which brought any charm to her fancy, though it was a removal from the vicinity of Norland beyond her wishes, she made no attempt to dissuade her mother from sending a letter of acquiescence.

Chapter 5

No sooner was her answer dispatched, than Mrs. Dashwood indulged herself in the pleasure of announcing to her son-in-law and his wife that she was provided with a house. Mrs. John Dashwood said nothing; but her husband civilly hoped that she would not be settled far from Norland. She had great satisfaction in replying that she was going into Devonshire. Edward turned hastily towards her, on hearing this, and, in a voice of surprise and concern, repeated, "Devonshire! Are you, indeed, going there? So far from hence! And to what part of it?" She explained the situation. It was within four miles northward of Exeter.

"It is but a cottage," she continued, "but I hope to see many of my friends in it."

She concluded with a very kind invitation to Mr. and Mrs. John Dashwood to visit her at Barton; and to Edward she gave one with still greater affection. To separate Edward and Elinor was as far from being her object as ever; and she wished to show Mrs. John Dashwood, how totally she disregarded her disapprobation of the match.

Mrs. Dashwood took the house for a twelvemonth; it was ready furnished, and she might have immediate possession. No difficulty arose on either side in the agreement; and she waited only for the disposal of her effects at Norland, and to determine her future household, before she set off for the west.

Her eagerness to be gone from Norland was preserved from diminution by the evident satisfaction of her daughter-in-law in the prospect of her removal; a satisfaction which was but feebly attempted to be concealed under a cold invitation to her to defer her departure. Now was the time when her son-in-law's promise to his father might with particular propriety be fulfilled. But Mrs. Dashwood began shortly to give over every hope of the kind, and to be convinced, from the general drift of his discourse, that his assistance extended no farther than their maintenance for six months at Norland. He so frequently talked of the increasing expenses of housekeeping that he seemed rather to stand in need of more money himself than to have any design of giving money away.

In a very few weeks from the day which brought Sir John Middleton's first letter to Norland, everything was so far settled in their future abode as to enable Mrs. Dashwood and her daughters to begin their journey.

Many were the tears shed by them in their last adieus to a place so much beloved. "Dear, dear Norland!" said Marianne, as she wandered alone before the house, on the last evening of their being there. "Oh! happy house, could you know what I suffer in now viewing you from this spot, from whence perhaps I may view you no more!—And you, ye well-known trees!—but you will continue the same.—No leaf will decay because we are removed, nor any branch become motionless although we can observe you no longer!—No; you will continue the same; and insensible of any change in those who walk under your shade!—But who will remain to enjoy you?"

Chapter 6

The first part of their journey was performed in too melancholy a disposition to be otherwise than tedious and unpleasant. But as they drew towards the end of it, their interest in the appearance of a country which they were to inhabit overcame their dejection, and a view of Barton Valley as they entered it gave them cheerfulness. It was a pleasant fertile spot, well wooded, and rich in pasture. After winding along it for more than a mile, they reached their own house.

As a house, Barton Cottage, though small, was comfortable and compact; but as a cottage it was defective, for the building was regular, the roof was tiled, the window shutters were not painted green, nor were the walls covered with honeysuckles. In comparison of Norland, it was poor and small indeed!— but the tears which recollection called forth as they entered the house were soon dried away. It was very early in September; the season was fine, and from first seeing the place under the advantage of good weather, they received an impression in its favour which was of material service in recommending it to their lasting approbation.

The situation of the house was good. High hills rose immediately behind, and at no great distance on each side. The village of Barton was chiefly on one of these hills, and formed a pleasant view from the cottage windows. The prospect in front was more extensive; it commanded the whole of the valley, and reached into the country beyond.

With the size and furniture of the house Mrs. Dashwood was upon the whole well satisfied; she had at this time ready money enough to supply all that was wanted of greater elegance to the apartments. "As for the house itself, to be sure," said she, "it is too small for our family, but we will make ourselves tolerably comfortable for the present, as it is too late in the year for improvements. Perhaps in the spring, if I have plenty of money, as I dare say I shall, we may think about building."

In the mean time, they were wise enough to be contented with the house as it was; and each of them was busy in arranging their particular concerns, and endeavoring to form themselves a home. Marianne's pianoforte was unpacked and properly disposed of; and Elinor's drawings were affixed to the walls of their sitting room.

In such employments as these they were interrupted soon after breakfast the next day by the entrance of their landlord, who called to welcome them to Barton, and to offer them every accommodation from his own house and garden in which theirs might at present be deficient. Sir John Middleton was a good looking man about forty. His countenance was thoroughly good-humoured; and his manners were as friendly as the style of his letter. Their arrival seemed to afford him real satisfaction, and their comfort to be an object of real solicitude to him. Within an hour after he left them, a large basket full of garden stuff and fruit arrived from the park, which was followed before the end of the day by a present of game.

Lady Middleton had sent a very civil message by him, denoting her intention of waiting on Mrs. Dashwood as soon as she could be assured that her visit would be no inconvenience; and as this message was answered by an invitation equally polite, her ladyship was introduced to them the next day.

Lady Middleton was not more than six or seven and twenty; her face was handsome, her figure tall and striking, and her address graceful. Her manners had all the elegance which her husband's wanted. But they would have been improved by some share of his frankness and warmth; and her visit was long enough to detract something from their first admiration, by showing that, though perfectly well-bred, she was reserved, cold, and had nothing to say for herself beyond the most common-place inquiry or remark.

Conversation however was not wanted, for Sir John was very chatty, and Lady Middleton had taken the wise precaution of bringing with her their eldest child, a fine little boy about six years old, by which means there was one subject always to be recurred to by the ladies in case of extremity, for they had to enquire his name and age, admire his beauty, and ask him questions which his mother answered for him, while he hung about her and held down his head.

An opportunity was soon to be given to the Dashwoods of debating on the rest of the children, as Sir John would not leave the house without securing their promise of dining at the park the next day.

Chapter 7

Barton Park was about half a mile from the cottage. The house was large and handsome; and the Middletons lived in a style of equal hospitality and elegance. They were scarcely ever without some friends staying with them in the house, and they kept more company of every kind than any other family in the neighbourhood. It was necessary to the happiness of both; for however dissimilar in temper and outward behaviour, they strongly resembled each other in that total want of talent and taste which confined their employments within a very narrow compass. Sir John was a sportsman, Lady Middleton a mother. He hunted and shot, and she humoured her children; and these were their only resources.

Lady Middleton piqued herself upon the elegance of her table, and of all her domestic arrangements; and from this kind of vanity was her greatest enjoyment in any of their parties. Sir John delighted in collecting about him more young people than his house would hold, and the noisier they were the better was he pleased.

The arrival of a new family in the country was always a matter of joy to him, and in every point of view he was charmed with the inhabitants he had now procured for his cottage at Barton. The Miss Dashwoods were young, pretty, and unaffected. The friendliness of his disposition made him happy in accommodating those, whose situation might be considered, in comparison with the past, as unfortunate.

Mrs. Dashwood and her daughters were met at the door of the house by Sir John, who welcomed them to Barton Park with unaffected sincerity; and as he attended them to the drawing room repeated to the young ladies the concern which the same subject had drawn from him the day before, at being unable to get any smart young men to meet them. They would see, he said, only one gentleman there besides himself; a particular friend who was staying at the park, but who was neither very young nor very gay. Lady Middleton's mother had arrived at Barton within the last hour, and as she was a very cheerful agreeable woman, he hoped the young ladies would not find it so very dull as they might imagine. The young ladies, as well as their mother, were perfectly satisfied with having two entire strangers of the party, and wished for no more.

Mrs. Jennings, Lady Middleton's mother, was a good-humoured, merry, fat, elderly woman, who talked a great deal, seemed very happy, and rather vulgar. She was full of jokes and laughter, and before dinner was over had said many witty things on the subject of lovers and husbands; hoped they had not left their hearts behind them in Sussex, and pretended to see them blush whether they did or not.

Colonel Brandon, the friend of Sir John was silent and grave. His appearance however was not unpleasing, in spite of his being in the opinion of Marianne and Margaret an absolute old bachelor, for he was on the wrong side of five and thirty; but though his face was not handsome, his countenance was sensible, and his address was particularly gentlemanlike.

There was nothing in any of the party which could recommend them as companions to the Dashwoods; but the cold insipidity of Lady Middleton was so particularly repulsive, that in comparison of it the gravity of Colonel Brandon, and even the boisterous mirth of Sir John and his mother-in-law was interesting.

In the evening, as Marianne was discovered to be musical, she was invited to play. The instrument was unlocked, everybody prepared to be charmed, and Marianne, who sang very well, at their request went through the chief of the songs which Lady Middleton had brought into the family on her marriage, and which perhaps had lain ever since in the same position on the pianoforte.

Marianne's performance was highly applauded. Sir John was loud in his admiration at the end of every song, and as loud in his conversation with the others while every song lasted. Lady Middleton frequently called him to order, wondered how any one's attention could be diverted from music for a moment, and asked Marianne to sing a particular song which Marianne had just finished. Colonel Brandon alone, of all the party, heard her without being in raptures. He paid her only the compliment of attention; and she felt a respect for him on the occasion, which the others had reasonably forfeited by their shameless want of taste. His pleasure in music was estimable when contrasted against the horrible insensibility of the others; and she was reasonable enough to allow that a man of five and thirty might well have outlived all acuteness of feeling and every exquisite power of enjoyment. She was perfectly disposed to make every allowance for the colonel's advanced state of life which humanity required.

Chapter 8

Mrs. Jennings was a widow with an ample jointure. She had only two daughters, both of whom she had lived to see respectably married, and she had now therefore nothing to do but to marry all the rest of the world. She was remarkably quick in the discovery of attachments, and this kind of discernment enabled her soon after her arrival at Barton decisively to pronounce that Colonel Brandon was very much in love with Marianne Dashwood. She rather suspected it to be so, on the very first evening of their being together, from his listening so attentively while she sang to them. It would be an excellent match, for *he* was rich, and *she* was handsome. Mrs. Jennings had been anxious to see Colonel Brandon well married, ever since her connection with Sir John first brought him to her knowledge; and she was always anxious to get a good husband for every pretty girl.

The immediate advantage to herself was by no means inconsiderable, for it supplied her with endless jokes against them both. At the park she laughed at the colonel, and in the cottage at Marianne. To the former her raillery was probably, as far as it regarded only himself, perfectly indifferent; but to the latter it was at first incomprehensible; and when its object was understood, she hardly knew whether most to laugh at its absurdity, or censure its impertinence, for she considered it as an unfeeling reflection on the colonel's advanced years, and on his forlorn condition as an old bachelor.

Mrs. Dashwood, who could not think a man five years younger than herself, so exceedingly ancient as he appeared to the youthful fancy of her daughter, ventured to clear Mrs. Jennings from the probability of wishing to throw ridicule on his age.

"But at least, Mama, you cannot deny the absurdity of the accusation. Colonel Brandon is old enough to be *my* father; and if he were ever animated enough to be in love, must have long outlived every sensation of the kind. When is a man to be safe from such wit, if age and infirmity will not protect him?"

"My dearest child," said her mother, laughing, "at this rate you must be in continual terror of *my* decay; and it must seem to you a miracle that my life has been extended to the advanced age of forty."

"I know very well that Colonel Brandon is not old enough to make his friends yet apprehensive of losing him in the course of nature. But thirty-five has nothing to do with matrimony."

"Perhaps," said Elinor, "thirty-five and seventeen had better not have anything to do with matrimony together. But if there should by any chance happen to be a woman who is single at seven and twenty, I should not think Colonel Brandon's being thirty-five any objection to his marrying *her*."

"A woman of seven and twenty," said Marianne, after pausing a moment, "can never hope to feel or inspire affection again, and if her home be uncomfortable, or her fortune small, I can suppose that she might bring herself to submit to the offices of a nurse, for the sake of the provision and security of a wife."

"It would be impossible, I know," replied Elinor, "to convince you that a woman of seven and twenty could feel for a man of thirty-five anything near enough to love, to make him a desirable companion to her. But I must object to your dooming Colonel Brandon and his wife to the constant confinement of a sick chamber, merely because he chanced to complain yesterday of a slight rheumatic feel in one of his shoulders."

"But he talked of flannel waistcoats," said Marianne; "and with me a flannel waistcoat is invariably connected with aches, cramps, rheumatisms, and every species of ailment that can afflict the old and the feeble."

"Had he been only in a violent fever, you would not have despised him half so much. Confess, Marianne, is not there something interesting to you in the flushed cheek, hollow eye, and quick pulse of a fever?"

Soon after this, upon Elinor's leaving the room, "Mama," said Marianne, "I have an alarm on the subject of illness which I cannot conceal from you. I am sure Edward Ferrars is not well. We have now been here almost a fortnight, and yet he does not come."

"Had you any idea of his coming so soon?" said Mrs. Dashwood. "*I* had none. On the contrary, if I have felt any anxiety at all on the subject, it has been in recollecting that he sometimes showed a want of pleasure and readiness in accepting my invitation, when I talked of his coming to Barton. Does Elinor expect him already?"

"I have never mentioned it to her, but of course she must."

"I rather think you are mistaken, for when I was talking to her yesterday of getting a new grate for the spare bedchamber, she observed that there was no immediate hurry for it, as it was not likely that the room would be wanted for some time."

"How strange this is! What can be the meaning of it! But the whole of their behaviour to each other has been unaccountable! In Edward's farewell there was no distinction between Elinor and me: it was the good wishes of an affectionate brother to both. And Elinor, in quitting Norland and Edward, cried not as I did. Even now her self-command is invariable. When is she dejected or melancholy? When does she try to avoid society, or appear restless and dissatisfied in it?"

Chapter 9

The Dashwoods were now settled at Barton with tolerable comfort to themselves. Sir John Middleton, who called on them every day for the first fortnight, and who was not in the habit of seeing much occupation at home, could not conceal his amazement on finding them always employed.

Their visitors were not many; for, in spite of Sir John's urgent entreaties that they would mix more in the neighbourhood, and repeated assurances of his carriage being always at their service, the independence of Mrs. Dashwood's spirit overcame the wish of society for her children; and she was resolute in declining to visit any family beyond the distance of a walk. There were but few who could be so classed; and it was not all of them that were attainable. About a mile and a half from the cottage, the girls had discovered an ancient respectable looking mansion which interested their imagination and made them wish to be better acquainted with it. But they learnt, on enquiry, that its possessor, an elderly lady of very good character, was unfortunately too infirm to mix with the world, and never stirred from home.

The whole country about them abounded in beautiful walks. The high downs which invited them from almost every window of the cottage to seek the exquisite enjoyment of air on their summits, were a happy alternative when the dirt of the valleys beneath shut up their superior beauties; and towards one of these hills did Marianne and Margaret one memorable morning direct their steps.

They gaily ascended the downs, rejoicing in their own penetration at every glimpse of blue sky.

They pursued their way against the wind, resisting it with laughing delight for about twenty minutes longer, when suddenly the clouds united over their heads, and a driving rain set full in their face. Chagrined and surprised, they were obliged, though unwillingly, to turn back, for no shelter was nearer than their own house. One consolation however remained for them: it was that of running with all possible speed down the steep side of the hill which led immediately to their garden gate.

They set off. Marianne had at first the advantage, but a false step brought her suddenly to the ground; and Margaret, unable to stop herself to assist her, was involuntarily hurried along, and reached the bottom in safety.

A gentleman carrying a gun, with two pointers playing round him, was passing up the hill and within a few yards of Marianne, when her accident happened. He put down his gun and ran to her assistance. She had raised herself from the ground, but her foot had been twisted in her fall, and she was scarcely able to stand. The gentleman offered his services; and perceiving that her modesty declined what her situation rendered necessary, took her up in his arms without farther delay, and carried her down the hill. Then passing through the garden, the gate of which had been left open by Margaret, he bore her directly into the house, whither Margaret was just arrived, and quitted not his hold till he had seated her in a chair in the parlour.

Elinor and her mother rose up in amazement at their entrance, and while the eyes of both were fixed on him with an evident wonder, he apologized for his intrusion by relating its cause, in a manner so frank and so graceful that his person, which was uncommonly handsome, received additional charms from his voice and expression.

Mrs. Dashwood then begged to know to whom she was obliged. His name, he replied, was Willoughby, and his present home was at Allenham, from whence he hoped she would allow him the honour of calling tomorrow to enquire after Miss Dashwood. The honour was readily granted, and he then departed, to make himself still more interesting, in the midst of a heavy rain.

His manly beauty and more than common gracefulness were instantly the theme of general admiration. Marianne herself had seen less of his person than the rest, for the confusion which crimsoned over her face, on his lifting her up, had robbed her of the power of regarding him after their entering the house. But she had seen enough of him to join in all the admiration of the others, and with an energy which always adorned her praise. Every circumstance belonging to him was interesting. His name was good, his residence was in their favourite village, and she soon found out that of all manly dresses a shooting-jacket was the most becoming.

Sir John called on them as soon as the next interval of fair weather that morning allowed him to get out of doors; and Marianne's accident being related to him, he was eagerly asked whether he knew any gentleman of the name of Willoughby at Allenham.

"Willoughby!" cried Sir John; "what, is *he* in the country? That is good news however; I will ride over tomorrow, and ask him to dinner on Thursday."

"You know him then," said Mrs. Dashwood.

"Know him! To be sure I do."

"And what sort of a young man is he?"

"As good a kind of fellow as ever lived, I assure you. A very decent shot, and there is not a bolder rider in England."

"And is that all you can say for him?" cried Marianne, indignantly. "But what are his manners on more intimate acquaintance? What his pursuits, his talents, and genius?"

Sir John was rather puzzled.

"Upon my soul," said he, "I do not know much about him as to all *that*. But he is a pleasant, good-humoured fellow, and has got the nicest little black bitch of a pointer I ever saw."

But Marianne could no more satisfy him as to the colour of Mr. Willoughby's pointer, than he could describe to her the shades of his mind.

"But who is he?" said Elinor. "Where does he come from? Has he a house at Allenham?"

On this point Sir John could give more certain intelligence; and he told them that Mr. Willoughby had no property of his own in the country; that he resided there only while he was visiting the old lady at Allenham Court, to whom he was related, and whose possessions he was to inherit; adding, "Yes, yes, he is very well worth catching I can tell you, Miss Dashwood; he has a pretty little estate of his own in Somersetshire besides; and if I were you, I would not give him up to my younger sister, in spite of all this tumbling down hills. Miss Marianne must not expect to have all the men to herself. Brandon will be jealous, if she does not take care."

"I do not believe," said Mrs. Dashwood, with a good humoured smile, "that Mr. Willoughby will be incommoded by the attempts of either of *my* daughters towards what you call *catching* him. I am glad to find, however, from what you say, that he is a respectable young man."

"He is as good a sort of fellow, I believe, as ever lived," repeated Sir John. "I remember last Christmas at a little hop at the park, he danced from eight o'clock till four, without once sitting down."

"Did he indeed?" cried Marianne with sparkling eyes, "and with elegance, with spirit?"

"Yes; and he was up again at eight to ride to covert."

"That is what I like; that is what a young man ought to be."

"Aye, aye, I see how it will be," said Sir John, "I see how it will be. You will be setting your cap at him now, and never think of poor Brandon."

"That is an expression, Sir John," said Marianne, warmly, "which I particularly dislike. I abhor every common-place phrase by which wit is intended; and 'setting one's cap at a man,' or 'making a conquest,' are the most odious of all."

Sir John did not much understand this reproof; but he laughed as heartily as if he did, and then replied, "Ay, you will make conquests enough, I dare say, one way or other. Poor Brandon! he is quite smitten already, and he is very well worth setting your cap at, I can tell you, in spite of all this tumbling about and spraining of ankles."

Chapter 10

Marianne's preserver called at the cottage early the next morning to make his personal enquiries. He was received by Mrs. Dashwood with a kindness which Sir John's account of him and her own gratitude prompted; and everything that passed during the visit tended to assure him of the sense, elegance, mutual affection, and domestic comfort of the family to whom accident had now introduced him. Of their personal charms he had not required a second interview to be convinced.

Miss Dashwood had a delicate complexion, regular features, and a remarkably pretty figure. Marianne was still handsomer. Her face was so lovely, that when in the common cant of praise, she was called a beautiful girl, truth was less violently outraged than usually happens. Her features were all good; her smile was sweet and attractive; and in her eyes, which were very dark, there was a life, a spirit, an eagerness, which could hardly be seen without delight. From Willoughby their expression was at first held back, by the embarrassment which the remembrance of his assistance created. But when this passed away, when her spirits became collected, when she saw that to the perfect good-breeding of the gentleman, he united frankness and vivacity, and above all, when she heard him declare, that of music and dancing he was passionately fond, she gave him such a look of approbation as secured the largest share of his discourse to herself for the rest of his stay.

They speedily discovered that their enjoyment of dancing and music was mutual. Encouraged by this to a further examination of his opinions, she proceeded to question him on the subject of books. Their taste was strikingly alike. The same books, the same passages were idolized by each—or if any difference appeared, any objection arose, it lasted no longer than till the force of her arguments and the brightness of her eyes could be displayed. He acquiesced in all her decisions, caught all her enthusiasm; and long before his visit concluded, they conversed with the familiarity of a long-established acquaintance.

"Well, Marianne," said Elinor, as soon as he had left them, "for *one* morning I think you have done pretty well. You have already ascertained Mr. Willoughby's opinion in almost every matter of importance. You know what he thinks of Cowper and Scott; you are certain of his estimating their beauties as he ought, and you have received every assurance of his admiring Pope no more than is proper. But how is your acquaintance to be long supported, under such extraordinary dispatch of every subject for discourse? You will soon have exhausted each favourite topic."

"Elinor," cried Marianne, "Are my ideas so scanty? But I see what you mean. I have been too much at my ease, too happy, too frank. I have been open and sincere where I ought to have been reserved, spiritless, dull, and deceitful."

"My love," said her mother, "you must not be offended with Elinor—she was only in jest. I should scold her myself, if she were capable of wishing to check the delight of your conversation with our new friend."

Willoughby gave every proof of his pleasure in their acquaintance, which an evident wish of improving it could offer. He came to them every day. He was a young man of good abilities, quick imagination, lively spirits, and open, affectionate manners. He was exactly formed to engage Marianne's heart, for with all this, he joined not only a captivating person, but a natural ardour of mind which was now roused and increased by the example of her own, and which recommended him to her affection beyond everything else.

In Mrs. Dashwood's estimation he was as faultless as in Marianne's; and Elinor saw nothing to censure in him but a propensity of saying too much what he thought on every occasion, without attention to persons or circumstances. In hastily forming and giving his opinion of other people, in sacrificing general politeness to the enjoyment of undivided attention where his heart was engaged, he displayed a want of caution which Elinor could not approve.

Marianne began now to perceive that the desperation which had seized her at sixteen and a half, of ever seeing a man who could satisfy her ideas of perfection, had been rash and unjustifiable. Willoughby was all that her fancy had delineated in that unhappy hour and in every brighter period, as capable of attaching her; and his behaviour declared his wishes to be in that respect as earnest, as his abilities were strong.

Her mother too, in whose mind not one speculative thought of their marriage had been raised, by his prospect of riches, was led before the end of a week to hope and expect it.

Colonel Brandon's partiality for Marianne now first became perceptible to Elinor, when it ceased to be noticed by them. She was obliged, though unwillingly, to believe that the sentiments which Mrs. Jennings had assigned him for her own satisfaction, were now actually excited by her sister. She saw it with concern; for what could a silent man of five and thirty hope, when opposed to a very lively one of five and twenty? She liked him— in spite of his gravity and reserve, she beheld in him an object of interest. His manners, though serious, were mild; and his reserve appeared rather the result of some oppression of spirits than of any natural gloominess of temper.

Perhaps she pitied and esteemed him the more because he was slighted by Willoughby and Marianne, who, prejudiced against him for being neither lively nor young, seemed resolved to undervalue his merits.

"Brandon is just the kind of man," said Willoughby one day, when they were talking of him together, "whom everybody speaks well of, and nobody cares about."

"That is exactly what I think of him," cried Marianne.

"Do not boast of it, however," said Elinor, "for it is injustice in both of you. He is highly esteemed by all the family at the park, and I never see him myself without taking pains to converse with him."

"That he is patronised by *you*," replied Willoughby, "is certainly in his favour; but as for the esteem of the others, it is a reproach in itself. Who would submit to the indignity of being approved by such a woman as Lady Middleton and Mrs. Jennings, that could command the indifference of anybody else?"

"But perhaps the abuse of such people as yourself and Marianne will make amends for the regard of Lady Middleton and her mother. If their praise is censure, your censure may be praise, for they are not more undiscerning, than you are prejudiced and unjust."

"In defence of your protégé you can even be saucy."

"My protégé, as you call him, is a sensible man; and sense will always have attractions for me. He has seen a great deal of the world; has been abroad, has read, and has a thinking mind. I have found him capable of giving me much information on various subjects; and he has always answered my inquiries with readiness of good-breeding and good nature."

"That is to say," cried Marianne contemptuously, "he has told you, that in the East Indies the climate is hot, and the mosquitoes are troublesome."

"Perhaps," said Willoughby, "his observations may have extended to the existence of nabobs, gold mohrs, and palanquins."

"I may venture to say that *his* observations have stretched much further than your candour. But why should you dislike him?"

"I do not dislike him. I consider him, on the contrary, as a very respectable man who has more money than he can spend and more time than he knows how to employ."

"Add to which," cried Marianne, "that he has neither genius, taste, nor spirit."

"You decide on his imperfections so much in the mass," replied Elinor, "that the commendation I am able to give of him is comparatively cold and insipid. I can only pronounce him to be a sensible man, well-bred, well-informed, of gentle address, and, I believe, possessing an amiable heart."

"Miss Dashwood," cried Willoughby, "you are endeavouring to disarm me by reason. But it will not do. You shall find me as stubborn as you can be artful. I have three unanswerable reasons for disliking Colonel Brandon; he threatened me with rain when I wanted it to be fine; he has found fault with the hanging of my curricle, and I cannot persuade him to buy my brown mare. If it will be any satisfaction to you, however, to be told, that I believe his character to be in other respects irreproachable, I am ready to confess it. And in return for an acknowledgment, which must give me some pain, you cannot deny me the privilege of disliking him as much as ever."

Chapter 11

Little had Mrs. Dashwood or her daughters imagined when they first came into Devonshire that so many engagements would arise to occupy their time. When Marianne was recovered, the schemes of amusement at home and abroad, which Sir John had been previously forming, were put into execution. The private balls at the park then began. Willoughby was included; and the ease and familiarity which naturally attended these parties were exactly calculated to give increasing intimacy to his acquaintance with the Dashwoods, to afford him opportunity of witnessing the excellencies of Marianne, and of receiving, in her behaviour to himself, the most pointed assurance of her affection.

Elinor could only wish that it were less openly shown; and once or twice did venture to suggest the propriety of some self-command to Marianne. But Marianne abhorred all concealment where no real disgrace could attend unreserved. Willoughby thought the same; and their behaviour at all times, was an illustration of their opinions.

When he was present she had no eyes for anyone else. Everything he did was right. Everything he said was clever. If their evenings at the park were concluded with cards, he cheated himself and all the rest of the party to get her a good hand. If dancing formed the amusement of the night, they were partners for half the time; and when obliged to separate for a couple of dances, were careful to stand together and scarcely spoke a word to anybody else.

This was the season of happiness to Marianne. Her heart was devoted to Willoughby, and the fond attachment to Norland was more likely to be softened than she had thought it possible before, by the charms which his society bestowed on her present home.

Elinor's happiness was not so great. Her heart was not so much at ease, nor her satisfaction in their amusements so pure. They afforded her no companion that could make amends for what she had left behind. Neither Lady Middleton nor Mrs. Jennings could supply to her the conversation she missed; although the latter was an everlasting talker. Lady Middleton was more agreeable than her mother only in being more silent. Elinor needed little observation to perceive that her reserve was a mere calmness of manner with which sense had nothing to do. Her insipidity was invariable, and though she did not oppose the parties arranged by her husband, provided everything were conducted in style and her two eldest children attended her, she never appeared to receive more enjoyment from them than she might have experienced in sitting at home.

In Colonel Brandon alone, of all her new acquaintance, did Elinor find a person who could give pleasure as a companion. Willoughby was out of the question. Her admiration and regard, even her sisterly regard, was all his own; but he was a lover; his attentions were wholly Marianne's. Colonel Brandon, unfortunately for himself, had no such encouragement to think only of Marianne, and in conversing with Elinor he found the greatest consolation for the indifference of her sister.

Elinor's compassion for him increased, as she had reason to suspect that the misery of disappointed love had already been known to him. This suspicion was given by some words which accidently dropped from him one evening at the park, when they were sitting down together by mutual consent, while the others were dancing. His eyes were fixed on Marianne, and, after a silence of some minutes, he said, with a faint smile, "Your sister, I understand, does not approve of second attachments."

"No," replied Elinor, "her opinions are all romantic."

"Or rather, as I believe, she considers them impossible to exist."

"I believe she does. A few years however will settle her opinions on the reasonable basis of common sense and observation; and then they may be more easy to define and to justify than they now are, by anybody but herself."

"This will probably be the case," he replied; "and yet there is something so amiable in the prejudices of a young mind, that one is sorry to see them give way to the reception of more general opinions."

"I cannot agree with you there," said Elinor. "There are inconveniences attending such feelings as Marianne's, which all the charms of enthusiasm and ignorance of the world cannot atone for."

After a short pause he resumed the conversation by saying, "Does your sister make no distinction in her objections against a second attachment? Or is it equally criminal in everybody? Are those who have been disappointed in their first choice, whether from the inconstancy of its object, or the perverseness of circumstances, to be equally indifferent during the rest of their lives?"

"Upon my word, I am not acquainted with the minutiae of her principles. I only know that I never yet heard her admit any instance of a second attachment's being pardonable."

"This," said he, "cannot hold; but a change, a total change of sentiments—No, no, do not desire it; for when the romantic refinements of a young mind are obliged to give way, how frequently are they succeeded by such opinions as are but too common, and too dangerous! I speak from experience. I once knew a lady who in temper and mind greatly resembled your sister, who thought and judged like her, but who from an inforced change—from a series of unfortunate circumstances—" Here he stopped suddenly; appeared to think that he had said too much, and by his countenance gave rise to conjectures, which might not otherwise have entered Elinor's head. The lady would probably have passed without suspicion, had he not convinced Miss Dashwood that what concerned her ought not to escape his lips. As it was, it required but a slight effort of fancy to connect his emotion with the tender recollection of past regard.

Chapter 12

As Elinor and Marianne were walking together the next morning the latter communicated a piece of news to her sister, which in spite of all that she knew before of Marianne's imprudence and want of thought, surprised her by its extravagant testimony of both. Marianne told her, with the greatest delight, that Willoughby had given her a horse. Without considering that it was not in her mother's plan to keep any horse, that if she were to alter her resolution in favour of this gift, she must buy another for the servant, and keep a servant to ride it, and after all, build a stable to receive them, she had accepted the present without hesitation.

"He intends to send his groom into Somersetshire immediately for it," she added, "and when it arrives we will ride every day. Imagine to yourself, my dear Elinor, the delight of a gallop on some of these downs."

Most unwilling was she to comprehend all the unhappy truths which attended the affair; and for some time she refused to submit to them. As to an additional servant, the expense would be a trifle and any horse would do for *him*; as to a stable, the merest shed would be sufficient. Elinor then ventured to doubt the propriety of her receiving such a present from a man so little, or at least so lately known to her. This was too much.

"You are mistaken, Elinor," said she warmly, "in supposing I know very little of Willoughby. I have not known him long indeed, but I am much better acquainted with him, than I am with any other creature in the world, except yourself and mama. I should hold myself guilty of greater impropriety in accepting a horse from my brother, than from Willoughby."

Elinor knew her sister's temper. Opposition on so tender a subject would only attach her the more to her own opinion. But by an appeal to her affection for her mother, by representing the inconveniences which that indulgent mother must draw on herself, if she consented to this increase of establishment, Marianne was shortly subdued; and she promised not to tempt her mother to such imprudent kindness by mentioning the offer, and to tell Willoughby that it must be declined.

She was faithful to her word; and when Willoughby called at the cottage, the same day, Elinor heard her express her disappointment to him in a low voice, on being obliged to forego the acceptance of his present. His concern was very apparent; and after expressing it with earnestness, he added, in the same low voice, —"But, Marianne, the horse is still yours, though you cannot use it now. I shall keep it only till you can claim it. When you leave Barton to form your own establishment in a more lasting home, Queen Mab shall receive you."

This was all overheard by Miss Dashwood; and in the whole of the sentence, she instantly saw an intimacy so decided, a meaning so direct, as marked a perfect agreement between them. From that moment she doubted not of their being engaged to each other; and the belief of it created no other surprise than that she, or any of their friends, should be left by tempers so frank, to discover it by accident.

Margaret related something to her the next day, which placed this matter in a still clearer light. Willoughby had spent the preceding evening with them, and Margaret, by being left some time in the parlour with only him and Marianne, had had opportunity for observations, which, with a most important face, she communicated to her eldest sister, when they were next by themselves.

"Oh, Elinor!" she cried, "I have such a secret to tell you about Marianne. I am sure she will be married to Mr. Willoughby very soon."

"You have said so," replied Elinor, "almost every day since they first met on High-church Down; and they had not known each other a week, I believe, before you were certain that Marianne wore his picture round her neck; but it turned out to be only the miniature of our great uncle."

"But indeed this is quite another thing. I am sure they will be married very soon, for he has got a lock of her hair."

"Take care, Margaret. It may be only the hair of some great uncle of *his*."

"But, indeed, Elinor, it is Marianne's. Last night after tea, when you and mama went out of the room, they were whispering and talking together as fast as could be, and he seemed to be begging something of her, and presently he took up her scissors and cut off a long lock of her hair, and folded it up in a piece of white paper; and put it into his pocket-book."

For such particulars, stated on such authority, Elinor could not withhold her credit.

Margaret's sagacity was not always displayed in a way so satisfactory to her sister. When Mrs. Jennings attacked her one evening at the park, to give the name of the young man who was Elinor's particular favourite, Margaret answered by looking at her sister, and saying, "I must not tell, may I, Elinor?"

This of course made everybody laugh; and Elinor tried to laugh too. But the effort was painful. She was convinced that Margaret had fixed on a person whose name she could not bear with composure to become a standing joke with Mrs. Jennings.

Marianne felt for her most sincerely; but she did more harm than good to the cause, by turning very red and saying in an angry manner to Margaret, "Remember that whatever your conjectures may be, you have no right to repeat them."

"Oh! pray, Miss Margaret, let us know all about it," said Mrs. Jennings. "What is the gentleman's name?"

"I must not tell, ma'am. But I know very well what it is; and I know where he is too."

"Yes, yes, we can guess where he is; at his own house at Norland to be sure. He is the curate of the parish I dare say."

"No, *that* he is not. He is of no profession at all."

"Margaret," said Marianne with great warmth, "you know that there is no such person in existence."

"Well, then, he is lately dead, Marianne, for I am sure there was such a man once, and his name begins with an F."

Most grateful did Elinor feel to Lady Middleton for observing, at this moment, "that it rained very hard." The idea however started by her, was immediately pursued by Colonel Brandon, who was on every occasion mindful of the feelings of others; and much was said on the subject of rain by both of them. Willoughby opened the piano-forte, and asked Marianne to sit down to it; and thus amidst the various endeavours of different people to quit the topic, it fell to the ground. But not so easily did Elinor recover from the alarm into which it had thrown her.

A party was formed this evening for going on the following day to see a very fine place about twelve miles from Barton, belonging to a brother-in-law of Colonel Brandon. The grounds were declared to be highly beautiful. They contained a noble piece of water; a sail on which was to a form a great part of the morning's amusement; cold provisions were to be taken, open carriages only to be employed, and every thing conducted in the usual style of a complete party of pleasure.

To some few of the company it appeared rather a bold undertaking, considering the time of year, and Mrs. Dashwood, who had already a cold, was persuaded by Elinor to stay at home.

Chapter 13

By ten o'clock the whole party was assembled at the park. They were all in high spirits and good humour, eager to be happy, and determined to submit to the greatest inconveniences and hardships rather than be otherwise.

While they were at breakfast the letters were brought in. Among the rest there was one for Colonel Brandon; he took it, looked at the direction, changed colour, and immediately left the room.

In about five minutes he returned.

"No bad news, Colonel, I hope;" said Mrs. Jennings, as soon as he entered the room.

"None at all, ma'am, I thank you."

"Was it from Avignon? I hope it is not to say that your sister is worse."

"No, ma'am. It came from town, and is merely a letter of business which requires my immediate attendance in town."

"In town!" cried Mrs. Jennings. "What can you have to do in town at this time of year?"

"My own loss is great," he continued, "in being obliged to leave so agreeable a party; but I am the more concerned, as I fear my presence is necessary to gain your admittance at Whitwell."

"But if you write a note to the housekeeper, Mr. Brandon," said Marianne, eagerly, "will it not be sufficient?"

He shook his head.

"We must go," said Sir John. "You cannot go to town till tomorrow, Brandon, that is all."

"I wish it could be so easily settled. But it is not in my power to delay my journey for one day!"

"You would not be six hours later," said Willoughby, "if you were to defer your journey till our return."

"I cannot afford to lose *one* hour."

Elinor then heard Willoughby say, in a low voice to Marianne, "There are some people who cannot bear a party of pleasure. Brandon is one of them. I would lay fifty guineas the letter was of his own writing."

"I have no doubt of it," replied Marianne.

"There is no persuading you to change your mind, Brandon, I know of old," said Sir John, "But, however, I hope you will think better of it. Consider, here are the two Miss Careys come over from Newton, the three Miss Dashwoods walked up from the cottage, and Mr. Willoughby got up two hours before his usual time, on purpose to go to Whitwell."

Colonel Brandon again repeated his sorrow at being the cause of disappointing the party; but at the same time declared it to be unavoidable.

"Well then, when will you come back again?"

"I hope we shall see you at Barton," added her ladyship, "as soon as you can conveniently leave town; and we must put off the party to Whitwell till you return."

"You are very obliging. But it is so uncertain, when I may have it in my power to return, that I dare not engage for it at all."

Colonel Brandon's horses were announced and he then took leave of the whole party.

"Is there no chance of my seeing you and your sisters in town this winter, Miss Dashwood?"

"I am afraid, none at all."

"Then I must bid you farewell for a longer time than I should wish to do."

To Marianne, he merely bowed and said nothing.

"Come Colonel," said Mrs. Jennings, "before you go, do let us know what you are going about."

He wished her a good morning, and, attended by Sir John, left the room.

The complaints and lamentations which politeness had hitherto restrained, now burst forth universally; and they all agreed again and again how provoking it was to be so disappointed.

"I can guess what his business is, however," said Mrs. Jennings exultingly. "It is about Miss Williams, I am sure."

"And who is Miss Williams?" asked Marianne.

"What! Do not you know who Miss Williams is? She is a relation of the Colonel's, my dear; a very near relation." Then, lowering her voice a little, she said to Elinor, "She is his natural daughter."

"Indeed!"

"Oh, yes; and as like him as she can stare. I dare say the Colonel will leave her all his fortune."

When Sir John returned, he joined most heartily in the general regret on so unfortunate an event; concluding however by observing, that as they were all got together, they must do something by way of being happy; and after some consultation it was agreed that they might procure a tolerable composure of mind by driving about the country. The carriages were then ordered; Willoughby's was first, and Marianne never looked happier than when she got into it. He drove through the park very fast, and they were soon out of sight; and nothing more of them was seen till their return. They both seemed delighted with their drive; but said only in general terms that they had kept in the lanes, while the others went on the downs.

It was settled that there should be a dance in the evening. Some more of the Careys came to dinner, and they had the pleasure of sitting down nearly twenty to table. Willoughby took his usual place between the two elder Miss Dashwoods. Mrs. Jennings sat on Elinor's right hand; and they had not been long seated, before she leant behind her and Willoughby, and said to Marianne, loud enough for them both to hear, "I have found you out in spite of all your tricks. I know where you spent the morning."

Marianne coloured, and replied very hastily, "Where, pray?"

"Did not you know," said Willoughby, "that we had been out in my curricle?"

"Yes, yes, Mr. Impudence, I know that very well, and I was determined to find out *where* you had been to. I hope you like your house, Miss Marianne. It is a very large one, I know; and when I come to see you, I hope you will have new-furnished it."

Marianne turned away in great confusion. Mrs. Jennings laughed heartily; and Elinor found that in her resolution to know where they had been, she had actually made her own woman inquire of Mr. Willoughby's groom; and that she had by that method been informed that they had gone to Allenham, and spent a considerable time there in walking about the garden and going all over the house.

As soon as they left the dining-room, Elinor enquired of her about it; and great was her surprise when she found that every circumstance related by Mrs. Jennings was perfectly true.

"Why should you imagine, Elinor, that we did not go there, or that we did not see the house? Is not it what you have often wished to do yourself?"

"Yes, Marianne, but I would not go while Mrs. Smith was there, and with no other companion than Mr. Willoughby."

"Mr. Willoughby however is the only person who can have a right to show that house; and as he went in an open carriage, it was impossible to have any other companion. If there had been any real impropriety in what I did, I should have been sensible of it at the time."

"But, my dear Marianne, as it has already exposed you to some very impertinent remarks, do you not now begin to doubt the discretion of your own conduct?"

"I am not sensible of having done anything wrong in walking over Mrs. Smith's grounds, or in seeing her house. They will one day be Mr. Willoughby's, and—"

"If they were one day to be your own, Marianne, you would not be justified in what you have done."

She blushed at this hint; but it was even visibly gratifying to her; and after a ten minutes' interval of earnest thought, she came to her sister again, and said with great good humour, "Perhaps, Elinor, it *was* rather ill-judged in me to go to Allenham; but Mr. Willoughby wanted particularly to show me the place; and it is a charming house, I assure you."

Chapter 14

The sudden termination of Colonel Brandon's visit at the park, with his steadiness in concealing its cause, filled the mind, and raised the wonder of Mrs. Jennings for two or three days. She wondered, with little intermission what could be the reason of it; and thought over every kind of distress that could have befallen him, with a fixed determination that he should not escape them all.

"Something very melancholy must be the matter, I am sure," said she. "I could see it in his face. I do think he must have been sent for about money matters, for what else can it be? I would give anything to know the truth of it. I would lay any wager it is about Miss Williams. I wonder what it can be! May be his sister is worse at Avignon, and has sent for him over. Well, I wish him out of all his trouble with all my heart, and a good wife into the bargain."

So wondered, so talked Mrs. Jennings. Elinor, though she felt really interested in the welfare of Colonel Brandon, could not bestow all the wonder on his going so suddenly away, which Mrs. Jennings was desirous of her feeling; her wonder was otherwise disposed of. It was engrossed by the extraordinary silence of her sister and Willoughby on the subject, which they must know to be peculiarly interesting to them all. As this silence continued, every day made it appear more strange and more incompatible with the disposition of both.

She could easily conceive that marriage might not be immediately in their power; for though Willoughby was independent, there was no reason to believe him rich. His estate had been rated by Sir John at about six or seven hundred a year; but he lived at an expense to which that income could hardly be equal, and he had himself often complained of his poverty. But for this strange kind of secrecy maintained by them relative to their engagement, she could not account; and it was so wholly contradictory to their general opinions and practice, that a doubt sometimes entered her mind of their being really engaged.

Nothing could be more expressive of attachment to them all, than Willoughby's behaviour. To Marianne it had all the distinguishing tenderness which a lover's heart could give, and to the rest of the family it was the affectionate attention of a son and a brother.

One evening in particular, about a week after Colonel Brandon left the country, his heart seemed more than usually open to every feeling of attachment to the objects around him; and on Mrs. Dashwood's happening to mention her design of improving the cottage in the spring, he warmly opposed every alteration of a place which affection had established as perfect with him.

"What!" he exclaimed. "Improve this dear cottage! No. *That* I will never consent to."

"Do not be alarmed," said Miss Dashwood, "nothing of the kind will be done; for my mother will never have money enough to attempt it."

"I am heartily glad of it," he cried. "May she always be poor, if she can employ her riches no better."

"Thank you, Willoughby. But you may be assured that I would not sacrifice one sentiment of local attachment of yours, or of any one whom I loved, for all the improvements in the world. But are you really so attached to this place as to see no defect in it?"

"I am," said he. "To me it is faultless, and were I rich enough, I would instantly pull Combe down, and build it up again in the exact plan of this cottage."

"With dark narrow stairs and a kitchen that smokes, I suppose," said Elinor.

"Yes," cried he in the same eager tone, "with all and everything belonging to it."

"I flatter myself," replied Elinor, "that even under the disadvantage of better rooms and a broader staircase, you will hereafter find your own house as faultless as you now do this."

"There certainly are circumstances," said Willoughby, "which might greatly endear it to me; but this place will always have one claim of my affection, which no other can possibly share."

Mrs. Dashwood looked with pleasure at Marianne, whose fine eyes were fixed so expressively on Willoughby, as plainly denoted how well she understood him.

"How often did I wish," added he, "when I was at Allenham this time twelvemonth, that Barton cottage were inhabited! How little did I then think that the very first news I should hear from Mrs. Smith, when I next came into the country, would be that Barton cottage was taken: and I felt an immediate satisfaction and interest in the event, which nothing but a kind of prescience of what happiness I should experience from it, can account for. Must it not have been so, Marianne?" speaking to her in a lowered voice. Then continuing his former tone, he said, "And yet this house you would spoil, Mrs. Dashwood? You would rob it of its simplicity by imaginary improvement! And this dear parlour in which our acquaintance first began, you would degrade to the condition of a common entrance."

Mrs. Dashwood again assured him that no alteration of the kind should be attempted.

"You are a good woman," he warmly replied. "Your promise makes me easy. Extend it a little farther, and it will make me happy. Tell me that not only your house will remain the same, but that I shall ever find you and yours as unchanged as your dwelling; and that you will always consider me with the kindness which has made everything belonging to you so dear to me."

The promise was readily given, and Willoughby's behaviour during the whole of the evening declared at once his affection and happiness.

"Shall we see you tomorrow to dinner?" said Mrs. Dashwood, when he was leaving them. "I do not ask you to come in the morning, for we must walk to the park, to call on Lady Middleton."

He engaged to be with them by four o'clock.

Chapter 15

Mrs. Dashwood's visit to Lady Middleton took place the next day, and two of her daughters went with her; but Marianne excused herself from being of the party, under some trifling pretext of employment; and her mother, who concluded that a promise had been made by Willoughby the night before of calling on her while they were absent, was perfectly satisfied with her remaining at home.

On their return from the park they found Willoughby's curricle and servant in waiting at the cottage, and Mrs. Dashwood was convinced that her conjecture had been just. They were no sooner in the passage than Marianne came hastily out of the parlour apparently in violent affliction, with her handkerchief at her eyes; and without noticing them ran up stairs. Surprised and alarmed they proceeded directly into the room she had just quitted, where they found only Willoughby.

"Is anything the matter with her?" cried Mrs. Dashwood as she entered. "Is she ill?"

"I hope not," he replied, trying to look cheerful; and with a forced smile presently added, "It is I who may rather expect to be ill—for I am now suffering under a very heavy disappointment!"

"Disappointment?"

"Yes, for I am unable to keep my engagement with you. Mrs. Smith has this morning exercised the privilege of riches upon a poor dependent cousin, by sending me on business to London."

"To London! And are you going this morning?"

"Almost this moment."

"This is very unfortunate. But Mrs. Smith must be obliged; and her business will not detain you from us long I hope."

He coloured as he replied, "You are very kind, but I have no idea of returning into Devonshire immediately. My visits to Mrs. Smith are never repeated within the twelvemonth."

"And is Mrs. Smith your only friend? For shame, Willoughby, can you wait for an invitation here?"

His colour increased; and with his eyes fixed on the ground he only replied, "You are too good."

Mrs. Dashwood looked at Elinor with surprise. Elinor felt equal amazement. For a few moments everyone was silent. Mrs. Dashwood first spoke.

"I have only to add, my dear Willoughby, that at Barton cottage you will always be welcome; for I will not press you to return here immediately, because you only can judge how far *that* might be pleasing to Mrs. Smith."

"My engagements at present," replied Willoughby, confusedly, "are of such a nature—that—I dare not flatter myself—"

He stopped. Mrs. Dashwood was too much astonished to speak, and another pause succeeded. This was broken by Willoughby, who said with a faint smile, "It is folly to linger in this manner. I will not torment myself any longer by remaining among friends whose society it is impossible for me now to enjoy." He then hastily took leave of them all and left the room.

Mrs. Dashwood felt too much for speech, and instantly quitted the parlour to give way in solitude to the concern and alarm which this sudden departure occasioned.

Elinor's uneasiness was at least equal to her mother's. She thought of what had just passed with anxiety and distrust. Willoughby's behaviour in taking leave of them, his embarrassment, and affectation of cheerfulness, and, above all, his unwillingness to accept her mother's invitation greatly disturbed her. One moment she feared that no serious design had ever been formed on his side; and the next that some unfortunate quarrel had taken place between him and her sister; though when she considered what Marianne's love for him was, a quarrel seemed almost impossible.

In about half an hour her mother returned, and though her eyes were red, her countenance was not uncheerful.

"Our dear Willoughby is now some miles from Barton, Elinor," said she, as she sat down to work, "and with how heavy a heart does he travel?"

"It is all very strange. So suddenly to be gone! It seems but the work of a moment. And last night he was with us so happy, so cheerful, so affectionate? And now, after only ten minutes notice—gone too without intending to return! Something more than what he owned to us must have happened. What can it be? Can they have quarrelled? Why else should he have shown such unwillingness to accept your invitation here?"

"He had not the power of accepting it. I have thought it all over I assure you, and I can perfectly account for everything that at first seemed strange to me as well as to you."

"Can you, indeed!"

"Yes. I have explained it to myself in the most satisfactory way. It will not satisfy *you*, I know; but you shall not talk *me* out of my trust in it. I am persuaded that Mrs. Smith suspects his regard for Marianne, disapproves of it, and on that account is eager to get him away. He is, moreover, aware that she *does* disapprove the connection, he dares not therefore at present confess to her his engagement with Marianne, and he feels himself obliged, from his dependent situation, to give into her schemes, and absent himself from Devonshire for a while. You will tell me, I know, that this may or may NOT have happened; but I will listen to no cavil, unless you can point out any other method of understanding the affair as satisfactory at this. And now, Elinor, what have you to say?"

"Nothing, for you have anticipated my answer."

"Oh, Elinor, how incomprehensible are your feelings! You had rather look out for misery for Marianne, and guilt for poor Willoughby, than an apology for the latter. Is nothing due to the man whom we have all such reason to love, and no reason in the world to think ill of? And, after all, what is it you suspect him of?"

"I can hardly tell myself. But suspicion of something unpleasant is the inevitable consequence of such an alteration as we just witnessed in him. Willoughby may undoubtedly have very sufficient reasons for his conduct, and I will hope that he has. But it would have been more like Willoughby to acknowledge them at once. Secrecy may be advisable; but still I cannot help wondering at its being practiced by him."

"Do not blame him, however, for departing from his character, where the deviation is necessary. But you really do admit the justice of what I have said in his defence?"

"Not entirely. It may be proper to conceal their engagement (if they *are* engaged) from Mrs. Smith. But this is no excuse for their concealing it from us."

"My dear child, do you accuse Willoughby and Marianne of concealment? This is strange indeed, when your eyes have been reproaching them every day for incautiousness."

"I want no proof of their affection," said Elinor; "but of their engagement I do."

"My Elinor, is it possible to doubt their engagement? How is it to be supposed that Willoughby, persuaded as he must be of your sister's love, should leave her, and leave her perhaps for months, without telling her of his affection; that they should part without a mutual exchange of confidence?"

"I confess," replied Elinor, "that every circumstance except *one* is in favour of their engagement; but that *one* is the total silence of both on the subject."

"How strange this is! You must think wretchedly indeed of Willoughby, if, after all that has openly passed between them, you can doubt the nature of the terms on which they are together. Do you suppose him really indifferent to her?"

"No, I cannot think that. He must and does love her, I am sure."

"But with a strange kind of tenderness, if he can leave her with such indifference, such carelessness of the future, as you attribute to him."

"You must remember, my dear mother, that I have never considered this matter as certain. I have had my doubts, I confess; but they are fainter than they were. If we find they correspond, every fear of mine will be removed."

"A mighty concession indeed! If you were to see them at the altar, you would suppose they were going to be married. But I require no such proof. Nothing in my opinion has ever passed to justify doubt. You cannot doubt your sister's wishes. It must be Willoughby therefore whom you suspect. But why? Has there been any inconsistency on his side to create alarm? Can he be deceitful?"

"I hope not, I believe not," cried Elinor. "I love Willoughby, sincerely love him. I was startled, I confess, by the alteration in his manners this morning; he did not speak like himself, and did not return your kindness with any cordiality. But all this may be explained by such a situation of his affairs as you have supposed. He had just parted from my sister, had seen her leave him in the greatest affliction; and if he felt obliged, to resist the temptation of returning here soon, he might well be embarrassed and disturbed. In such a case, a plain and open avowal of his difficulties would have been more to his honour I think; but I will not raise objections against any one's conduct on so illiberal a foundation."

"You speak very properly. Willoughby certainly does not deserve to be suspected. Had he been in a situation to act independently and marry immediately, it might have been odd that he should leave us without acknowledging everything to me at once: but this is not the case. It is an engagement in some respects not prosperously begun, for their marriage must be at a very uncertain distance; and even secrecy, as far as it can be observed, may now be very advisable."

They saw nothing of Marianne till dinner time, when she entered the room and took her place at the table without saying a word. Her eyes were red and swollen. She avoided the looks of them all, could neither eat nor speak, and after some time, on her mother's silently pressing her hand with tender compassion, her small degree of fortitude was quite overcome, she burst into tears and left the room.

This violent oppression of spirits continued the whole evening. The slightest mention of anything relative to Willoughby overpowered her in an instant; and though her family were most anxiously attentive to her comfort, it was impossible for them, if they spoke at all, to keep clear of every subject which her feelings connected with him.

Chapter 16

Marianne was awake the whole night, and she wept the greatest part of it. She got up with a headache, was unable to talk, and unwilling to take any nourishment; giving pain every moment to her mother and sisters, and forbidding all attempt at consolation from either. Her sensibility was potent enough!

When breakfast was over she walked out by herself, and wandered about the village of Allenham, indulging the recollection of past enjoyment and crying over the present reverse for the chief of the morning.

The evening passed off in the equal indulgence of feeling. She played over every favourite song that she had been used to play to Willoughby, and sat at the instrument gazing on every line of music that he had written out for her, till her heart was so heavy that no farther sadness could be gained; and this nourishment of grief was every day applied. In books too she courted the misery which a contrast between the past and present was certain of giving. She read nothing but what they had been used to read together.

Such violence of affliction indeed could not be supported for ever; it sunk within a few days into a calmer melancholy; but these employments, to which she daily recurred still produced occasional effusions of sorrow as lively as ever.

No letter from Willoughby came; and none seemed expected by Marianne. Her mother was surprised, and Elinor again became uneasy. But Mrs. Dashwood could find explanations whenever she wanted them, which at least satisfied herself.

"Remember, Elinor," said she, "how very often Sir John fetches our letters himself from the post, and carries them to it. We have already agreed that secrecy may be necessary, and we must acknowledge that it could not be maintained if their correspondence were to pass through Sir John's hands."

Elinor could not deny the truth of this, and she tried to find in it a motive sufficient for their silence. But there was one method so direct, so simple, that she could not help suggesting it to her mother.

"Why do you not ask Marianne at once," said she, "whether she is or is not engaged to Willoughby?"

"I would not ask such a question for the world. Supposing it possible that they are not engaged, what distress would not such an enquiry inflict! I know Marianne's heart: I know that she dearly loves me, and that I shall not be the last to whom the affair is made known, when circumstances make the revealment of it eligible."

Elinor thought this generosity overstrained, considering her sister's youth, and urged the matter further, but in vain; common sense, common care, common prudence, were all sunk in Mrs. Dashwood's romantic delicacy.

It was several days before Willoughby's name was mentioned before Marianne by any of her family; Sir John and Mrs. Jennings, indeed, were not so nice; their witticisms added pain to many a painful hour; but one evening, Mrs. Dashwood, accidentally taking up a volume of Shakespeare, exclaimed, "We have never finished Hamlet, Marianne; our dear Willoughby went away before we could get through it. We will put it by, that when he comes again . . . But it may be months, perhaps, before *that* happens."

"Months!" cried Marianne, with strong surprise. "No–nor many weeks."

Mrs. Dashwood was sorry for what she had said; but it gave Elinor pleasure, as it produced a reply from Marianne so expressive of confidence in Willoughby and knowledge of his intentions.

One morning, about a week after his leaving the country, Marianne was prevailed on to join her sisters in their usual walk, instead of wandering away by herself. They walked along the road through the valley, and chiefly in silence, for Marianne's *mind* could not be controlled, and Elinor, satisfied with gaining one point, would not then attempt more. A long stretch of the road which they had travelled on first coming to Barton, lay before them; and on reaching that point, they stopped to look around them.

Amongst the objects in the scene, they soon discovered a man on horseback riding towards them. In a few minutes they could distinguish him to be a gentleman; and in a moment afterwards Marianne rapturously exclaimed,

"It is he; it is indeed; I know it is!" She was hastening to meet him, when Elinor cried out, "Indeed, Marianne, I think you are mistaken. It is not Willoughby. The person is not tall enough for him, and has not his air."

"He has, he has," cried Marianne, "His air, his coat, his horse. I knew how soon he would come."

She walked eagerly on as she spoke and Elinor quickened her pace and kept up with her. Marianne looked again; her heart sunk within her; and abruptly turning round, she was hurrying back, when the voices of both her sisters were raised to detain her; a third, almost as well known as Willoughby's, joined them in begging her to stop, and she turned round with surprise to see and welcome Edward Ferrars.

He was the only person in the world who could at that

moment be forgiven for not being Willoughby; the only one who could have gained a smile from her; but she dispersed her tears to smile on *him*, and in her sister's happiness forgot for a time her own disappointment.

He dismounted, and giving his horse to his servant, walked back with them to Barton, whither he was purposely coming to visit them.

He was welcomed by them all with great cordiality, but especially by Marianne, who showed more warmth of regard in her reception of him than even Elinor herself. To Marianne, indeed, the meeting between Edward and her sister was but a continuation of that unaccountable coldness which she had often observed at Norland in their mutual behaviour. On Edward's side, more particularly, there was a deficiency of all that a lover ought to look and say on such an occasion. He seemed scarcely sensible of pleasure in seeing them, said little but what was forced from him by questions, and distinguished Elinor by no mark of affection. Marianne began almost to feel a dislike of Edward; and it ended, as every feeling must end with her, by carrying back her thoughts to Willoughby, whose manners formed a contrast sufficiently striking to those of his brother elect.

After a short silence which succeeded the first surprise and enquiries of meeting, Marianne asked Edward if he came directly from London. No, he had been in Devonshire a fortnight.

"A fortnight!" she repeated, surprised at his being so long in the same county with Elinor without seeing her before.

He looked rather distressed as he added, that he had been staying with some friends near Plymouth.

"Have you been lately in Sussex?" said Elinor.

"I was at Norland about a month ago."

"And how does dear, dear Norland look?" cried Marianne.

"Dear, dear Norland," said Elinor, "probably looks much

as it always does at this time of the year. The woods and walks thickly covered with dead leaves."

"Oh," cried Marianne, "with what transporting sensation have I formerly seen them fall! How have I delighted, as I walked, to see them driven in showers about me by the wind!"

"It is not every one," said Elinor, "who has your passion for dead leaves."

"No; my feelings are not often shared, not often understood. But *sometimes* they are." She sank into a reverie for a few moments; but rousing herself again, "Now, Edward, look at those hills! Did you ever see their equals?"

"It is a beautiful country," he replied; "but these bottoms must be dirty in winter."

"How can you think of dirt, with such objects before you?"

"Because," replied he, smiling, "among the rest of the objects before me, I see a very dirty lane."

"How strange!" said Marianne to herself as she walked on.

"Have you an agreeable neighbourhood here? Are the Middletons pleasant people?"

"No, not all," answered Marianne; "we could not be more unfortunately situated."

"Marianne," cried her sister, "how can you say so? Have you forgot, Marianne, how many pleasant days we have owed to them?"

"No," said Marianne, in a low voice, "nor how many painful moments."

Elinor took no notice of this; and directed her attention to their visitor. His coldness and reserve mortified her severely but she avoided every appearance of resentment or displeasure, and treated him as she thought he ought to be treated from the family connection.

Chapter 17

Mrs. Dashwood was surprised only for a moment at seeing him. He received the kindest welcome from her; and shyness, coldness, reserve could not stand against such a reception. Indeed a man could not very well be in love with either of her daughters, without extending the passion to her; and Elinor had the satisfaction of seeing him soon become more like himself. He praised their house, admired its prospect, was attentive, and kind; but still he was not in spirits. The whole family perceived it, and Mrs. Dashwood, attributing it to some want of liberality in his mother, sat down to table indignant against all selfish parents.

"What are Mrs. Ferrars's views for you at present, Edward?" said she, "Are you still to be a great orator in spite of yourself?"

"No. I hope my mother is now convinced that I have no more talents than inclination for a public life!"

"You have no ambition, I well know. Your wishes are all moderate."

"As moderate as those of the rest of the world, I believe. I wish as well as everybody else to be perfectly happy; but, like everybody else it must be in my own way. Greatness will not make me so."

"Strange that it would!" cried Marianne. "What have wealth or grandeur to do with happiness?"

"Grandeur has but little," said Elinor, "but wealth has much to do with it."

"Elinor, for shame!" said Marianne, "money can only give happiness where there is nothing else to give it. Beyond a competence, it can afford no real satisfaction, as far as mere self is concerned."

"Perhaps," said Elinor, smiling, "we may come to the same point. *Your* competence and *my* wealth are very much alike, I dare say; and without them, as the world goes now, we shall both agree that every kind of external comfort must be wanting. Come, what is your competence?"

"About eighteen hundred or two thousand a year; not more than *that*."

Elinor laughed. "*Two* thousand a year! *One* is my wealth! I guessed how it would end."

"And yet two thousand a-year is a very moderate income," said Marianne. "A proper establishment of servants, a carriage, perhaps two, and hunters, cannot be supported on less."

Elinor smiled again, to hear her sister describing so accurately their future expenses at Combe Magna.

"Hunters!" repeated Edward–"but why must you have hunters? Everybody does not hunt."

Marianne coloured as she replied, "But most people do."

"I wish," said Margaret, striking out a novel thought, "that somebody would give us all a large fortune apiece!"

"Oh that they would!" cried Marianne, her eyes sparkling with animation.

"I should be puzzled to spend so large a fortune myself," said Mrs. Dashwood, "if my children were all to be rich without my help."

"You must begin your improvements on this house," observed Elinor, "and your difficulties will soon vanish."

"What magnificent orders would travel from this family to London," said Edward, "in such an event! What a happy day for booksellers, music-sellers, and print-shops! You, Miss Dashwood, would give a general commission for every new print of merit to be sent you—and as for Marianne, I know her greatness of soul, there would not be music enough in London to content her. And books! Thomson, Cowper, Scott—she would buy them all over and over again: Should not you, Marianne? Forgive me, if I am very saucy. But I was willing to show you that I had not forgot our old disputes."

"I love to be reminded of the past, Edward. You are very right in supposing how my money would be spent—some of it, at least—my loose cash would certainly be employed in improving my collection of music and books."

"And the bulk of your fortune would be laid out in annuities on the authors or their heirs."

"No, Edward, I should have something else to do with it."

"Perhaps, then, you would bestow it as a reward on that person who wrote the ablest defence of your favourite maxim, that no one can ever be in love more than once in their life—your opinion on that point is unchanged, I presume?"

"Undoubtedly. At my time of life opinions are tolerably fixed. It is not likely that I should now see or hear anything to change them."

"Marianne is as steadfast as ever, you see," said Elinor, "she is not at all altered."

"She is only grown a little more grave than she was."

"Nay, Edward," said Marianne, "*you* need not reproach me. You are not very gay yourself."

"Why should you think so!" replied he, with a sigh. "But gaiety never was a part of *my* character."

"Nor do I think it a part of Marianne's," said Elinor; "I should hardly call her a lively girl—she is very earnest, very eager in all she does—sometimes talks a great deal and always with animation—but she is not often really merry."

"I believe you are right," he replied, "and yet I have always set her down as a lively girl."

"I have frequently detected myself in such kind of mistakes," said Elinor, "in a total misapprehension of character in some point or other. Sometimes one is guided by what they say of themselves, and very frequently by what other people say of them, without giving oneself time to deliberate and judge."

"But I thought it was right, Elinor," said Marianne, "to be guided wholly by the opinion of other people. I thought our judgments were given us merely to be subservient to those of neighbours. This has always been your doctrine, I am sure."

"No, Marianne, never. My doctrine has never aimed at the subjection of the understanding. All I have ever attempted to influence has been the behaviour. You must not confound my meaning. I am guilty, I confess, of having often wished you to treat our acquaintance in general with greater attention; but when have I advised you to adopt their sentiments or to conform to their judgment in serious matters?"

"You have not been able to bring your sister over to your plan of general civility," said Edward to Elinor, "Do you gain no ground?"

"Quite the contrary," replied Elinor, looking expressively at Marianne.

"My judgment," he returned, "is all on your side of the question; but I am afraid my practice is much more on your sister's. I never wish to offend, but I am so foolishly shy, that I often seem negligent, when I am only kept back by my natural awkwardness."

"Marianne has not shyness to excuse any inattention of hers," said Elinor.

"She knows her own worth too well for false shame," replied

77

Edward. "Shyness is only the effect of a sense of inferiority in some way or other. If I could persuade myself that my manners were perfectly easy and graceful, I should not be shy."

"But you would still be reserved," said Marianne, "and that is worse."

Edward started—"Reserved! Am I reserved, Marianne?"

"Yes, very."

"I do not understand you," replied he, colouring. "Reserved!—how, in what manner? What am I to tell you? What can you suppose?"

Elinor looked surprised at his emotion; but trying to laugh off the subject, she said to him, "Do not you know my sister well enough to understand what she means? Do not you know she calls every one reserved who does not talk as fast, and admire what she admires as rapturously as herself?"

Edward made no answer. His gravity and thoughtfulness returned on him in their fullest extent—and he sat for some time silent and dull.

Chapter 18

Elinor saw, with great uneasiness the low spirits of her friend. It was evident that he was unhappy; she wished it were equally evident that he still distinguished her by the same affection which once she had felt no doubt of inspiring; but the reservedness of his manner towards her contradicted one moment what a more animated look had intimated the preceding one.

He joined her and Marianne in the breakfast-room the next morning before the others were down; and Marianne, who was always eager to promote their happiness as far as she could, soon left them to themselves. But before she was half way upstairs she heard the parlour door open, and, turning round, was astonished to see Edward himself come out.

"I am going into the village to see my horses," said he, "I shall be back again presently."

Edward returned to them with fresh admiration of the surrounding country; in his walk to the village, he had seen many parts of the valley to advantage. This was a subject which ensured Marianne's attention, and she was beginning to describe her own admiration of these scenes, when Edward interrupted her by saying, "You must not enquire too far, Marianne—remember I have no knowledge in the picturesque, and I shall offend you by my ignorance and want of taste if we come to particulars. You must be satisfied with such admiration as I can honestly give. I call it a very fine country—the hills are steep, the woods seem full of fine timber, and the valley looks comfortable and snug. I can easily believe it to be full of rocks and promontories, grey moss and brush wood, but these are all lost on me. I know nothing of the picturesque."

"I am afraid it is but too true," said Marianne; "but why should you boast of it?"

"I suspect," said Elinor, "that to avoid one kind of affectation, Edward here falls into another. Because he believes many people pretend to more admiration of the beauties of nature than they really feel, and is disgusted with such pretensions, he affects greater indifference and less discrimination in viewing them himself than he possesses."

"It is very true," said Marianne, "that admiration of landscape scenery is become a mere jargon. Sometimes I have kept my feelings to myself, because I could find no language to describe them in but what was worn and hackneyed out of all sense and meaning."

"I am convinced," said Edward, "that you really feel all the delight in a fine prospect which you profess to feel. I like a fine prospect, but not on picturesque principles. I do not like crooked, twisted, blasted trees. I admire them much more if they are tall, straight, and flourishing. I do not like ruined, tattered cottages, and a troop of tidy, happy villages please me better than the finest banditti in the world."

The subject was continued no further; and Marianne remained thoughtfully silent, till a new object suddenly engaged her attention. She was sitting by Edward, and in taking his tea from Mrs. Dashwood, his hand passed so directly before her, as to make a ring, with a plait of hair in the centre, very conspicuous on one of his fingers.

"I never saw you wear a ring before, Edward," she cried. "Is that Fanny's hair? I remember her promising to give you some. But I should have thought her hair had been darker."

He coloured very deeply, and giving a momentary glance at Elinor, replied, "Yes; it is my sister's hair. The setting always casts a different shade on it, you know."

Elinor had met his eye, and looked conscious likewise. That the hair was her own, she instantaneously felt as well satisfied as Marianne; the only difference in their conclusions was, that what Marianne considered as a free gift from her sister, Elinor was conscious must have been procured by some theft or contrivance unknown to herself. She was not in a humour, however, to regard it as an affront, and affecting to take no notice of what passed, by instantly talking of something else.

Edward was particularly grave the whole morning. Marianne severely censured herself for what she had said; but her own forgiveness might have been more speedy had she known how little offence it had given her sister.

Before the middle of the day, they were visited by Sir John and Mrs. Jennings, who came to take a survey of the guest. With the assistance of his mother-in-law, Sir John was not long in discovering that the name of Ferrars began with an F. And this prepared a future mine of raillery against the devoted Elinor, which nothing but the newness of their acquaintance with Edward could have prevented from being immediately sprung.

"You *must* drink tea with us tonight," said he, "for we shall be quite alone—and tomorrow you must absolutely dine with us, for we shall be a large party."

Mrs. Jennings enforced the necessity. "And who knows but you may raise a dance," said she. "And that will tempt *you*, Miss Marianne."

"A dance!" cried Marianne. "Impossible! Who is to dance?"

"Who! Why yourselves, and the Careys, and Whitakers to be sure. What! You thought nobody could dance because a certain person that shall be nameless is gone!"

"I wish with all my soul," cried Sir John, "that Willoughby were among us again."

This, and Marianne's blushing, gave new suspicions to Edward. "And who is Willoughby?" said he, in a low voice, to Miss Dashwood, by whom he was sitting.

She gave him a brief reply. Edward saw enough to comprehend, not only the meaning of others, but such of Marianne's expressions as had puzzled him before; and when their visitors left them, he went immediately round her, and said, in a whisper, "I have been guessing. Shall I tell you my guess?"

"Certainly."

"Well then; I guess that Mr. Willoughby hunts."

Marianne was surprised and confused, yet she could not help smiling at the quiet archness of his manner, and after a moment's silence, said,

"Oh, Edward! How can you?—But the time will come I hope . . . I am sure you will like him."

"I do not doubt it," replied he.

Chapter 19

Edward remained a week at the cottage; he was earnestly pressed by Mrs. Dashwood to stay longer; but he seemed resolved to be gone when his enjoyment among his friends was at the height. His spirits, during the last two or three days, though still very unequal, were greatly improved—he grew more and more partial to the house and environs—never spoke of going away without a sigh—declared his time to be wholly disengaged—even doubted to what place he should go when he left them—but still, go he must. He valued their kindness beyond anything, and his greatest happiness was in being with them. Yet, he must leave them at the end of a week, in spite of their wishes and his own, and without any restraint on his time.

Elinor placed all that was astonishing in this way of acting to his mother's account; and it was happy for her that he had a mother whose character was so imperfectly known to her, as to be the general excuse for everything strange on the part of her son. His want of spirits, of openness, and of consistency, were most usually attributed to his want of independence, and his better knowledge of Mrs. Ferrars's disposition and designs. The old well-established grievance of duty against will, parent against child, was the cause of all. She would have been glad to know when these difficulties were to cease, when Mrs. Ferrars would be reformed, and her son be at liberty to be happy. But from such vain wishes she was forced to turn for comfort to the renewal of her confidence in Edward's affection.

"I think, Edward," said Mrs. Dashwood, as they were at breakfast the last morning, "you would be a happier man if you had any profession to engage your time and give an interest to your plans and actions. Some inconvenience to your friends, indeed, might result from it—you would not be able to give them so much of your time. But you would know where to go when you left them."

"I do assure you," he replied, "that I have long thought on this point, as you think now. It has been, and is, and probably will always be a heavy misfortune to me, that I have had no necessary business to engage me, no profession to give me employment, or afford me anything like independence. I always preferred the church, as I still do. But that was not smart enough for my family. They recommended the army. That was a great deal too smart for me. The law was allowed to be genteel enough but I had no inclination for the law, even in this less abstruse study of it, which my family approved. I was therefore entered at Oxford and have been properly idle ever since."

"The consequence of which, I suppose, will be," said Mrs. Dashwood, "that your sons will be brought up to as many pursuits, employments, professions, and trades as Columella's."

"They will be brought up," said he, in a serious accent, "to be as unlike myself as is possible.

"Come, come, Edward. You are in a melancholy humour, and fancy that any one unlike yourself must be happy. But remember that the pain of parting from friends will be felt by everybody at times, whatever be their education or state. Know your own happiness. Your mother will secure to you, in time, that independence you are so anxious for. How much may not a few months do?"

"I think," replied Edward, "that I may defy many months to produce any good to me."

This desponding turn of mind gave additional pain to them all in the parting, which shortly took place, and left an uncomfortable impression on Elinor's feelings especially, which required some trouble and time to subdue. But she did not adopt the method so judiciously employed by Marianne, on a similar occasion, to augment and fix her sorrow, by seeking silence, solitude and idleness.

Elinor sat down to her drawing-table as soon as he was out of the house, busily employed herself the whole day, appearing to interest herself almost as much as ever in the general concerns of the family, and if, by this conduct, she did not lessen her own grief, it was at least prevented from unnecessary increase, and her mother and sisters were spared much solicitude on her account.

Without shutting herself up from her family, or leaving the house in determined solitude to avoid them, Elinor found every day afforded her leisure enough to think of Edward, and of Edward's behaviour, in every possible variety which the different state of her spirits at different times could produce: with tenderness, pity, approbation, censure, and doubt. Her thoughts could not be chained elsewhere; and the past and the future, on a subject so interesting, must be before her, must force her attention, and engross her memory, her reflection, and her fancy.

From a reverie of this kind, as she sat at her drawing-table, she was roused one morning, soon after Edward's leaving them, by the arrival of company. The closing of the little gate drew her eyes to the window, and she saw a large party walking up to the door. Amongst them were Sir John and Lady Middleton and Mrs. Jennings, but there were two others, a gentleman and lady, who were quite unknown to her. As soon as Sir John perceived her, he left the rest of the party to the ceremony of knocking at the door, and stepping across the turf, obliged her to open the casement to speak to him.

"Well," said he, "We have brought you some strangers. How do you like them?"

"Hush! They will hear you."

"Never mind if they do. It is only the Palmers. Charlotte is very pretty, I can tell you. You may see her if you look this way."

They were now joined by Mrs. Jennings, who came hallooing to the window, "How do you do, my dear? How does Mrs. Dashwood do? And where are your sisters? What! All alone! You will be glad of a little company to sit with you. I have brought my other son and daughter to see you. I thought I heard a carriage last night, while we were drinking our tea, but it never entered my head that it could be them. I said to Sir John, I do think I hear a carriage; perhaps it is Colonel Brandon come back again—"

Elinor was obliged to turn from her, in the middle of her story, to receive the rest of the party; Lady Middleton introduced the two strangers; Mrs. Dashwood and Margaret came down stairs at the same time, and they all sat down to look at one another.

Mrs. Palmer was several years younger than Lady Middleton, and totally unlike her in every respect. She was short and plump, had a very pretty face, and the finest expression of good humour in it that could possibly be. She came in with a smile, smiled all the time of her visit, except when she laughed, and smiled when she went away. Her husband was a grave looking young man of five or six and twenty. He entered the room with a look of self-consequence, slightly bowed to the ladies, without speaking a word, and, after briefly surveying them and their apartments, took up a newspaper from the table, and continued to read it as long as he stayed.

Mrs. Palmer, on the contrary, was hardly seated before her admiration of the parlour and everything in it burst forth.

"Well! What a delightful room this is! I never saw anything so charming! Only think, sister, how delightful everything is! How I should like such a house for myself! Should not you, Mr. Palmer?"

Mr. Palmer made her no answer, and did not even raise his eyes from the newspaper.

Mrs. Jennings, in the meantime, talked on as loud as she could, and continued her account of their surprise, the evening before, on seeing their friends, without ceasing till everything was told. Mrs. Palmer laughed heartily at the recollection of their astonishment, and everybody agreed, two or three times over, that it had been quite an agreeable surprise.

"You may believe how glad we all were to see them," added Mrs. Jennings, leaning forward towards Elinor, "but, however, I can't help wishing they had not made such a long journey of it, for they came all round by London upon account of some business, for you know (nodding significantly and pointing to her daughter) it was wrong in her situation. I wanted her to stay at home and rest this morning, but she would come with us; she longed so much to see you all!"

Mrs. Palmer laughed, and said it would not do her any harm.

"She expects to be confined in February," continued Mrs. Jennings.

"Here comes Marianne," cried Sir John. "Now, Palmer, you shall see a monstrous pretty girl."

He immediately went into the passage, opened the front door, and ushered her in himself. Mr. Palmer looked up on her entering the room, stared at her some minutes, and then returned to his newspaper. Mrs. Palmer's eye was now caught by the drawings which hung round the room. She got up to examine them.

"Oh, dear! How beautiful these are! Do but look, mama, how sweet! I could look at them forever." And then sitting down again, she very soon forgot that there were any such things in the room.

When Lady Middleton rose to go away, Mr. Palmer rose also,

laid down the newspaper, stretched himself and looked at them all around.

"My love, have you been asleep?" said his wife, laughing.

He made her no answer; and only observed, after again examining the room, that it was very low pitched, and that the ceiling was crooked. He then made his bow, and departed with the rest.

Sir John had been very urgent with them all to spend the next day at the park. Mrs. Dashwood, absolutely refused on her own account; her daughters might do as they pleased They attempted, therefore, likewise, to excuse themselves; the weather was uncertain, and not likely to be good. But Sir John would not be satisfied—the carriage should be sent for them and they must come. Lady Middleton too, though she did not press their mother, pressed them. Mrs. Jennings and Mrs. Palmer joined their entreaties, all seemed equally anxious to avoid a family party; and the young ladies were obliged to yield.

"Why should they ask us?" said Marianne, as soon as they were gone. "The rent of this cottage is said to be low; but we have it on very hard terms, if we are to dine at the park whenever any one is staying either with them, or with us."

"They mean no less to be civil and kind to us now," said Elinor, "by these frequent invitations, than by those which we received from them a few weeks ago. The alteration is not in them, if their parties are grown tedious and dull. We must look for the change elsewhere."

Chapter 20

As the Miss Dashwoods entered the drawing-room of the park the next day, at one door, Mrs. Palmer came running in at the other, looking as good-humoured and merry as before.

"I am so glad to see you!" said she, seating herself between Elinor and Marianne, "for it is so bad a day I was afraid you might not come, which would be a shocking thing, as we go away again tomorrow. I am so sorry we cannot stay longer; however we shall meet again in town very soon, I hope."

They were obliged to put an end to such an expectation.

"Not go to town!" cried Mrs. Palmer, with a laugh, "I shall be quite disappointed if you do not. I could get the nicest house in world for you, next door to ours, in Hanover-square."

They thanked her; but were obliged to resist all her entreaties.

"Oh, my love," cried Mrs. Palmer to her husband, who just then entered the room—"you must help me to persuade the Miss Dashwoods to go to town this winter."

Her love made no answer; and after slightly bowing to the ladies, began complaining of the weather.

"How horrid all this is!" said he. "Such weather makes everything and everybody disgusting. Dullness is as much produced within doors as without, by rain. What the devil does Sir John mean by not having a billiard room in his house?"

The rest of the company soon dropt in.

"I am afraid, Miss Marianne," said Sir John, "you have not been able to take your usual walk to Allenham today."

Marianne looked very grave and said nothing.

"Oh, don't be so sly before us," said Mrs. Palmer; "for we know all about it, I assure you; and I admire your taste very much, for I think he is extremely handsome. We do not live a great way from him in the country, you know. I never was at his house; but they say it is a sweet pretty place."

"As vile a spot as I ever saw in my life," said Mr. Palmer.

Marianne remained perfectly silent, though her countenance betrayed her interest in what was said.

"Is it very ugly?" continued Mrs. Palmer—"then it must be some other place that is so pretty I suppose."

When they were seated in the dining room, Sir John observed with regret that they were only eight all together.

"My dear," said he to his lady, "it is very provoking that we should be so few. Why did not you ask the Gilberts to come to us today?"

"Did not I tell you, Sir John, when you spoke to me about it before, that it could not be done? They dined with us last."

"You and I, Sir John," said Mrs. Jennings, "should not stand upon such ceremony."

"Then you would be very ill-bred," cried Mr. Palmer.

"My love you contradict everybody," said his wife with her usual laugh. "Do you know that you are quite rude?"

"I did not know I contradicted anybody in calling your mother ill-bred."

"Ay, you may abuse me as you please," said the good-natured old lady, "you have taken Charlotte off my hands, and cannot give her back again.

Charlotte laughed heartily to think that her husband could not get rid of her; and exultingly said, she did not care how cross he was to her, as they must live together. The studied indifference, insolence, and discontent of her husband gave her no pain; and when he scolded or abused her, she was highly diverted.

"Mr. Palmer is so droll!" said she, in a whisper, to Elinor. "He is always out of humour."

Elinor was not inclined, after a little observation, to give him credit for being so genuinely and unaffectedly ill-natured or ill-bred as he wished to appear. His temper might perhaps be a little soured by finding, like many others of his sex, that through some unaccountable bias in favour of beauty, he was the husband of a very silly woman, but she knew that this kind of blunder was too common for any sensible man to be lastingly hurt by it. It was rather a wish of distinction, she believed, which produced his contemptuous treatment of everybody, and his general abuse of everything before him. It was the desire of appearing superior to other people.

"Oh, my dear Miss Dashwood," said Mrs. Palmer soon afterwards, "Will you come and spend some time at Cleveland this Christmas? Now, pray do—and come while the Westons are with us. My love," applying to her husband, "don't you long to have the Miss Dashwoods come to Cleveland?"

They both eagerly and resolutely declined her invitation.

"But indeed you must and shall come. You cannot think what a sweet place Cleveland is; and we are so gay now, for Mr. Palmer is always going about the country canvassing against the election. But, poor fellow! It is very fatiguing to him, for he is forced to make everybody like him."

Elinor could hardly keep her countenance as she assented to the hardship of such an obligation.

"How charming it will be," said Charlotte, "when he is in Parliament! Won't it? But do you know, he says, he will never frank for me? He declares he won't. Don't you, Mr. Palmer?"

Mr. Palmer took no notice of her.

"He cannot bear writing, you know," she continued, "he says it is quite shocking."

"No," said he, "I never said anything so irrational. Don't palm all your abuses of languages upon me."

"There now; you see how droll he is. Sometimes he won't speak to me for half a day together, and then he comes out with something so droll—all about anything in the world."

She surprised Elinor very much as they returned into the drawing-room, by asking her whether she did not like Mr. Palmer excessively.

"Certainly," said Elinor; "he seems very agreeable."

"Well—I am so glad you do. Mr. Palmer is excessively pleased with you and your sisters I can tell you, and you can't think how disappointed he will be if you don't come to Cleveland."

Elinor was again obliged to decline her invitation; and by changing the subject, put a stop to her entreaties. She thought it probable that as they lived in the same county, Mrs. Palmer might be able to give some more particular account of Willoughby's general character, than could be gathered from the Middletons' partial acquaintance with him. She began by inquiring if they saw much of Mr. Willoughby at Cleveland, and whether they were intimately acquainted with him.

"Oh dear, yes; I know him extremely well," replied Mrs. Palmer; "Not that I ever spoke to him, indeed; but I have seen him forever in town. Mama saw him here once before; but I was with my uncle at Weymouth. However, I dare say we should have seen a great deal of him in Somersetshire, if it had not happened very unluckily that we should never have been in the country together. I know why you inquire about him, very well; your sister is to marry him."

"My dear Mrs. Palmer!"

"Upon my honour, I did. I met Colonel Brandon Monday morning in Bond-street, just before we left town, and he told me of it directly."

"Colonel Brandon tell you of it! Surely you must be mistaken. To give such intelligence to a person who could not be interested in it, even if it were true, is not what I should expect Colonel Brandon to do."

"But I do assure you it was so. When we met him, we began talking of my brother and sister, and one thing and another, and I said to him, 'So, Colonel, there is a new family come to Barton cottage, I hear, and mama sends me word they are very pretty, and that one of them is going to be married to Mr. Willoughby of Combe Magna. Is it true, pray?'"

"And what did the Colonel say?"

"Oh—he did not say much; but he looked as if he knew it to be true."

"Mr. Brandon was very well, I hope?"

"Oh! Yes, quite well; and so full of your praises, he did nothing but say fine things of you."

"I am flattered by his commendation. He seems an excellent man; and I think him uncommonly pleasing."

"So do I. He is such a charming man, that it is quite a pity he should be so grave and so dull. Mama says *he* was in love with your sister too."

"Is Mr. Willoughby much known in your part of Somersetshire?" said Elinor.

"Oh! yes, extremely well. That is, I do not believe many people are acquainted with him, because Combe Magna is so far off; but they all think him extremely agreeable I assure you. Nobody is more liked than Mr. Willoughby wherever he goes, and so you may tell your sister."

Mrs. Palmer's information respecting Willoughby was not very material; but any testimony in his favour, however small, was pleasing to her.

"I am so glad we are got acquainted at last," continued Charlotte. "And now I hope we shall always be great friends. And

I am so glad your sister is going to be well married! I hope you will be a great deal at Combe Magna."

"You have been long acquainted with Colonel Brandon, have not you?"

"Yes, a great while; ever since my sister married. He was a particular friend of Sir John's. I believe," she added in a low voice, "he would have been very glad to have had me, if he could. But mama did not think the match good enough for me, otherwise Sir John would have mentioned it to the Colonel, and we should have been married immediately."

"Did not Colonel Brandon know of Sir John's proposal to your mother before it was made? Had he never owned his affection to yourself?"

"Oh, no! But if mama had not objected to it, I dare say he would have liked it of all things. However, I am much happier as I am. Mr. Palmer is the kind of man I like."

Chapter 21

The Palmers returned to Cleveland the next day, and the two families at Barton were again left to entertain each other. But this did not last long; Elinor had hardly got their last visitors out of her head before Sir John's and Mrs. Jennings's active zeal in the cause of society, procured her some other new acquaintance to see and observe.

In a morning's excursion to Exeter, they had met with two young ladies, whom Mrs. Jennings had the satisfaction of discovering to be her relations, and this was enough for Sir John to invite them directly to the park. Their engagements at Exeter instantly gave way before such an invitation, and Lady Middleton was thrown into no little alarm on the return of Sir John, by hearing that she was very soon to receive a visit from two girls whom she had never seen in her life, and of whose elegance, whose tolerable gentility even, she could have no proof. As it was impossible, however, now to prevent their coming, Lady Middleton resigned herself to the idea.

The young ladies arrived: their appearance was by no means ungenteel or unfashionable. Their dress was very smart, their manners very civil, they were delighted with the house, and in raptures with the furniture, and they happened to be so doatingly fond of children that Lady Middleton's good opinion was engaged in their favour before they had been an hour at the Park.

She declared them to be very agreeable girls indeed, which for her ladyship was enthusiastic admiration. Sir John's confidence in his own judgment rose with this animated praise, and he set off directly for the cottage to tell the Miss Dashwoods of the Miss Steeles' arrival, and to assure them of their being the sweetest girls in the world. Sir John wanted the whole family to walk to the Park directly and look at his guests. Benevolent, philanthropic man! It was painful to him even to keep a third cousin to himself.

"Do come now," said he, "You can't think how you will like them. Lucy is monstrous pretty, and so good humoured and agreeable! And they both long to see you of all things, for they have heard at Exeter that you are the most beautiful creatures in the world. How can you be so cross as not to come? Why they are your cousins, you know, after a fashion. *You* are my cousins, and they are my wife's, so you must be related."

But Sir John could not prevail. He could only obtain a promise of their calling at the Park within a day or two, and then left them in amazement at their indifference, to walk home and boast anew of their attractions to the Miss Steeles.

When their promised visit to the Park and consequent introduction to these young ladies took place, they found in the appearance of the eldest, who was nearly thirty, with a very plain and not a sensible face, nothing to admire; but in the other, who was not more than two or three and twenty, they acknowledged considerable beauty; her features were pretty, and she had a sharp quick eye, and a smartness of air, which gave distinction to her person. —Their manners were particularly civil, and Elinor saw with what constant and judicious attention they were making themselves agreeable to Lady Middleton. With her children they were in continual raptures, extolling their beauty, courting their notice, and humouring their whims; and such of their time as could be spared from the importunate demands which this politeness made on it, was spent in admiration of whatever her ladyship was doing, if she happened to be doing anything. Lady Middleton saw with maternal complacency all the impertinent encroachments and mischievous tricks to which her cousins submitted. She saw their sashes untied, their hair pulled about their ears, their work-bags searched, and their knives and scissors stolen away, and felt no doubt of its being a reciprocal enjoyment.

"John is in such spirits today!" said she, on his taking Miss Steeles's pocket handkerchief, and throwing it out of window. "He is full of monkey tricks."

"And here is my sweet little Annamaria," she added, tenderly caressing a little girl of three years old, who had not made a noise for the last two minutes; "And she is always so gentle and quiet— Never was there such a quiet little thing!"

But unfortunately in bestowing these embraces, a pin in her ladyship's head dress slightly scratching the child's neck, produced from this pattern of gentleness such violent screams, as could hardly be outdone by any creature professedly noisy. She was seated in her mother's lap, covered with kisses, her wound bathed with lavender-water, by one of the Miss Steeles, who was on her knees to attend her, and her mouth stuffed with sugar plums by the other. She still screamed and sobbed lustily, till Lady Middleton luckily remembering that in a scene of similar distress last week, some apricot marmalade had been successfully applied for a bruised temple, the same remedy was eagerly proposed for this unfortunate scratch, and a slight intermission of screams in the young lady on hearing it, gave them reason to hope that it would not be rejected. She was carried out of the room therefore in her mother's arms, in quest of this medicine.

"Poor little creatures!" said Miss Steele, as soon as they were gone. "It might have been a very sad accident."

"Yet I hardly know how," cried Marianne, "unless it had been under totally different circumstances. But this is the usual way of heightening alarm, where there is nothing to be alarmed at in reality."

"What a sweet woman Lady Middleton is!" said Lucy Steele.

Marianne was silent; it was impossible for her to say what she did not feel, however trivial the occasion; and upon Elinor therefore the whole task of telling lies when politeness required it, always fell. She did her best when thus called on, by speaking of Lady Middleton with more warmth than she felt, though with far less than Miss Lucy.

"And Sir John too," cried the elder sister, "what a charming man he is! And what a charming little family they have! I never saw such fine children in my life. —I declare I quite dote upon them already, and indeed I am always distractedly fond of children."

"I should guess so," said Elinor, with a smile, "from what I have witnessed this morning."

"I have a notion," said Lucy, "you think the little Middletons rather too much indulged. For my part, I love to see children full of life and spirits; I cannot bear them if they are tame and quiet."

"I confess," replied Elinor, "that while I am at Barton Park, I never think of tame and quiet children with any abhorrence."

A short pause succeeded this speech, which was first broken by Miss Steele, who seemed very much disposed for conversation, and who now said rather abruptly, "And how do you like Devonshire, Miss Dashwood? I suppose you were very sorry to leave Sussex."

In some surprise at the familiarity of this question, Elinor replied that she was.

"Norland is a prodigious beautiful place, is not it?" added Miss Steele.

"We have heard Sir John admire it excessively," said Lucy, who seemed to think some apology necessary for the freedom of her sister.

"I think everyone *must* admire it," replied Elinor, "who ever saw the place."

"And had you a great many smart beaux there? I suppose you have not so many in this part of the world; for my part, I think they are a vast addition always."

"But why should you think," said Lucy, looking ashamed of her sister, "that there are not as many genteel young men in Devonshire as Sussex?"

"Nay, my dear, I'm sure I don't pretend to say that there aren't. I was only afraid the Miss Dashwoods might find it dull at Barton, if they had not so many as they used to have. But perhaps you young ladies may not care about the beaux. For my part, I think they are vastly agreeable, provided they dress smart and behave civil. I suppose your brother was quite a beau, Miss Dashwood, before he married, as he was so rich?"

"Upon my word," replied Elinor, "I cannot tell you, for I do not perfectly comprehend the meaning of the word. But this I can say, that if he ever was a beau before he married, he is one still for there is not the smallest alteration in him."

"Oh! dear! One never thinks of married men's being beaux— they have something else to do."

"Lord! Anne," cried her sister, "you can talk of nothing but beaux;—you will make Miss Dashwood believe you think of nothing else."

This specimen of the Miss Steeles was enough. The vulgar freedom and folly of the eldest left her no recommendation, and as Elinor was not blinded by the beauty, or the shrewd look of the youngest, to her want of real elegance and artlessness, she left the house without any wish of knowing them better.

Not so the Miss Steeles. They came from Exeter, well provided with admiration for the use of Sir John Middleton, his family, and all his relations, and no niggardly proportion was now dealt out to his fair cousins, whom they declared to be the most beautiful, elegant, accomplished, and agreeable girls they had ever beheld, and with whom they were particularly anxious to be better acquainted. And to be better acquainted therefore, Elinor soon found was their inevitable lot, for as Sir John was entirely on the side of the Miss Steeles, their party would be too strong for opposition, and that kind of intimacy must be submitted to, which consists of sitting an hour or two together in the same room almost every day.

To do him justice, he did everything in his power to promote their unreserve, by making the Miss Steeles acquainted with whatever he knew or supposed of his cousins' situations in the most delicate particulars, and Elinor had not seen them more than twice, before the eldest of them wished her joy on her sister's having been so lucky as to make a conquest of a very smart beau since she came to Barton.

"'Twill be a fine thing to have her married so young to be sure," said she, "And I hope you may have as good luck yourself soon, but perhaps you may have a friend in the corner already."

Elinor could not suppose that Sir John would be more nice in proclaiming his suspicions of her regard for Edward, than he had been with respect to Marianne; indeed it was rather his favourite joke of the two, as being somewhat newer and more conjectural; and since Edward's visit, they had never dined together without his drinking to her best affections with so much significancy and so many nods and winks, as to excite general attention. The letter F—had been likewise invariably brought forward, and found productive of such countless jokes, that its character as the wittiest letter in the alphabet had been long established with Elinor.

The Miss Steeles, as she expected, had now all the benefit of these jokes, and in the eldest of them they raised a curiosity to know the name of the gentleman alluded to. But Sir John did not sport long with the curiosity which he delighted to raise, for he had at least as much pleasure in telling the name, as Miss Steele had in hearing it.

"His name is Ferrars," said he, in a very audible whisper; "but pray do not tell it, for it's a great secret."

"Ferrars!" repeated Miss Steele; "Mr. Ferrars is the happy man, is he? What! your sister-in-law's brother, Miss Dashwood? a very agreeable young man to be sure; I know him very well."

"How can you say so, Anne?" cried Lucy, who generally made an amendment to all her sister's assertions. "Though we have seen him once or twice at my uncle's, it is rather too much to pretend to know him very well."

Elinor heard all this with attention and surprise. "And who was this uncle? Where did he live? How came they acquainted?" The manner in which Miss Steele had spoken of Edward, increased her curiosity; for it struck her as being rather ill-natured, and suggested the suspicion of that lady's knowing, or fancying herself to know something to his disadvantage.

Chapter 22

Marianne, who had never much toleration for anything like impertinence, vulgarity, inferiority of parts, or even difference of taste from herself, was at this time particularly ill-disposed, from the state of her spirits, to be pleased with the Miss Steeles, or to encourage their advances; and to the invariable coldness of her behaviour towards them, Elinor principally attributed that preference of herself which soon became evident in the manners of both, but especially of Lucy, who missed no opportunity of striving to improve their acquaintance by an easy and frank communication of her sentiments.

Lucy was naturally clever; her remarks were often just and amusing; and as a companion for half an hour Elinor frequently found her agreeable; but her powers had received no aid from education: she was ignorant and illiterate; and her deficiency of all mental improvement, could not be concealed from Miss Dashwood. Elinor saw, and pitied her for, the neglect of abilities which education might have rendered so respectable; but she saw, with less tenderness of feeling, the thorough want of delicacy, of rectitude, and integrity of mind, which her attentions, her assiduities, her flatteries at the Park betrayed; and she could have no lasting satisfaction in the company of a person who joined insincerity with ignorance.

"You will think my question an odd one, I dare say," said Lucy to her one day, as they were walking together from the park to the cottage—"but pray, are you personally acquainted with your sister-in-law's mother, Mrs. Ferrars?"

Elinor *did* think the question a very odd one, and her countenance expressed it, as she answered that she had never seen Mrs. Ferrars.

"Indeed!" replied Lucy; "I wonder at that, for I thought you must have seen her at Norland sometimes. Then, perhaps, you cannot tell me what sort of a woman she is?"

"No," returned Elinor, cautious of giving her real opinion of Edward's mother. "I know nothing of her."

"I am sure you think me very strange, for enquiring about her in such a way," said Lucy, eyeing Elinor attentively as she spoke; "but perhaps there may be reasons—I wish I might venture; but however I hope you will do me the justice of believing that I do not mean to be impertinent."

They walked on for a few minutes in silence. It was broken by Lucy, who renewed the subject again by saying, with some hesitation, "I cannot bear to have you think me impertinently curious. Indeed, I should be very glad of your advice how to manage in such an uncomfortable situation as I am; but, however, there is no occasion to trouble *you*. I am sorry you do not happen to know Mrs. Ferrars."

"I am sorry I do *not*," said Elinor, in great astonishment, "if it could be of any use to *you* to know my opinion of her. But really I never understood that you were at all connected with that family, and therefore I am a little surprised, I confess, at so serious an inquiry into her character."

"If I dared tell you all, you would not be so much surprised. Mrs. Ferrars is certainly nothing to me at present, but the time *may* come, how soon it will come must depend upon herself, when we may be very intimately connected."

She looked down as she said this, amiably bashful, with only one side glance at her companion to observe its effect on her.

"Good heavens!" cried Elinor, "what do you mean? Are you acquainted with Mr. Robert Ferrars? Can you be?"

"No," replied Lucy, "not to Mr. *Robert* Ferrars—but his eldest brother."

What felt Elinor at that moment? Astonishment, that would have been as painful as it was strong, had not an immediate disbelief of the assertion attended it.

"You may well be surprised," continued Lucy; "for to be sure you could have had no idea of it before; for I dare say he never dropped the smallest hint of it to you or any of your family; because it was always meant to be a great secret, and I am sure has been faithfully kept so by me to this hour. Not a soul of all my relations know of it but Anne, and I never should have mentioned it to you, if I had not felt the greatest dependence in the world upon your secrecy; and I really thought my behaviour in asking so many questions about Mrs. Ferrars must seem so odd, that it ought to be explained."

Elinor for a few moments remained silent. At length forcing herself to speak, and to speak cautiously, she said, with calmness of manner, which tolerably well concealed her surprise and solicitude. "May I ask if your engagement is of long standing?"

"We have been engaged these four years."

"I did not know," said she, "that you were even acquainted till the other day!"

"Our acquaintance, however, is of many years date. He was under my uncle's care, you know, a considerable while."

"Your uncle!"

"Yes; Mr. Pratt. Did you never hear him talk of Mr. Pratt?"

"I think I have," replied Elinor.

"He was four years with my uncle, who lives at Longstaple, near Plymouth. It was there our acquaintance began, and it was there our engagement was formed, though not till a year after he had quitted as a pupil. I was very unwilling to enter into it, as you may imagine, without the knowledge and approbation of his mother; but I was too young, and loved him too well, to be so prudent as I ought to have been. You must have seen enough of him to be sensible he is very capable of making a woman sincerely attached to him."

"Certainly," answered Elinor, without knowing what she said; but after a moment's reflection, she added, with revived security of Edward's honour and love, and her companion's falsehood. "Engaged to Mr. Edward Ferrars! I beg your pardon; but surely there must be some mistake of person or name. We cannot mean the same Mr. Ferrars."

"We can mean no other," cried Lucy, smiling. "Mr. Edward Ferrars, the eldest son of Mrs. Ferrars, of Park Street, and brother of your sister-in-law, Mrs. John Dashwood, is the person I mean."

"It is strange," replied Elinor, in a most painful perplexity, "that I should never have heard him even mention your name."

"Our first care has been to keep the matter secret. You knew nothing of me, or my family, and, therefore, there could be no *occasion* for ever mentioning my name to you."

She was silent. Elinor's security sunk; but her self-command did not sink with it.

"Four years you have been engaged," said she with a firm voice.

"Yes; and heaven knows how much longer we may have to wait. Poor Edward! It puts him quite out of heart." Then taking a small miniature from her pocket, she added, "To prevent the possibility of mistake, be so good as to look at this face."

She put it into her hands as she spoke; and when Elinor saw the painting, whatever other doubts her fear of a too hasty decision, or her wish of detecting falsehood might suffer to linger in her mind, she could have none of its being Edward's face. She returned it almost instantly, acknowledging the likeness.

"I have never been able," continued Lucy, "to give him my picture in return, which I am very much vexed at, for he has been always so anxious to get it! But I am determined to set for it the very first opportunity."

"You are quite in the right," replied Elinor calmly. They then proceeded a few paces in silence. Lucy spoke first.

"I am sure," said she, "I have no doubt in the world of your faithfully keeping this secret, because you must know of what importance it is to us, not to have it reach his mother."

"I certainly did not seek your confidence," said Elinor; "but you do me no more than justice in imagining that I may be depended on. Your secret is safe with me; but pardon me if I express some surprise at so unnecessary a communication. You must at least have felt that my being acquainted with it could not add to its safety."

"I was afraid you would think I was taking a great liberty with you," said she, "in telling you all this. I really thought some explanation was due to you after my making such particular inquiries about Edward's mother; and Anne is the only person that knows of it, and she has no judgment at all; indeed, she does me a great deal more harm than good, for I am in constant fear of her betraying me. I only wonder that I am alive after what I have suffered for Edward's sake these last four years. Everything in such suspense and uncertainty; and seeing him so seldom—we can hardly meet above twice a-year. I am sure I wonder my heart is not quite broke."

Here she took out her handkerchief; but Elinor did not feel very compassionate.

"Sometimes." continued Lucy, after wiping her eyes, "I think whether it would not be better for us both to break off the matter entirely." As she said this, she looked directly at her companion.

"But then at other times I have not resolution enough for it. I cannot bear the thoughts of making him so miserable, as I know the very mention of such a thing would do. What would you advise me to do in such a case, Miss Dashwood?"

"Pardon me," replied Elinor, startled by the question; "but I can give you no advice under such circumstances. Your own judgment must direct you."

"To be sure," continued Lucy, after a few minutes silence on both sides, "his mother must provide for him sometime or other; but poor Edward is so cast down by it! Did you not think him dreadful low-spirited when he was at Barton? He was so miserable when he left us at Longstaple, to go to you, that I was afraid you would think him quite ill."

"Did he come from your uncle's, then, when he visited us?"

"Oh, yes; he had been staying a fortnight with us. Did you think he came directly from town?"

"No," replied Elinor, most feelingly sensible of every fresh circumstance in favour of Lucy's veracity; "I remember he told us, that he had been staying a fortnight with some friends near Plymouth."

"Did not you think him sadly out of spirits?" repeated Lucy.

"We did, indeed, particularly so when he first arrived."

"Poor fellow! I am afraid it is just the same with him now; for he writes in wretched spirits. I heard from him just before I left Exeter;" taking a letter from her pocket and carelessly showing the direction to Elinor. "You know his hand, I dare say, a charming one it is; but that is not written so well as usual. He was tired, I dare say, for he had just filled the sheet to me as full as possible."

Elinor saw that it *was* his hand, and she could doubt no longer. For a few moments, she was almost overcome—her heart sunk within her, and she could hardly stand; but exertion was indispensably necessary; and she struggled so resolutely against the oppression of her feelings, that her success was speedy, and for the time complete.

"Writing to each other," said Lucy, returning the letter into her pocket, "is the only comfort we have in such long separations. Yes, I have one other comfort in his picture, but poor Edward has not even *that*. If he had but my picture, he says he should be easy. I gave him a lock of my hair set in a ring when he was at Longstaple last, and that was some comfort to him, he said, but not equal to a picture. Perhaps you might notice the ring when you saw him?"

"I did," said Elinor, with a composure of voice, under which was concealed an emotion and distress beyond anything she had ever felt before.

Fortunately for her, they had now reached the cottage, and the conversation could be continued no further. After sitting with them a few minutes, the Miss Steeles returned to the Park, and Elinor was then at liberty to think and be wretched.

Chapter 23

What Lucy had asserted to be true, therefore, Elinor could not, dared not longer doubt. Their opportunity of acquaintance in the house of Mr. Pratt was a foundation for the rest, at once indisputable and alarming; and Edward's visit near Plymouth, his melancholy state of mind, his dissatisfaction at his own prospects, his uncertain behaviour towards herself, the picture, the letter, the ring, formed altogether such a body of evidence, as overcame every fear of condemning him unfairly, and established as a fact, which no partiality could set aside, his ill-treatment of herself. Had Edward been intentionally deceiving her? Had he feigned a regard for her which he did not feel? Was his engagement to Lucy an engagement of the heart? No; whatever it might once have been, she could not believe it such at present. His affection was all her own. She could not be deceived in that. Her mother, sisters, Fanny, all had been conscious of his regard for her at Norland. He certainly loved her. He had been blamable, highly blamable, in remaining at Norland after he first felt her influence over him to be more than it ought to be. In that, he could not be defended; but if he had injured her, how much more had he injured himself; if her case were pitiable, his was hopeless. His imprudence had made her miserable for a while; but it seemed to have deprived himself of all chance of ever being otherwise. Could he ever be tolerably happy with Lucy Steele; could he, were his affection for herself out of the question, with his integrity, his delicacy, and well-informed mind, be satisfied with a wife like her—illiterate, artful, and selfish?

If in the supposition of his seeking to marry herself, his difficulties from his mother had seemed great, how much greater were they now likely to be, when the object of his engagement was undoubtedly inferior in connections, and probably inferior in fortune to herself.

As these considerations occurred to her in painful succession, she wept for him, more than for herself. Supported by the conviction of having done nothing to merit her present unhappiness, and consoled by the belief that Edward had done nothing to forfeit her esteem, she thought she could even now, command herself enough to guard every suspicion of the truth from her mother and sisters. And so well was she able to answer her own expectations, that when she joined them at dinner only two hours after she had first suffered the extinction of all her dearest hopes, no one would have supposed from the appearance of the sisters, that Elinor was mourning in secret over obstacles which must divide her for ever from the object of her love, and that Marianne was internally dwelling on the perfections of a man, of whose whole heart she felt thoroughly possessed, and whom she expected to see in every carriage which drove near their house.

The necessity of concealing from her mother and Marianne, what had been entrusted in confidence to herself, though it obliged her to unceasing exertion, was no aggravation of Elinor's distress. On the contrary it was a relief to her, to be spared the communication of what would give such affliction to them, and to be saved likewise from hearing that condemnation of Edward, which would probably flow from the excess of their partial affection for herself.

She was stronger alone, and her own good sense so well

supported her, that her firmness was as unshaken, her appearance of cheerfulness as invariable, as with regrets so poignant and so fresh, it was possible for them to be.

Much as she had suffered from her first conversation with Lucy on the subject, she soon felt an earnest wish of renewing it. She particularly wanted to convince Lucy, by her readiness to enter on the matter again, and her calmness in conversing on it, that she was no otherwise interested in it than as a friend. That Lucy was disposed to be jealous of her appeared very probable: it was plain that Edward had always spoken highly in her praise, not merely from Lucy's assertion, but from her venturing to trust her on so short a personal acquaintance, with a secret so confessedly and evidently important. But indeed, while Elinor remained so well assured within herself of being really beloved by Edward, it required no other consideration of probabilities to make it natural that Lucy should be jealous. What other reason for the disclosure of the affair could there be, but that Elinor might be informed by it of Lucy's superior claims on Edward, and be taught to avoid him in future? She had little difficulty in understanding thus much of her rival's intentions, and while she was firmly resolved to act by her as every principle of honour and honesty directed, to combat her own affection for Edward and to see him as little as possible; she could not deny herself the comfort of endeavouring to convince Lucy that her heart was unwounded. And as she could now have nothing more painful to hear on the subject than had already been told, she did not mistrust her own ability of going through a repetition of particulars with composure.

But it was not immediately that an opportunity of doing so could be commanded; for the weather was not often fine enough to allow of their joining in a walk, where they might most easily separate themselves from the others; and though they met at least every other evening either at the park or cottage, and chiefly at the former, they could not be supposed to meet for the sake of conversation.

One or two meetings of this kind had taken place, without affording Elinor any chance of engaging Lucy in private, when Sir John called at the cottage one morning, to beg that they would all dine with Lady Middleton that day, as he was obliged to attend the club at Exeter. Elinor, who foresaw a fairer opening for the point she had in view, in such a party as this was likely to be, more at liberty among themselves under the tranquil and well-bred direction of Lady Middleton than when her husband united them together in one noisy purpose, immediately accepted the invitation; Margaret, with her mother's permission, was equally compliant, and Marianne, though always unwilling to join any of their parties, was persuaded by her mother, who could not bear to have her seclude herself from any chance of amusement, to go likewise.

The insipidity of the meeting was exactly such as Elinor had expected; and nothing could be less interesting than the whole of their discourse both in the dining parlour and drawing room: to the latter, the children accompanied them, and while they remained there, she was too well convinced of the impossibility of engaging Lucy's attention to attempt it. They quitted it only with the removal of the tea-things. The card-table was then placed, and Elinor began to wonder at herself for having ever entertained a hope of finding time for conversation at the park.

"I am glad," said Lady Middleton to Lucy, "you are not going to finish poor little Annamaria's basket this evening; for I am sure it must hurt your eyes to work filigree by candlelight. And we will make the dear little love some amends for her disappointment to-morrow."

Lucy recollected herself instantly and replied, "Indeed you are very much mistaken, Lady Middleton; I am only waiting to know whether you can make your party without me, or I should have been at my filigree already."

"You are very good, I hope it won't hurt your eyes—will you ring the bell for some working candles."

Lucy directly drew her work table near her and reseated herself with an alacrity and cheerfulness which seemed to infer that she could taste no greater delight than in making a filigree basket for a spoilt child.

Lady Middleton proposed a rubber of Casino to the others. No one made any objection but Marianne, who with her usual inattention to the forms of general civility, exclaimed, "Your Ladyship will have the goodness to excuse *me*—you know I detest cards. I shall go to the piano-forte; I have not touched it since it was tuned

Lady Middleton looked as if she thanked heaven that *she* had never made so rude a speech.

The remaining five were now to draw their cards.

"Perhaps," continued Elinor, "if I should happen to cut out, I may be of some use to Miss Lucy Steele, in rolling her papers for her; and there is so much still to be done to the basket, that it must be impossible I think for her labour singly, to finish it this evening."

"Indeed I shall be very much obliged to you for your help," cried Lucy, "for I find there is more to be done to it than I thought there was."

"Oh! that would be terrible, indeed," said Miss Steele— "Dear little soul, how I do love her!"

"You are very kind," said Lady Middleton to Elinor; "and as you really like the work, perhaps you will be as well pleased not to cut in till another rubber, or will you take your chance now?"

Elinor joyfully profited by the first of these proposals. Lucy made room for her with ready attention, and the two fair rivals were thus seated side by side at the same table, and, with the utmost harmony, engaged in forwarding the same work. The pianoforte at which Marianne, wrapped up in her own music and her own thoughts, had by this time forgotten that any body was in the room besides herself, was luckily so near them that Miss Dashwood now judged she might safely, under the shelter of its noise, introduce the interesting subject, without any risk of being heard at the card-table.

Chapter 24

In a firm, though cautious tone, Elinor thus began.

"I should be undeserving of the confidence you have honoured me with, if I felt no desire for its continuance, or no farther curiosity on its subject. I will not apologize therefore for bringing it forward again."

"Thank you," cried Lucy warmly, "for breaking the ice; you have set my heart at ease by it; for I was somehow or other afraid I had offended you by what I told you."

"Offended me! How could you suppose so? Believe me," and Elinor spoke it with the truest sincerity, "nothing could be further from my intention than to give you such an idea."

"And yet I do assure you," replied Lucy, her little sharp eyes full of meaning, "there seemed to me to be a coldness and displeasure in your manner that made me quite uncomfortable. But I am very glad to find it was only my own fancy, and that you really do not blame me. If you knew what a consolation it was to me to relieve my heart speaking to you of what I am always thinking of every moment of my life."

"Indeed, I can easily believe that it was a very great relief to you, to acknowledge your situation to me, and be assured that you shall never have reason to repent it. You seem to me to be surrounded with difficulties, and you will have need of all your mutual affection to support you under them. Mr. Ferrars, I believe, is entirely dependent on his mother."

"He has only two thousand pounds of his own; it would be madness to marry upon that, though for my own part, I could give up every prospect of more without a sigh. I have been always used to a very small income, and could struggle with any poverty for him; but I love him too well to be the selfish means of robbing him, perhaps, of all that his mother might give him if he married to please her. We must wait, it may be for many years. With almost every other man in the world, it would be an alarming prospect; but Edward's affection and constancy nothing can deprive me of I know."

"That conviction must be everything to you; and he is undoubtedly supported by the same trust in yours."

"Edward's love for me," said Lucy, "has been pretty well put to the test, by our long, very long absence since we were first engaged. I can safely say that he has never gave me one moment's alarm on that account from the first."

Elinor hardly knew whether to smile or sigh at this assertion.

Lucy went on. "I am rather of a jealous temper too by nature, and our continual separation, I was enough inclined for suspicion, to have found out the truth in an instant, if there had been the slightest alteration in his behaviour to me when we met."

"All this," thought Elinor, "is very pretty; but it can impose upon neither of us."

"But what," said she after a short silence, "are your views? or have you none but that of waiting for Mrs. Ferrars's death. Is her son determined to submit to this, and to all the tediousness of the many years of suspense in which it may involve you, rather than run the risk of her displeasure for a while by owning the truth?"

"If we could be certain that it would be only for a while! But Mrs. Ferrars is a very headstrong proud woman, and in her first fit of anger upon hearing it, would very likely secure everything to Robert, and the idea of that, for Edward's sake, frightens away all my inclination for hasty measures."

"And for your own sake too, or you are carrying your disinterestedness beyond reason."

Lucy looked at Elinor again, and was silent.

"Do you know Mr. Robert Ferrars?" asked Elinor.

"Not at all—I never saw him; but I fancy he is very unlike his brother—silly and a great coxcomb."

"A great coxcomb!" repeated Miss Steele, whose ear had caught those words by a sudden pause in Marianne's music. "Oh, they are talking of their favourite beaux, I dare say."

"No sister," cried Lucy, "you are mistaken there, our favourite beaux are *not* great coxcombs."

"I can answer for it that Miss Dashwood's is not," said Mrs. Jennings, laughing heartily; "for he is one of the modestest, prettiest-behaved young men I ever saw; but as for Lucy, she is such a sly little creature, there is no finding out who *she* likes."

"Oh," cried Miss Steele, looking significantly round at them, "I dare say Lucy's beau is quite as modest and pretty behaved as Miss Dashwood's."

Elinor blushed in spite of herself. Lucy bit her lip, and looked angrily at her sister. A mutual silence took place for some time. Lucy first put an end to it by saying in a lower tone—

"I will honestly tell you of one scheme which has lately come into my head. I dare say you have seen enough of Edward to know that he would prefer the church to every other profession; now my plan is that he should take orders as soon as he can, and then through your interest, which I am sure you would be kind enough to use out of friendship for him, your brother might be persuaded to give him Norland living. That would be enough for us to marry upon, and we might trust to time and chance for the rest."

"I should always be happy," replied Elinor, "to show any mark of my esteem and friendship for Mr. Ferrars; but do you not perceive that my interest on such an occasion would be perfectly unnecessary? He is brother to Mrs. John Dashwood—*that* must be recommendation enough to her husband."

"But Mrs. John Dashwood would not much approve of Edward's going into orders."

"Then I rather suspect that my interest would do very little."

They were again silent for many minutes. At length Lucy exclaimed with a deep sigh, "I believe it would be the wisest way to put an end to the business at once by dissolving the engagement. We seem so beset with difficulties on every side, that though it would make us miserable for a time, we should be happier perhaps in the end. But you will not give me your advice, Miss Dashwood?"

"No," answered Elinor, with a smile, which concealed very agitated feelings, "You know very well that my opinion would have no weight with you, unless it were on the side of your wishes."

"Indeed you wrong me," replied Lucy, with great solemnity; "I do really believe, that if you was to say to me, 'I advise you by all means to put an end to your engagement with Edward Ferrars, it will be more for the happiness of both of you,' I should resolve upon doing it immediately."

Elinor blushed for the insincerity of Edward's future wife, and replied, "This compliment would effectually frighten me from giving any opinion on the subject had I formed one. It raises my influence much too high; the power of dividing two people so tenderly attached is too much for an indifferent person."

"'Tis because you are an indifferent person," said Lucy, with some pique, "that your judgment might justly have such weight with me."

Another pause therefore of many minutes' duration, succeeded this speech, and Lucy was still the first to end it.

"Shall you be in town this winter, Miss Dashwood?" said she.

"Certainly not."

"I am sorry for that," returned the other, while her eyes brightened at the information, "it would have gave me such pleasure to meet you there! But I dare say you will go for all that. To be sure, your brother and sister will ask you to come to them."

"It will not be in my power to accept their invitation if they do."

"How unlucky that is! I had quite depended upon meeting you there. But I only go for the sake of seeing Edward. He will be there in February."

Elinor was soon called to the card-table by the conclusion of the first rubber, and the confidential discourse of the two ladies was therefore at an end. She sat down to the card table with the melancholy persuasion that Edward was not only without affection for the person who was to be his wife; but that he had not even the chance of being tolerably happy in marriage, which sincere affection on *her* side would have given, for self-interest alone could induce a woman to keep a man to an engagement, of which she seemed so thoroughly aware that he was weary.

From this time the subject was never revived by Elinor, and when entered on by Lucy, who seldom missed an opportunity of introducing it, it was treated by the former with calmness and caution, and dismissed as soon as civility would allow; for she felt such conversations to be an indulgence which Lucy did not deserve, and which were dangerous to herself.

The visit of the Miss Steeles at Barton Park was lengthened far beyond what the first invitation implied. They were prevailed on to stay nearly two months at the park, and to assist in the due celebration of that festival which requires a more than ordinary share of private balls and large dinners to proclaim its importance.

Chapter 25

Though Mrs. Jennings was in the habit of spending a large portion of the year at the houses of her children and friends, she was not without a settled habitation of her own. Since the death of her husband, she had resided every winter in a house in one of the streets near Portman Square. Towards this home, she began on the approach of January to turn her thoughts, and thither she one day abruptly, and very unexpectedly by them, asked the elder Misses Dashwood to accompany her. Elinor immediately gave a grateful but absolute denial for both, in which she believed herself to be speaking their united inclinations. Mrs. Jennings received the refusal with some surprise, and repeated her invitation immediately.

"Oh, Lord! I am sure your mother can spare you very well. Don't fancy that you will be any inconvenience to me, for I shan't put myself at all out of my way for you. We three shall be able to go very well in my chaise; and when we are in town, if you do not like to go wherever I do, well and good, you may always go with one of my daughters. I am sure your mother will not object to it; for I have had such good luck in getting my own children off my hands that she will think me a very fit person to have the charge of you; and if I don't get one of you at least well married before I have done with you, it shall not be my fault."

"I have a notion," said Sir John, "that Miss Marianne would not object to such a scheme, if her elder sister would come into it. So I would advise you two, to set off for town, when you are tired of Barton, without saying a word to Miss Dashwood about it."

"Nay," cried Mrs. Jennings, "I am sure I shall be monstrous glad of Miss Marianne's company, whether Miss Dashwood will go or not. But one or the other, if not both of them, I must have. Come, Miss Marianne, let us strike hands upon the bargain, and if Miss Dashwood will change her mind by and bye, why so much the better."

"I thank you, ma'am, sincerely thank you," said Marianne, with warmth. "Your invitation has insured my gratitude for ever. But my mother, my dearest, kindest mother; oh! no, nothing should tempt me to leave her."

Mrs. Jennings repeated her assurance that Mrs. Dashwood could spare them perfectly well; and Elinor, who now understood her sister, and saw to what indifference to almost everything else she was carried by her eagerness to be with Willoughby again, made no further direct opposition to the plan, and merely referred it to her mother's decision. Whatever Marianne was desirous of, her mother would be eager to promote—she could not expect to influence the latter to cautiousness of conduct in an affair respecting which she had never been able to inspire her with distrust; and she dared not explain the motive of her own disinclination for going to London. That Marianne, thoroughly acquainted with Mrs. Jennings' manners, and invariably disgusted by them, should overlook every inconvenience of that kind, in her pursuit of one object, was such a proof, so strong, so full, of the importance of that object to her, as Elinor, in spite of all that had passed, was not prepared to witness.

On being informed of the invitation, Mrs. Dashwood, would not hear of their declining the offer upon *her* account; insisted on their both accepting it directly; and then began to foresee, with her usual cheerfulness, a variety of advantages that would accrue to them all, from this separation.

"I am delighted with the plan," she cried, "it is exactly what I could wish. Margaret and I shall be as much benefited by it as yourselves. We shall go on so quietly and happily together with our books and our music! You will be under the care of a motherly good sort of woman, of whose kindness to you I can have no doubt. And in all probability you will see your brother, and whatever may be his faults, or the faults of his wife, when I consider whose son he is, I cannot bear to have you so wholly estranged from each other."

"Though with your usual anxiety for our happiness," said Elinor, "you have been obviating every impediment to the present scheme which occurred to you, there is still one objection which, in my opinion, cannot be so easily removed."

Marianne's countenance sunk.

"And what," said Mrs. Dashwood, "is my dear prudent Elinor going to suggest? What formidable obstacle is she now to bring forward?"

"My objection is this; though I think very well of Mrs. Jennings's heart, she is not a woman whose society can afford us pleasure, or whose protection will give us consequence."

"That is very true," replied her mother, "but of her society, you will scarcely have anything at all, and you will almost always appear in public with Lady Middleton."

"If Elinor is frightened away by her dislike of Mrs. Jennings," said Marianne, "at least it need not prevent *my* accepting her invitation. I could put up with every unpleasantness of that kind with very little effort."

Elinor resolved within herself, that if her sister persisted in going, she would go likewise, as she did not think it proper that Marianne should be left to the sole guidance of her own judgment, or that Mrs. Jennings should be abandoned to the mercy of Marianne for all the comfort of her domestic hours. To this determination she was the more easily reconciled by recollecting that Edward Ferrars, by Lucy's account, was not to be in town before February.

"I will have you *both* go," said Mrs. Dashwood. "These objections are nonsensical; and if Elinor would ever condescend to anticipate enjoyment, she would foresee it there from a variety of sources; she would perhaps, expect some from improving her acquaintance with her sister-in-law's family."

Elinor had often wished for an opportunity of attempting to weaken her mother's dependence on the attachment of Edward and herself, that the shock might be less when the whole truth were revealed, she forced herself to begin her design by saying, as calmly as she could, "I like Edward Ferrars very much, and shall always be glad to see him; but as to the rest of the family, it is a matter of perfect indifference to me, whether I am ever known to them or not."

After very little farther discourse, it was finally settled that the invitation should be fully accepted.

Elinor submitted to the arrangement which counteracted her wishes with less reluctance than she had expected to feel. When she saw her mother so thoroughly pleased with the plan, and her sister exhilarated by it in look, voice, and manner, restored to all her usual animation, she could not be dissatisfied with the cause, and would hardly allow herself to distrust the consequence.

Marianne's joy was almost a degree beyond happiness, so great was her impatience to be gone. Her unwillingness to quit her mother was her only restorative to calmness; and at the moment of parting her grief on that score was excessive. Her mother's affliction was hardly less, and Elinor was the only one of the three, who seemed to consider the separation as anything short of eternal.

Chapter 26

Elinor could not find herself in the carriage with Mrs. Jennings, and beginning a journey to London under her protection, and as her guest, without wondering at her own situation, so short had their acquaintance with that lady been, so wholly unsuited were they in age and disposition, and so many had been her objections against such a measure only a few days before! But these objections had all, with that happy ardour of youth which Marianne and her mother equally shared, been overcome or overlooked; and Elinor, in spite of every occasional doubt of Willoughby's constancy, could not witness the rapture of delightful expectation which filled the whole soul and beamed in the eyes of Marianne, without feeling how blank was her own prospect. A short, a very short time however must now decide what Willoughby's intentions were; in all probability he was already in town. Marianne's eagerness to be gone declared her dependence on finding him there; and Elinor was resolved upon gaining every new light as to his character which her own observation or the intelligence of others could give her, but likewise upon watching his behaviour to her sister with such zealous attention, as to ascertain what he was and what he meant, before many meetings had taken place.

They reached town by three o'clock the third day, glad to be released, after such a journey, from the confinement of a carriage, and ready to enjoy all the luxury of a good fire.

The house was handsome, and handsomely fitted up, and the young ladies were immediately put in possession of a very comfortable apartment.

As dinner was not to be ready in less than two hours from their arrival, Elinor determined to employ the interval in writing to her mother, and sat down for that purpose. In a few moments Marianne did the same. "I am writing home, Marianne," said Elinor; "had not you better defer your letter for a day or two?"

"I am *not* going to write to my mother," replied Marianne, hastily, and as if wishing to avoid any farther inquiry. Elinor said no more; it immediately struck her that she must then be writing to Willoughby; and the conclusion which as instantly followed was, that, however mysteriously they might wish to conduct the affair, they must be engaged. Marianne's letter was finished in a very few minutes; in length it could be no more than a note; it was then folded up, sealed, and directed with eager rapidity. No sooner was it complete than Marianne, ringing the bell, requested the footman who answered it to get that letter conveyed for her to the two-penny post.

Her spirits still continued very high; but there was a flutter in them which prevented their giving much pleasure to her sister, and this agitation increased as the evening drew on. She could scarcely eat any dinner, and when they afterwards returned to the drawing room, seemed anxiously listening to the sound of every carriage.

It was a great satisfaction to Elinor that Mrs. Jennings, by being much engaged in her own room, could see little of what was passing. The tea things were brought in, and already had Marianne been disappointed more than once by a rap at a neighbouring door, when a loud one was suddenly heard which could not be mistaken for one at any other house, Elinor felt secure of its announcing Willoughby's approach, and Marianne, starting up, moved towards the door, could not help exclaiming, "Oh, Elinor, it is Willoughby, indeed it is!" and seemed almost ready to throw herself into his arms, when Colonel Brandon appeared.

It was too great a shock to be borne with calmness, and she immediately left the room. Elinor was disappointed too; but at the same time her regard for Colonel Brandon ensured his welcome with her; and she felt particularly hurt that a man so partial to her sister should perceive that she experienced nothing but grief and disappointment in seeing him.

"Is your sister ill?" said he.

Elinor answered in some distress that she was, and then talked of head-aches, low spirits, and over fatigues; and of everything to which she could decently attribute her sister's behaviour.

He heard her with the most earnest attention, but seeming to recollect himself, said no more on the subject, and began directly to speak of his pleasure at seeing them in London.

Elinor wished very much to ask whether Willoughby were then in town, but she was afraid of giving him pain by any enquiry after his rival; and at length, by way of saying something, she asked if he had been in London ever since she had seen him last. "Yes," he replied, with some embarrassment, "almost ever since; I have been once or twice at Delaford for a few days, but it has never been in my power to return to Barton."

This, and the manner in which it was said, immediately brought back to her remembrance all the circumstances of his quitting that place, with the uneasiness and suspicions they had caused to Mrs. Jennings, and she was fearful that her question had implied much more curiosity on the subject than she had ever felt.

Mrs. Jennings soon came in. "Oh! Colonel," said she, with her usual noisy cheerfulness, "I am monstrous glad to see you—sorry I could not come before—Lord, I have been as busy as a bee ever since dinner! But pray, Colonel, how came you to conjure out that I should be in town today?"

"I had the pleasure of hearing it at Mr. Palmer's, where I have been dining."

"Oh, you did; well, and how do they all do at their house? How does Charlotte do? I warrant you she is a fine size by this time."

"Mrs. Palmer appeared quite well, and I am commissioned to tell you, that you will certainly see her to-morrow."

"Well, Colonel, I have brought two young ladies with me, you see—that is, you see but one of them now, but there is another somewhere. Your friend, Miss Marianne, too—which you will not be sorry to hear. I do not know what you and Mr. Willoughby will do between you about her. Ay, it is a fine thing to be young and handsome. But Colonel, where have you been to since we parted? And how does your business go on?"

He replied with his accustomary mildness to all her inquiries, but without satisfying her in any. Elinor now began to make the tea, and Marianne was obliged to appear again.

After her entrance, Colonel Brandon became more thoughtful and silent than he had been before, and Mrs. Jennings could not prevail on him to stay long. No other visitor appeared that evening, and the ladies were unanimous in agreeing to go early to bed.

Marianne rose the next morning with recovered spirits and happy looks. The disappointment of the evening before seemed forgotten in the expectation of what was to happen that day. They had not long finished their breakfast before Mrs. Palmer's barouche stopped at the door, and in a few minutes she came laughing into the room: so delighted to see them all, that it was hard to say whether she received most pleasure from meeting her mother or the Miss Dashwoods again.

After an hour or two spent in what her mother called comfortable chat, it was proposed by Mrs. Palmer that they should all accompany her to some shops where she had business that morning, to which Mrs. Jennings and Elinor readily consented, as having likewise some purchases to make themselves; and Marianne, though declining it at first was induced to go likewise.

Wherever they went, she was evidently always on the watch. In Bond Street especially, where much of their business lay, her eyes were in constant inquiry. Restless and dissatisfied everywhere, her sister could never obtain her opinion of any article of purchase, however it might equally concern them both: she received no pleasure from anything; was only impatient to be at home again.

It was late in the morning before they returned home; and no sooner had they entered the house than Marianne flew eagerly up stairs, and when Elinor followed, she found her turning from the table with a sorrowful countenance, which declared that no Willoughby had been there.

"Has no letter been left here for me since we went out?" said she to the footman. "Are you quite sure of it?" she replied. "Are you certain that no servant, no porter has left any letter or note?"

The man replied that none had.

"How very odd!" said she in a low and disappointed voice.

"How odd, indeed!" repeated Elinor within herself, regarding her sister with uneasiness. "If she had not known him to be in town she would not have written to him, as she did; she would have written to Combe Magna; and if he is in town, how odd that he should neither come nor write!"

She determined, after some consideration, that if appearances continued many days longer as unpleasant as they now were, she would represent in the strongest manner to her mother the necessity of some serious enquiry into the affair.

Mrs. Palmer and two elderly ladies of Mrs. Jennings's intimate acquaintance dined with them. The former left them soon after tea to fulfill her evening engagements; and Elinor was obliged to assist in making a whist table for the others. Marianne was of no use on these occasions, as she would never learn the game;

but though her time was therefore at her own disposal, the evening was spent in all the anxiety of expectation and the pain of disappointment.

Chapter 27

"If this open weather holds much longer," said Mrs. Jennings, when they met at breakfast the following morning, "Sir John will not like leaving Barton next week; 'tis a sad thing for sportsmen to lose a day's pleasure."

"That is true," cried Marianne, in a cheerful voice. "I had not thought of *that*. This weather will keep many sportsmen in the country."

It was a lucky recollection, all her good spirits were restored by it. "It is charming weather for *them* indeed," she continued, as she sat down to the breakfast table with a happy countenance. "How much they must enjoy it! But" (with a little return of anxiety) "it cannot be expected to last long. But frosts will soon set in, and in all probability with severity. Perhaps it may freeze tonight!"

"At any rate," said Elinor, wishing to prevent Mrs. Jennings from seeing her sister's thoughts as clearly as she did, "I dare say we shall have Sir John and Lady Middleton in town by the end of next week."

"Ay, my dear, I'll warrant you we do. Mary always has her own way."

"And now," silently conjectured Elinor, "she will write to Combe by this day's post."

But if she *did*, the letter was written and sent away with

a privacy which eluded all her watchfulness to ascertain the fact. Whatever the truth of it might be, and far as Elinor was from feeling thorough contentment about it, yet while she saw Marianne in spirits, she could not be very uncomfortable herself.

The morning was chiefly spent in leaving cards at the houses of Mrs. Jennings's acquaintance to inform them of her being in town; and Marianne was all the time busy in observing the direction of the wind, watching the variations of the sky and imagining an alteration in the air.

"Don't you find it colder than it was in the morning, Elinor? There seems to me a very decided difference. I can hardly keep my hands warm even in my muff."

Elinor was alternately diverted and pained; but Marianne persevered, and saw every night in the brightness of the fire, and every morning in the appearance of the atmosphere, the certain symptoms of approaching frost.

The Miss Dashwoods had no greater reason to be dissatisfied with Mrs. Jennings's style of living, and set of acquaintance, than with her behaviour to themselves, which was invariably kind. Everything in her household arrangements was conducted on the most liberal plan, and excepting a few old city friends, whom an introduction could at all discompose the feelings of her young companions. Pleased to find herself more comfortably situated in that particular than she had expected, Elinor was very willing to compound for the want of much real enjoyment from any of their evening parties, which formed only for cards, could have little to amuse her.

Colonel Brandon, who had a general invitation to the house, was with them almost every day; he came to look at Marianne and talk to Elinor, who often derived more satisfaction from conversing with him than from any other daily occurrence, but who saw at the same time with much concern his continued regard for her sister.

About a week after their arrival, it became certain that Willoughby was also arrived. His card was on the table when they came in from the morning's drive.

"Good God!" cried Marianne, "he has been here while we were out." Elinor, rejoiced to be assured of his being in London, now ventured to say, "Depend upon it, he will call again tomorrow." But Marianne seemed hardly to hear her, and on Mrs. Jennings's entrance, escaped with the precious card.

This event, while it raised the spirits of Elinor, restored to those of her sister all, and more than all, their former agitation. From this moment her mind was never quiet; the expectation of seeing him every hour of the day, made her unfit for anything. She insisted on being left behind, the next morning, when the others went out.

Elinor's thoughts were full of what might be passing in Berkeley Street during their absence; but a moment's glance at her sister when they returned was enough to inform her, that Willoughby had paid no second visit there. A note was just then brought in, and laid on the table.

"For me!" cried Marianne, stepping hastily forward.

"No, ma'am, for my mistress."

"You are expecting a letter, then?" said Elinor, unable to be longer silent.

"Yes, a little—not much."

After a short pause. "You have no confidence in me, Marianne."

"Nay, Elinor, this reproach from *you*—you who have confidence in no one!"

"Me!" returned Elinor in some confusion; "indeed, Marianne, I have nothing to tell."

"Nor I," answered Marianne with energy, "our situations then are alike. We have neither of us anything to tell; you, because you do not communicate, and I, because I conceal nothing."

Elinor, distressed by this charge of reserve in herself, which she was not at liberty to do away, knew not how, under such circumstances, to press for greater openness in Marianne.

The note was from Lady Middleton, announcing their arrival in Conduit Street the night before, and requesting the company of her mother and cousins the following evening. The invitation was accepted; but when the hour of appointment drew near, Elinor had some difficulty in persuading her sister to go, for still she had seen nothing of Willoughby.

Sir John had contrived to collect around him, nearly twenty young people, and to amuse them with a ball. Mr. and Mrs. Palmer were of the party; from the former, they received no mark of recognition on their entrance. He looked at them slightly, without seeming to know who they were, and merely nodded to Mrs. Jennings from the other side of the room. Marianne gave one glance round the apartment as she entered: it was enough—*he* was not there—and she sat down, equally ill-disposed to receive or communicate pleasure. After they had been assembled about an hour, Mr. Palmer sauntered towards the Miss Dashwoods to express his surprise on seeing them in town, though Colonel Brandon had been first informed of their arrival at his house.

Never had Marianne been so unwilling to dance in her life, as she was that evening, and never so much fatigued by the exercise. She complained of it as they returned to Berkeley Street.

"Aye, aye," said Mrs. Jennings, "we know the reason of all that very well; if a certain person who shall be nameless, had been there, you would not have been a bit tired: and to say the truth it was not very pretty of him not to give you the meeting when he was invited."

"Invited!" cried Marianne.

"So my daughter Middleton told me, for it seems Sir John met him somewhere in the street this morning." Marianne said no more, but looked exceedingly hurt. Impatient in this situation to be doing something that might lead to her sister's relief, Elinor resolved to write the next morning to her mother, and hoped by awakening her fears for the health of Marianne, to procure those inquiries which had been so long delayed; and she was still more eagerly bent on this measure by perceiving after breakfast on the morrow, that Marianne was again writing to Willoughby, for she could not suppose it to be to any other person.

About the middle of the day, Mrs. Jennings went out by herself on business, and Elinor began her letter directly. She was very earnest in her application to her mother, relating all that had passed, her suspicions of Willoughby's inconstancy, urging her by every plea of duty and affection to demand from Marianne an account of her real situation with respect to him.

Her letter was scarcely finished, when a rap foretold a visitor, and Colonel Brandon was announced. Marianne, who had seen him from the window, and who hated company of any kind, left the room before he entered it. He looked more than usually grave, and sat for some time without saying a word. Elinor, persuaded that he had some communication to make in which her sister was concerned, impatiently expected its opening. After a pause of several minutes, their silence was broken, by his asking her in a voice of some agitation, when he was to congratulate her on the acquisition of a brother? Elinor was not prepared for such a question, and having no answer ready, was obliged to adopt the simple and common expedient, of asking what he meant? He tried to smile as he replied, "your sister's engagement to Mr. Willoughby is very generally known."

"It cannot be generally known," returned Elinor, "for her own family do not know it."

He looked surprised and said, "I beg your pardon, I am afraid my inquiry has been impertinent; but I had not supposed any secrecy intended, as they openly correspond, and their marriage is universally talked of."

"How can that be? By whom can you have heard it mentioned?"

"By many—by Mrs. Jennings, Mrs. Palmer, and the Middletons. But still I might not have believed it, if I had not, when the servant let me in today, accidentally seen a letter in his hand, directed to Mr. Willoughby in your sister's writing. I came to inquire, but I was convinced before I could ask the question. Is everything finally settled? I believe I have been wrong in saying so much, but I hardly know what to do, and on your prudence I have the strongest dependence. Tell me that it is all absolutely resolved on, that any attempt, that in short concealment, if concealment be possible, is all that remains."

These words, which conveyed to Elinor a direct avowal of his love for her sister, affected her very much. The real state of things between Willoughby and her sister was so little known to herself, that in endeavouring to explain it, she might be as liable to say too much as too little. Yet as she was convinced that Marianne's affection for Willoughby, could leave no hope of Colonel Brandon's success, whatever the event of that affection might be, and at the same time wished to shield her conduct from censure, she thought it most prudent and kind, after some consideration, to say more than she really knew or believed. She acknowledged, therefore, that though she had never been informed by themselves of the terms on which they stood with each other, of their mutual affection she had no doubt, and of their correspondence she was not astonished to hear.

He listened to her with silent attention, and on her ceasing to speak, rose directly from his seat, and after saying in a voice of emotion, "to your sister I wish all imaginable happiness; to Willoughby that he may endeavour to deserve her," took leave, and went away.

Elinor derived no comfortable feelings from this conversation, to lessen the uneasiness of her mind on other points; she was left, on the contrary, with a melancholy impression of Colonel Brandon's unhappiness, and was prevented even from wishing it removed, by her anxiety for the very event that must confirm it.

Chapter 28

Nothing occurred during the next three or four days, to make Elinor regret what she had done, in applying to her mother; for Willoughby neither came nor wrote. They were engaged about the end of that time to attend Lady Middleton to a party, from which Mrs. Jennings was kept away by the indisposition of her youngest daughter; and for this party, Marianne, wholly dispirited, careless of her appearance, and seeming equally indifferent whether she went or staid, prepared, without one look of hope or one expression of pleasure. She sat by the drawing-room fire after tea, without once stirring from her seat, or altering her attitude, and when at last they were told that Lady Middleton waited for them at the door, she started as if she had forgotten that any one was expected.

They arrived in due time at the place of destination, and as soon as the string of carriages before them would allow, alighted, ascended the stairs, heard their names announced from one landing-place to another in an audible voice, and entered a room splendidly lit up, quite full of company, and insufferably hot. When they had paid their tribute of politeness by curtsying to the lady of the house, they were permitted to mingle in the crowd. After some time spent in saying little or doing less, Lady Middleton sat down to Cassino, and as Marianne was not in spirits for moving about, she and Elinor luckily succeeding to chairs, placed themselves at no great distance from the table.

They had not remained in this manner long, before Elinor perceived Willoughby in earnest conversation with a very fashionable looking young woman. She soon caught his eye, and he immediately bowed, but without attempting to speak to her, or to approach Marianne, though he could not but see her. Elinor turned involuntarily to Marianne, to see whether it could be unobserved by her. At that moment she first perceived him, and her whole countenance glowing with sudden delight, she would have moved towards him instantly, had not her sister caught hold of her.

"Good heavens!" she exclaimed, "he is there—he is there—Oh! Why does he not look at me? Why cannot I speak to him?"

"Pray, pray be composed," cried Elinor, "and do not betray what you feel to every body present. Perhaps he has not observed you yet."

At last he turned round again, and regarded them both; she started up, and pronouncing his name in a tone of affection, held out her hand to him. He approached, and addressing himself rather to Elinor than Marianne, as if wishing to avoid her eye, and determined not to observe her attitude, inquired in a hurried manner after Mrs. Dashwood. Elinor was unable to say a word. But the feelings of her sister were instantly expressed. Her face was crimsoned over, and she exclaimed, in a voice of the greatest emotion, "Good God! Willoughby, what is the meaning of this? Have you not received my letters? Will you not shake hands with me?"

He could not then avoid it, but her touch seemed painful to him, and he held her hand only for a moment. During all this time he was evidently struggling for composure. Elinor watched his countenance and saw its expression becoming more tranquil. After a moment's pause, he spoke with calmness.

"I did myself the honour of calling in Berkeley Street last Tuesday, and very much regretted that I was not fortunate enough to find yourselves and Mrs. Jennings at home."

"But have you not received my notes?" cried Marianne in the wildest anxiety. Tell me, Willoughby; for heaven's sake tell me, what is the matter?"

He made no reply; his complexion changed and all his embarrassment returned; but he recovered himself again, and after saying, "Yes, I had the pleasure of receiving the information of your arrival in town," turned hastily away with a slight bow and joined his friend.

Marianne, now looking dreadfully white, and unable to stand, sunk into her chair, and Elinor, expecting every moment to see her faint, tried to screen her from the observation of others.

"Go to him, Elinor," she cried, as soon as she could speak, "and force him to come to me. Tell him I must see him again. I shall not have a moment's peace till this is explained. Oh go to him this moment."

"No, my dearest Marianne, you must wait. This is not the place for explanations. Wait only till tomorrow."

With difficulty however could she prevent her from following him herself; and to persuade her to check her agitation, to wait, at least, with the appearance of composure, till she might speak to him with more privacy and more effect, was impossible; for Marianne continued incessantly to give way in a low voice to the misery of her feelings. In a short time Elinor saw Willoughby quit the room, and telling Marianne that he was gone, urged the impossibility of speaking to him again that evening, as a fresh argument for her to be calm. She instantly begged her sister would entreat Lady Middleton to take them home.

Lady Middleton, on being informed that Marianne was unwell, was too polite to object for a moment to her wish of going away, and making over her cards to a friend, they departed as soon the carriage could be found. Marianne was in a silent agony, too much oppressed even for tears; but as Mrs. Jennings was luckily not come home, they could go directly to their own room. She was soon undressed and in bed, and as she seemed desirous of being alone, her sister had leisure enough for thinking over the past.

That some kind of engagement had subsisted between Willoughby and Marianne she could not doubt; and that Willoughby was weary of it, seemed equally clear. Nothing but a thorough change of sentiment could account for it. Her indignation would have been still stronger than it was, had she not witnessed that embarrassment which seemed to speak a consciousness of his own misconduct. Absence might have weakened his regard, and convenience might have determined him to overcome it, but that such a regard had formerly existed she could not bring herself to doubt.

As for Marianne, on the pangs which so unhappy a meeting must already have given her, she could not reflect without the deepest concern. Her own situation gained in the comparison; for while she could *esteem* Edward as much as ever, however they might be divided in future, her mind might be always supported. But every circumstance that could embitter such an evil seemed uniting to heighten the misery of Marianne in a final separation from Willoughby—in an immediate and irreconcilable rupture with him.

Chapter 29

Before the house-maid had lit their fire the next day, Marianne, only half dressed, was kneeling against one of the window-seats for the sake of all the little light she could command from it, and writing as fast as a continual flow of tears would permit her. In this situation, Elinor, roused from sleep by her agitation and sobs, first perceived her; and said, in a tone of the most considerate gentleness, "Marianne, may I ask—?"

"No, Elinor," she replied, "ask nothing; you will soon know all."

The sort of desperate calmness with which this was said, lasted no longer than while she spoke, and was immediately followed by a return of the same excessive affliction. It was some minutes before she could go on with her letter, and the frequent bursts of grief which still obliged her, at intervals, to withhold her pen, were proofs enough of her feeling how more than probable it was that she was writing for the last time to Willoughby.

Elinor paid her every quiet and unobtrusive attention in her power; and she would have tried to sooth and tranquilize her still more, had not Marianne entreated her, not to speak to her for the world. The restless state of Marianne's mind not only prevented her from remaining in the room a moment after she was dressed, but made her wander about the house till breakfast time, avoiding the sight of everybody.

At breakfast she neither ate, nor attempted to eat anything; and Elinor's attention was then all employed in endeavouring to engage Mrs. Jennings's notice entirely to herself.

As this was a favourite meal with Mrs. Jennings, it lasted a considerable time, and they were just setting themselves, after it, round the common working table, when a letter was delivered to Marianne, which she eagerly caught from the servant, and instantly ran out of the room. Elinor, who saw that it must come from Willoughby, felt immediately such a sickness at heart as made her hardly able to hold up her head, and sat in such a general tremour as made her fear it impossible to escape Mrs. Jennings's notice. That good lady, however, saw only that Marianne had received a letter from Willoughby.

"Upon my word, I never saw a young woman so desperately in love in my life!" she said. "I hope, from the bottom of my heart, he won't keep her waiting much longer, for it is quite grievous to see her look so ill and forlorn. Pray, when are they to be married?"

Elinor obliged herself to answer such an attack as this, and, therefore, trying to smile, replied, "And have you really, Ma'am, talked yourself into a persuasion of my sister's being engaged to Mr. Willoughby? I must beg, therefore, that you will not deceive yourself any longer. I do assure you that nothing would surprise me more than to hear of their being going to be married."

"For shame, for shame, Miss Dashwood! How can you talk so? Don't we all know that it must be a match, that they were over head and ears in love with each other from the first moment they met? It has been known all over town this ever so long. I tell everybody of it and so does Charlotte."

"Indeed, Ma'am," said Elinor, very seriously, "you are mistaken. Indeed, you are doing a very unkind thing in spreading the report, and you will find that you have though you will not believe me now."

Mrs. Jennings laughed again, but Elinor had not spirits to say more, and eager at all events to know what Willoughby had written, hurried away to their room, where, on opening the door, she saw Marianne stretched on the bed, almost choked by grief, one letter in her hand, and two or three others laying by her. Elinor drew near, but without saying a word; and seating herself on the bed, took her hand, kissed her affectionately several times, and then gave way to a burst of tears, which at first was scarcely less violent than Marianne's. The latter seemed to feel all the tenderness of this behaviour, and after some time thus spent in joint affliction, she put all the letters into Elinor's hands; and then covering her face with her handkerchief, almost screamed with agony. Elinor watched by her till this excess of suffering had somewhat spent itself, and then turning eagerly to Willoughby's letter, read as follows:

Bond Street, January.

"MY DEAR MADAM,

"I have just had the honour of receiving your letter. I am much concerned to find there was anything in my behaviour last night that did not meet your approbation; and though I am quite at a loss to discover in what point I could be so unfortunate as to offend you, I entreat your forgiveness of what I can assure you to have been perfectly unintentional. My esteem for your whole family is very sincere; but if I have been so unfortunate as to give rise to a belief of more than I felt, or meant to express, I shall reproach myself for not having been more guarded in my professions of that esteem. That I should ever have meant more you will allow to be impossible, when you understand that my affections have been long engaged elsewhere, and it will not be many weeks, I believe, before this engagement is fulfilled. It is with great regret that I obey your commands in returning the letters with which I have been honoured from you, and the lock of hair, which you so obligingly bestowed on me.

I am, dear Madam,
Your most obedient
humble servant,

JOHN
WILLOUGHBY.

Though aware, before she began it, that it must bring a confession of his inconstancy, and confirm their separation forever, she was not aware that such language could be suffered to announce it; nor could she have supposed Willoughby capable of departing so far from the appearance of every honourable and delicate feeling—so as to send a letter so impudently cruel: a letter of which every line was an insult, and which proclaimed its writer to be deep in hardened villainy.

She read it again and again; but every perusal only served to increase her abhorrence of the man, and so bitter were her feelings against him, that she dared not trust herself to speak, lest she might wound Marianne still deeper by treating their disengagement an escape from the worst and most irremediable of all evils, a connection, for life, with an unprincipled man.

In her earnest meditations on the contents of the letter, on the depravity of that mind which could dictate it, Elinor forgot the immediate distress of her sister, forgot that she had three letters on her lap yet unread, and so entirely forgot how long she had been in the room, that when on hearing a carriage drive up to the door, she went to the window to see who could be coming so unreasonably early, she was all astonishment to perceive Mrs. Jennings's chariot, which she knew had not been ordered till one. Determined not to quit Marianne, she hurried away to excuse herself from attending Mrs. Jennings, on account of her sister being indisposed. Mrs. Jennings admitted the excuse most readily, and Elinor, after seeing her safe off, returned to Marianne, whom she found attempting to rise from the bed, and whom she reached just in time to prevent her from falling on the floor, faint and giddy from a long want of proper rest and food. A glass of wine, which Elinor procured for her directly, made her more comfortable, and she was at last able to express some sense of her kindness, by saying,

"Poor Elinor! How unhappy I make you!"

"I only wish," replied her sister, "there were any thing I *could* do, which might be of comfort to you."

This was too much for Marianne, who could only exclaim, in the anguish of her heart, "Oh! Elinor, I am miserable, indeed."

"Exert yourself, dear Marianne," she cried, "if you would not kill yourself and all who love you. Think of your mother; think of her misery while *you* suffer: for her sake you must exert yourself."

"I cannot, I cannot," cried Marianne; "Oh! How easy for those, who have no sorrow of their own to talk of exertion! Happy, happy Elinor, *you* cannot have an idea of what I suffer."

"Do you call *me* happy, Marianne? Ah! if you knew! And can you believe me to be so, while I see you so wretched!"

"Forgive me, forgive me," throwing her arms round her sister's neck; "I know you feel for me; but yet you are—you must be happy; Edward loves you—what, oh what, can do away such happiness as that?"

"Many, many circumstances," said Elinor, solemnly.

"No, no, no," cried Marianne wildly, "he loves you, and only you. You *can* have no grief."

"I can have no pleasure while I see you in this state."

"And you will never see me otherwise. Mine is a misery which nothing can do away."

"You must not talk so, Marianne. Much as you suffer now,

think of what you would have suffered if the discovery of his character had been delayed to a later period—if your engagement had been carried on for months and months, as it might have been, before he chose to put an end to it. Every additional day of unhappy confidence, on your side, would have made the blow more dreadful."

"Engagement!" cried Marianne, "there has been no engagement. He has broken no faith with me."

"No engagement! But he told you that he loved you."

"Yes—no—never absolutely. It was every day implied, but never professedly declared. Sometimes I thought it had been—but it never was."

"Yet you wrote to him?—"

"Yes—could that be wrong after all that had passed? "

Elinor said no more, and turning again to the three letters which now raised a much stronger curiosity than before, directly ran over the contents of all. The first, which was what her sister had sent him on their arrival in town, was to this effect.

Berkeley Street, January.

"How surprised you will be, Willoughby, on receiving this; and I think you will feel something more than surprise, when you know that I am in town. An opportunity of coming hither, though with Mrs. Jennings, was a temptation we could not resist. I wish you may receive this in time to come here to-night, but I will not depend on it. At any rate I shall expect you to-morrow. For the present, adieu.

M.D.

Her second note, which had been written on the morning after the dance at the Middletons', was in these words:

"I cannot express my disappointment in having missed you the day before yesterday, nor my astonishment at not having received any answer to a note which I sent you above a week ago. Pray call again as soon as possible, and explain the reason of my having expected this in vain. We were last night at Lady Middleton's, where there was a dance. I have been told that you were asked to be of the party. But could it be so? You must be very much altered indeed since we parted, if that could be the case, and you not there. But I will not suppose this possible, and I hope very soon to receive your personal assurance of its being otherwise.

M.D.

The contents of her last note to him were these:

"What am I to imagine, Willoughby, by your behaviour last night? I was prepared to meet you with the pleasure which our separation naturally produced. I was repulsed indeed! I have passed a wretched night in endeavouring to excuse a conduct which can scarcely be called less than insulting; but though I have not yet been able to form any reasonable apology for your behaviour, I am perfectly ready to hear your justification of it. You have perhaps been misinformed, or purposely deceived, in something concerning me, which may have lowered me in your opinion. Tell me what it is, explain the grounds on which you acted, and I shall be satisfied, in being able to satisfy you. It would grieve me indeed to be obliged to think ill of you; but if I am to do it, if I am to learn that you are not what we have hitherto believed you, that your regard for us all was insincere, that your behaviour to me was intended only to deceive, let it be told as soon as possible. If your sentiments are no longer what they were, you will return my notes, and the lock of my hair which is in your possession.

M.D.

That such letters, so full of affection and confidence, could have been so answered, Elinor, for Willoughby's sake, would have been unwilling to believe. But her condemnation of him did not blind her to the impropriety of their having been written at all; and she was silently grieving over the imprudence which had hazarded such unsolicited proofs of tenderness, when Marianne, perceiving that she had finished the letters, observed to her that they contained nothing but what anyone would have written in the same situation.

"I felt myself," she added, "to be as solemnly engaged to him, as if the strictest legal covenant had bound us to each other."

"I can believe it," said Elinor; "but unfortunately he did not feel the same."

"He *did* feel the same, Elinor—I was once as dear to him as my own soul could wish. This lock of hair, which now he can so readily give up, was begged of me with the most earnest supplication. Have you forgot the morning that we parted too! When he told me that it might be many weeks before we met again—his distress—can I ever forget his distress?"

For a moment or two she could say no more; but when this emotion had passed away, she added, in a firmer tone, "Elinor, I have been cruelly used; but not by Willoughby."

"Dearest Marianne, who but himself? By whom can he have been instigated?"

"By all the world, rather than by his own heart. I could rather believe every creature of my acquaintance leagued together to ruin me in his opinion, than believe his nature capable of such cruelty. This woman of whom he writes may have been so barbarous to bely me."

Elinor would not contend, and only replied, "Whoever may have been so detestably your enemy, let them be cheated of their malignant triumph, my dear sister, by seeing how nobly the consciousness of your own innocence and good intentions supports your spirits."

"No, no," cried Marianne, "misery such as mine has no pride. I care not who knows that I am wretched."

"But for my mother's sake and mine—"

"I would do more than for my own. But to appear happy when I am so miserable—Oh! Who can require it?"

Again they were both silent. Marianne, seated at the foot of the bed, with her head leaning against one of its posts, again took up Willoughby's letter, and, after shuddering over every sentence, exclaimed: "It is too much! Oh, Willoughby, Willoughby, could this be yours! Cruel, cruel—nothing can acquit you. Whatever he might have heard against me—ought he not to have suspended his belief? 'The lock of hair which you so obligingly bestowed on me'—That is unpardonable. Willoughby, where was your heart when you wrote those words? Elinor, can he be justified?"

"No, Marianne, in no possible way."

"And yet this woman—who knows what her art may have been? Whom did I ever hear him talk of as young and attractive among his female acquaintance?"

Another pause ensued; Marianne was greatly agitated, and it ended thus: "Elinor, I must go home. I must go and comfort mama. Cannot we be gone to-morrow?"

"It would be impossible to go to-morrow. We owe Mrs. Jennings much more than civility; and civility of the commonest kind must prevent such a hasty removal as that."

"Well then, another day or two, perhaps; but I cannot stay here long, I cannot stay to endure the questions and remarks of all these people. The Middletons and Palmers—how am I to bear their pity?"

Elinor advised her to lie down again, and for a moment she did so; but in restless pain of mind and body she moved from one posture to another, till growing more and more hysterical, her sister could with difficulty keep her on the bed at all. Some lavender drops, however, which she was at length persuaded to take, were of use; and from that time till Mrs. Jennings returned, she continued on the bed quiet and motionless.

Chapter 30

Mrs. Jennings came immediately to their room on her return, and without waiting to have her request of admittance answered, opened the door and walked in with a look of real concern.

"How do you do my dear?" said she in a voice of great compassion to Marianne, who turned away her face without attempting to answer.

"How is she, Miss Dashwood? Poor thing! She looks very bad. No wonder. Ay, it is but too true. He is to be married very soon—a good-for-nothing fellow! Mrs. Taylor told me of it half an hour ago, and she was told it by a particular friend of Miss Grey herself. Well, said I, all I can say is, that if this be true, he has used a young lady of my acquaintance abominably ill. If ever I meet him again, I will give him such a dressing as he has not had this many a day. But there is one comfort, my dear Miss Marianne; he is not the only young man in the world worth having; and with your pretty face you will never want admirers. Well, poor thing! I won't disturb her any longer, for she had better have her cry out at once and have done with. The Parrys and Sandersons luckily are coming tonight you know, and that will amuse her."

She then went away, walking on tiptoe out of the room, as if she supposed her young friend's affliction could be increased by noise.

Marianne, to the surprise of her sister, determined on dining with them. Elinor even advised her against it. But no, she would go down; she could bear it very well.

When there, though looking most wretchedly, she ate more and was calmer than her sister had expected. Had she tried to speak, or had she been conscious of half Mrs. Jennings's well-meant but ill-judged attentions to her, this calmness could not have been maintained; but not a syllable escaped her lips; and the abstraction of her thoughts preserved her in ignorance of everything that was passing before her.

Elinor, who did justice to Mrs. Jennings's kindness, though its effusions were often distressing, and returned her those civilities, which her sister could not make or return for herself. Their good friend saw that Marianne was unhappy. She treated her therefore, with all the indulgent fondness of a parent towards a favourite child on the last day of its holidays. Had not Elinor, in the sad countenance of her sister, seen a check to all mirth, she could have been entertained by Mrs. Jennings's endeavours to cure a disappointment in love, by a variety of sweetmeats and olives, and a good fire. As soon, however, as the consciousness of all this was forced by continual repetition on Marianne, she could stay no longer. With a hasty exclamation of Misery, and a sign to her sister not to follow her, she directly got up and hurried out of the room.

"Poor soul!" cried Mrs. Jennings, as soon as she was gone, "How it grieves me to see her! Well, it is the oddest thing to me, that a man should use such a pretty girl so ill! But when there is plenty of money on one side, and next to none on the other, Lord bless you! they care no more about such things!"

"The lady then—Miss Grey I think you called her—is very rich?"

"Fifty thousand pounds, my dear and by all accounts, it won't come before it's wanted; for they say he is all to pieces. No wonder, dashing about with his curricle and hunters! Well, it don't signify talking; but when a young man, be who he will, comes and makes love to a pretty girl, and promises marriage, he has no business to fly off from his word only because he grows poor, and a richer girl is ready to have him."

"Do you know what kind of a girl Miss Grey is? Is she said to be amiable?"

"I never heard any harm of her; indeed I hardly ever heard her mentioned; except that Mrs. Taylor did say this morning, that one day Miss Walker hinted to her, that she believed Mr. and Mrs. Ellison would not be sorry to have Miss Grey married, for she and Mrs. Ellison could never agree."

"And who are the Ellisons?"

"Her guardians, my dear. But now she is of age and may choose for herself; and a pretty choice she has made! What now," after pausing a moment, "your poor sister is gone to her own room, I suppose, to moan by herself. Is there nothing one can get to comfort her? Well, by-and-by we shall have a few friends, and that will amuse her a little."

"Dear ma'am, this kindness is quite unnecessary. Marianne, I dare say, will not leave her room again this evening. I shall persuade her if I can to go early to bed, for I am sure she wants rest."

"Aye, I believe that will be best for her. Lord! no wonder she has been looking so bad and so cast down this last week or two, for this matter I suppose has been hanging over her head as long as that. And so the letter that came today finished it! Lord! How concerned Sir John and my daughters will be when they hear it! If I had my senses about me I might have called in Conduit Street in my way home, and told them of it. But I shall see them tomorrow."

"It would be unnecessary I am sure, for you to caution Mrs. Palmer and Sir John against ever naming Mr. Willoughby, or making the slightest allusion to what has passed, before my sister. Their own good-nature must point out to them the real cruelty of appearing to know anything about it when she is present; and the less that may ever be said to myself on the subject, the more my feelings will be spared, as you my dear madam will easily believe."

"Oh! Lord! Yes, that I do indeed. It must be terrible for you to hear it talked of; and as for your sister, I am sure I would not mention a word about it to her for the world. For my part, I think the less that is said about such things, the better, the sooner 'tis blown over and forgot. And what does talking ever do you know?"

"In this affair it can only do harm; for it has been attended by circumstances which, for the sake of everyone concerned in it, make it unfit to become the public conversation. I must do *this* justice to Mr. Willoughby—he has broken no positive engagement with my sister."

"Law, my dear! Don't pretend to defend him. No positive engagement indeed! After taking her all over Allenham House, and fixing on the very rooms they were to live in hereafter!"

Elinor, for her sister's sake, could not press the subject further. After a short silence on both sides, Mrs. Jennings, with all her natural hilarity, burst forth again.

"Well, my dear, 'tis a true saying about an ill-wind, for it will be all the better for Colonel Brandon. He will have her at last; aye, that he will. I hope he will come tonight. It will be all to one a better match for your sister. Two thousand a year without debt or drawback—except the little love-child, indeed; aye, I had forgot her; but she may be 'prenticed out at a small cost, and then what does it signify? If we *can* but put Willoughby out of her head!"

"Ay, if we can do *that*, Ma'am," said Elinor, "we shall do very well with or without Colonel Brandon." And then rising, she went away to join Marianne, whom she found, as she expected, in her own room, leaning, in silent misery, over the small remains of a fire.

"You had better leave me," was all the notice that her sister received from her.

"I will leave you," said Elinor, "if you will go to bed." But this, from the momentary perverseness of impatient suffering, she at first refused to do. Her sister's earnest, though gentle persuasion, however, soon softened her to compliance, and Elinor saw her lay her aching head on the pillow, and as she hoped, in a way to get some quiet rest before she left her.

In the drawing-room, whither she then repaired, she was soon joined by Mrs. Jennings, with a wine-glass, full of something, in her hand.

"My dear," said she, entering, "I have just recollected that I have some of the finest old Constantia wine in the house that ever was tasted, so I have brought a glass of it for your sister."

"Dear Ma'am," replied Elinor, smiling at the difference of the complaints for which it was recommended, "How good you are! But I have just left Marianne in bed, and, I hope, almost asleep; and as I think nothing will be of so much service to her as rest, if you will give me leave, I will drink the wine myself."

Mrs. Jennings, though regretting that she had not been five minutes earlier, was satisfied with the compromise; and Elinor, as she swallowed the chief of it, reflected, that though its effects on a colicky gout were, at present, of little importance to her, its healing powers, on a disappointed heart might be as reasonably tried on herself as on her sister.

Colonel Brandon came in while the party were at tea, and by his manner of looking round the room for Marianne, Elinor immediately fancied that he neither expected nor wished to see her there, and, in short, that he was already aware of what occasioned her absence. Mrs. Jennings was not struck by the same thought; for soon after his entrance, she walked across the room to the tea-table where Elinor presided, and whispered, "The Colonel looks as grave as ever you see. He knows nothing of it; do tell him, my dear."

He shortly afterwards drew a chair close to hers, and, with a look which perfectly assured her of his good information, inquired after her sister.

"Marianne is not well," said she. "She has been indisposed all day, and we have persuaded her to go to bed."

"Perhaps, then," he hesitatingly replied, "What I heard this morning may be—there may be more truth in it than I could believe possible at first."

"What did you hear?"

"That a gentleman, whom I *knew* to be engaged—but how shall I tell you? If you know it already, as surely you must, I may be spared."

"You mean," answered Elinor, with forced calmness, "Mr. Willoughby's marriage with Miss Grey. Yes, we *do* know it all. Where did you hear it?"

"In a stationer's shop in Pall Mall, where I had business. Two ladies were waiting for their carriage, and one of them was giving the other an account of the intended match. The name of Willoughby, John Willoughby, frequently repeated, first caught my attention; and what followed was a positive assertion that everything was now finally settled respecting his marriage with Miss Grey. It would be impossible to describe what I felt. The communicative lady I learnt, on inquiry, for I stayed in the shop till they were gone, was a Mrs. Ellison, and that, as I have been since informed, is the name of Miss Grey's guardian."

"It is. But have you likewise heard that Miss Grey has fifty thousand pounds? In that, if in anything, we may find an explanation."

"It may be so; but Willoughby is capable—at least I think—"

he stopped a moment; then added in a voice which seemed to distrust itself, "And your sister—how did she—"

"Her sufferings have been very severe. Till yesterday, I believe, she never doubted his regard; and even now, perhaps—but *I* am almost convinced that he never was really attached to her. He has been very deceitful, and in some points, there seems a hardness of heart about him."

"Ah!" said Colonel Brandon, "there is, indeed! But your sister does not consider quite as you do?"

"You know her disposition, and may believe how eagerly she would still justify him if she could."

He made no answer; and soon afterwards the subject was necessarily dropped. Mrs. Jennings, who expected to see the effect of Miss Dashwood's communication, in such an instantaneous gaiety on Colonel Brandon's side, as might have become a man in the bloom of youth, of hope and happiness, saw him, with amazement, remain the whole evening more serious and thoughtful than usual.

Chapter 31

From a night of more sleep than she had expected, Marianne awoke the next morning to the same consciousness of misery in which she had closed her eyes.

Elinor encouraged her as much as possible to talk of what she felt; and before breakfast was ready, they had gone through the subject again and again. Sometimes she could believe Willoughby to be as unfortunate and as innocent as herself, and at others, lost every consolation in the impossibility of acquitting him. In one thing, however, she was uniform, when it came to the point, in avoiding, where it was possible, the presence of Mrs. Jennings, and in a determined silence when obliged to endure it. Her heart was hardened against the belief of Mrs. Jennings's entering into her sorrows with any compassion.

"No, no, no, it cannot be," she cried; "she cannot feel. Her kindness is not sympathy; her good-nature is not tenderness. All that she wants is gossip."

Elinor had not needed this to be assured of the injustice to which her sister was often led in her opinion of others, by the irritable refinement of her own mind, and the too great importance placed by her on the delicacies of a strong sensibility. Marianne expected from other people the same opinions and feelings as her own, and she judged of their motives by the immediate effect of their actions on herself. Thus a circumstance occurred, while the sisters were together in their own room after breakfast, which sunk the heart of Mrs. Jennings still lower in her estimation; because, through her own weakness, it chanced to prove a source of fresh pain to herself, though Mrs. Jennings was governed in it by an impulse of the utmost goodwill.

With a letter in her outstretched hand, and countenance gaily smiling, from the persuasion of bringing comfort, she entered their room, saying, "Now, my dear, I bring you something that I am sure will do you good."

Marianne heard enough. In one moment her imagination placed before her a letter from Willoughby, full of tenderness and contrition, instantly followed by Willoughby himself. The work of one moment was destroyed by the next. The hand writing of her mother, never till then unwelcome, was before her; and, in the acuteness of the disappointment which followed such an ecstasy of more than hope, she felt as if, till that instant, she had never suffered.

The cruelty of Mrs. Jennings no language, and now she could reproach her only by the tears which streamed from her eyes with passionate violence. But the letter, when she was calm enough to read it, brought little comfort. Willoughby filled every page. Her mother, still confident of their engagement, had only been roused by Elinor's application to entreat from Marianne greater openness towards them both; and this, with such tenderness towards her, such affection for Willoughby, and such a conviction of their future happiness in each other, that she wept with agony through the whole of it.

All her impatience to be at home again now returned; and she was wildly urgent to be gone. Elinor, unable herself to determine whether it were better for Marianne to be in London or at Barton, offered no counsel of her own except of patience till their mother's wishes could be known; and at length she obtain ed her sister's consent to wait for that knowledge.

Mrs. Jennings went out alone for the rest of the morning. Elinor then sat down to write her mother an account of what had passed, and entreat her directions for the future; while Marianne, who came into the drawing-room on Mrs. Jennings's going away, remained fixed at the table where Elinor wrote, watching the advancement of her pen, grieving over her for the hardship of such a task, and grieving still more fondly over its effect on her mother.

In this manner they had continued about a quarter of an hour, when Marianne, whose nerves could not then bear any sudden noise, was startled by a rap at the door.

"Who can this be?" cried Elinor. "So early too! I thought we *had* been safe."

Marianne moved to the window.

"It is Colonel Brandon!" said she, with vexation.

"He will not come in, as Mrs. Jennings is from home."

"I will not trust to *that*," retreating to her own room. "A man who has nothing to do with his own time has no conscience in his intrusion on that of others."

The event proved her conjecture right, though it was founded on injustice and error; for Colonel Brandon *did* come in.

"I met Mrs. Jennings in Bond Street," said he, after the first salutation, "and she encouraged me to come on; and I was the more easily encouraged, because I thought it probable that I might find you alone, which I was very desirous of doing. My object— my wish—my sole wish is giving comfort to your sister's mind. My regard for her, for yourself, for your mother—will you allow me to prove it, by relating some circumstances which nothing but a *very* sincere regard—I think I am justified—" He stopped.

"I understand you," said Elinor. "You have something to tell me of Mr. Willoughby. Your telling it will be the greatest act of friendship that can be shown Marianne. Pray, pray let me hear it."

"You will find me a very awkward narrator, Miss Dashwood; I

hardly know where to begin. A short account of myself, I believe, will be necessary, and it *shall* be a short one. On such a subject," sighing heavily, "can I have little temptation to be diffuse. You have probably entirely forgotten a conversation between us one evening at Barton Park in which I alluded to a lady I had once known, as resembling, in some measure, your sister Marianne."

"Indeed," answered Elinor, "I have *not* forgotten it."

He looked pleased by this remembrance, and added, "If I am not deceived by the uncertainty, the partiality of tender recollection, there is a very strong resemblance between them, as well in mind as person. This lady was one of my nearest relations, an orphan from her infancy, and under the guardianship of my father. Our ages were nearly the same, and from our earliest years we were playfellows and friends. I cannot remember the time when I did not love Eliza; and my affection for her, as we grew up, was such, as perhaps, judging from my present forlorn and cheerless gravity, you might think me incapable of having ever felt. Hers, for me, was, I believe, fervent as the attachment of your sister to Mr. Willoughby and it was, though from a different cause, no less unfortunate. At seventeen she was lost to me forever. She was married— married against her inclination to my brother. Her fortune was large, and our family estate much encumbered. My brother did not deserve her; he did not even love her. I had hoped that her regard for me would support her under any difficulty, and for some time it did; but at last the misery of her situation overcame all her resolution. We were within a few hours of eloping together for Scotland. The treachery, or the folly, of my cousin's maid betrayed us. I was banished to the house of a relation far distant, and she was allowed no liberty, no society, no amusement, till my father's point was gained. I had depended on her fortitude too far, and the blow was a severe one—but had her marriage been happy, so young as I then was, a few months must have reconciled me to it. This however was not the case. My brother had no regard for her; and from the first he treated her unkindly. She resigned herself at first to all the misery of her situation. But can we wonder that, with such a husband to provoke inconstancy, and without a friend to advise or restrain her (for my father lived only a few months after their marriage, and I was with my regiment in the East Indies) she should fall? Had I remained in England, perhaps—but I meant to promote the happiness of both by removing from her for years. The shock which her marriage had given me," he continued, in a voice of great agitation, "what I felt when I heard, about two years afterwards, of her divorce. It was *that* which threw this gloom—even now the recollection of what I suffered—"

Elinor, affected by his relation, and still more by his distress, could not speak. He saw her concern, and coming to her, took her hand, pressed it, and kissed it with grateful respect. A few minutes more of silent exertion enabled him to proceed with composure.

"It was nearly three years after this unhappy period before I returned to England. My first care, when I *did* arrive, was of course to seek for her. I could not trace her beyond her first seducer, and there was every reason to fear that she had removed from him only to sink deeper in a life of sin. At last, however, and after I had been six months in England, I *did* find her. Regard for a former servant of my own, who had since fallen into misfortune, carried me to visit him in a spunging-house, where he was confined for debt; and there, in the same house, under a similar confinement, was my unfortunate sister. So altered—so faded— worn down by acute suffering of every kind! That she was, to all appearance, in the last stage of a consumption, was—yes, in such a situation it was my greatest comfort. Life could do nothing for her, beyond giving time for a better preparation for death; and that was given. I saw her placed in comfortable lodgings, and under proper attendants; I visited her every day during the rest of her short life: I was with her in her last moments."

Again he stopped to recover himself; and Elinor spoke her feelings in an exclamation of tender concern.

"Your sister, I hope, cannot be offended," said he, "by the resemblance I have fancied between her and my poor disgraced relation. Ah! Miss Dashwood—a subject such as this—untouched for fourteen years—it is dangerous to handle it at all! I *will* be more collected—more concise. She left to my care her only child, a little girl, the offspring of her first guilty connection, who was then about three years old. It was a valued, a precious trust to me; and gladly would I have discharged it in the strictest sense, by watching over her education myself, had the nature of our situations allowed it; but I had no family, no home; and my little Eliza was therefore placed at school. I saw her there whenever I could, and after the death of my brother, she visited me at Delaford. It is now three years ago (she had just reached her fourteenth year,) that I removed her from school, to place her under the care of a very respectable woman, residing in Dorsetshire, who had the charge of four or five other girls of about the same time of life; and for two years I had every reason to be pleased with her situation. But last February, she suddenly disappeared. I had allowed her, at her earnest desire, to go to Bath with one of her young friends, who was attending her father there for his health. I knew him to be a very good sort of man, and I thought well of his daughter—better than she deserved, for, with a most obstinate and ill-judged secrecy, she would tell nothing, would give no clue, though she certainly knew all. He, her father, a well-meaning, but not a quick-sighted man, could really, I believe, give no information; for he had been generally confined to the house, while the girls were ranging over the town and making what acquaintance they chose. In short, I could learn nothing but that she was gone; all the rest, for eight long months, was left to conjecture. What I thought, what I feared, may be imagined."

"Good heavens!" cried Elinor, "Could it be—could Willoughby—!"

"The first news that reached me of her," he continued, "came in a letter from herself, last October. It was forwarded to me from Delaford, and I received it on the very morning of our intended party to Whitwell; and this was the reason of my leaving Barton so suddenly. Little did Mr. Willoughby imagine, I suppose, when his looks censured me for incivility in breaking up the party, that I was called away to the relief of one whom he had made poor and miserable; but *had* he known it, what would it have availed? Would he have been less gay or less happy in the smiles of your sister? No, he had already done that, which no man who *can* feel for another would do. He had left the girl whose youth and innocence he had seduced, in a situation of the utmost distress. He had left her, promising to return; he neither returned, nor wrote, nor relieved her."

"This is beyond everything!" exclaimed Elinor.

"His character is now before you; expensive, dissipated, and worse than both. Knowing all this, as I have now known it many weeks, guess what I must have felt on seeing your sister as fond of him as ever, and on being assured that she was to marry him. When I came to you last week and found you alone, I came determined to know the truth. To suffer you all to be so deceived; to see your sister—but what could I do? I had no hope of interfering with success; and sometimes I thought your sister's influence might yet reclaim him. But now, after such dishonorable usage, who can tell what were his designs on her. Whatever they may have been, however, she may now, and hereafter doubtless *will* turn with gratitude towards her own condition, when she compares it with that of my poor Eliza. Surely this comparison must have its use with her. She will feel her own sufferings to be nothing. They proceed from no misconduct, and can bring no disgrace. Use your own discretion, however, in communicating to her what I have told you. You must know best what will be its effect; but had I not seriously, and from my heart believed it might be of service, might lessen her regrets, I would not have suffered myself to trouble you with this account of my family afflictions."

Elinor's thanks followed this speech with grateful earnestness. "I have been more pained," said she, "by her endeavors to acquit him than by all the rest. Now, though at first she will suffer much, I am sure she will soon become easier. Have you," she continued, after a short silence, "ever seen Mr. Willoughby since you left him at Barton?"

"Yes," he replied gravely, "Once, I have."

Elinor, startled by his manner, looked at him anxiously, saying, "What? Have you met him to—"

"I could meet him no other way. Eliza had confessed to me, though most reluctantly, the name of her lover; and when he returned to town, which was within a fortnight after myself, we met by appointment, he to defend, I to punish his conduct... Such has been the unhappy resemblance between the fate of mother and daughter! and so imperfectly have I discharged my trust!"

"Is she still in town?"

"No; as soon as she recovered from her lying-in, for I found her near her delivery, I removed her and her child into the country, and there she remains."

Recollecting, soon afterwards, that he was probably dividing Elinor from her sister, he put an end to his visit, receiving from her again the same grateful acknowledgments, and leaving her full of compassion and esteem for him.

Chapter 32

When the particulars of this conversation were repeated by Miss Dashwood to her sister, as they very soon were, the effect on her was not entirely such as the former had hoped to see. Not that Marianne appeared to distrust the truth of any part of it, for she listened to it all with the most steady and submissive attention, made neither objection nor remark, attempted no vindication of Willoughby, and seemed to show by her tears that she felt it to be impossible. But though this behaviour assured Elinor that the conviction of this guilt *was* carried home to her mind, though she saw with satisfaction the effect of it, in her no longer avoiding Colonel Brandon when he called, in her speaking to him, she did not see her less wretched. She felt the loss of Willoughby's character yet more heavily than she had felt the loss of his heart; his seduction and desertion of Miss Williams, preyed altogether so much on her spirits, that she could not bring herself to speak of what she felt even to Elinor; and, brooding over her sorrows in silence, gave more pain to her sister than could have been communicated by the most open and most frequent confession of them.

To give the feelings or the language of Mrs. Dashwood on receiving and answering Elinor's letter would be only to give a repetition of what her daughters had already felt and said; of a disappointment hardly less painful than Marianne's, and an indignation even greater than Elinor's.

Against the interest of her own individual comfort, Mrs. Dashwood had determined that it would be better for Marianne to be anywhere, at that time, than at Barton, where everything within her view would be bringing back the past in the strongest and most afflicting manner. She recommended it to her daughters, therefore, by all means not to shorten their visit to Mrs. Jennings. A variety of occupations, of objects, and of company, which could not be procured at Barton, would be inevitable there, and might yet, she hoped, cheat Marianne, at times, into some interest beyond herself.

From all danger of seeing Willoughby again, her mother considered her to be at least equally safe in town as in the country, since his acquaintance must now be dropped by all who called themselves her friends.

She had yet another reason for wishing her children to remain where they were; a letter from her son-in-law had told her that he and his wife were to be in town before the middle of February, and she judged it right that they should sometimes see their brother.

Marianne had promised to be guided by her mother's opinion, and she submitted to it therefore without opposition, though it proved perfectly different from what she wished and expected, and that by requiring her longer continuance in London it deprived her of the only possible alleviation of her wretchedness, the personal sympathy of her mother.

But it was a matter of great consolation to her, that what brought evil to herself would bring good to her sister; and Elinor, on the other hand, suspecting that it would not be in her power to avoid Edward entirely, comforted herself by thinking, that though their longer stay would therefore militate against her own happiness, it would be better for Marianne than an immediate return into Devonshire.

Her carefulness in guarding her sister from ever hearing Willoughby's name mentioned, was not thrown away. Marianne, though without knowing it herself, reaped all its advantage; for neither Mrs. Jennings, nor Sir John, nor even Mrs. Palmer herself, ever spoke of him before her.

Sir John, could not have thought it possible. A man of whom he had always had such reason to think well! Such a good-natured fellow! It was an unaccountable business. He wished him at the devil with all his heart."

Mrs. Palmer, in her way, was equally angry. She was determined to drop his acquaintance immediately, and she was very thankful that she had never been acquainted with him at all; she hated him so much that she was resolved never to mention his name again, and she should tell everybody she saw, how good-for-nothing he was.

The calm and polite unconcern of Lady Middleton on the occasion was a happy relief to Elinor's spirits. It was a great comfort to her to be sure of exciting no interest in *one* person who would meet her without feeling any curiosity after particulars, or any anxiety for her sister's health.

Lady Middleton expressed her sense of the affair about once every day, or twice, if the subject occurred very often, by saying, "It is very shocking, indeed!" and by the means of this continual though gentle vent, was able not only to see the Miss Dashwoods from the first without the smallest emotion, but very soon to see them without recollecting a word of the matter; and having thus supported the dignity of her own sex, and spoken her decided censure of what was wrong in the other, she thought herself at liberty to attend to the interest of her own assemblies, and therefore determined that as Mrs. Willoughby would at once be a woman of elegance and fortune, to leave her card with her as soon as she married.

Colonel Brandon's delicate, unobtrusive enquiries were never unwelcome to Miss Dashwood. His chief reward for the painful exertion of disclosing past sorrows and present humiliations, was given in the pitying eye with which Marianne sometimes observed him, and the gentleness of her voice whenever (though it did not often happen) she was obliged, or could oblige herself to speak to him. *These* assured him that his exertion had produced an increase of good-will towards himself, and *these* gave Elinor hopes of its being further augmented hereafter.

Early in February, within a fortnight from the receipt of Willoughby's letter, Elinor had the painful office of informing her sister that he was married. She had taken care to have the intelligence conveyed to herself, as soon as it was known that the ceremony was over, as she was desirous that Marianne should not receive the first notice of it from the public papers.

She received the news with resolute composure; made no observation on it, and at first shed no tears; but after a short time they would burst out, and for the rest of the day, she was in a state hardly less pitiable than when she first learnt to expect the event.

The Willoughbys left town as soon as they were married; and Elinor now hoped, as there could be no danger of her seeing either of them, to prevail on her sister, who had never yet left the house since the blow first fell, to go out again by degrees as she had done before.

About this time the two Miss Steeles, lately arrived at their cousin's house in Bartlett's Buildings, Holburn, presented themselves again before their more grand relations in Conduit and Berkeley Streets.

Elinor only was sorry to see them. Their presence always gave her pain, and she hardly knew how to make a very gracious return to the overpowering delight of Lucy in finding her *still* in town.

"I should have been quite disappointed if I had not found you here *still*," said she repeatedly, with a strong emphasis on the word. It would have been such a great pity to have went away before your brother and sister came. And now to be sure you will be in no hurry to be gone."

"Well, my dear," said Mrs. Jennings, "and how did you travel?"

"Not in the stage, I assure you," replied Miss Steele, with quick exultation. "We came post all the way, and had a very smart beau to attend us. Dr. Davies was coming to town, and so we thought we'd join him in a post-chaise."

"Oh, oh!" cried Mrs. Jennings. "Very pretty, indeed! and the Doctor is a single man, I warrant you."

"There now," said Miss Steele, affectedly simpering, "everybody laughs at me so about the Doctor, and I cannot think why. My cousins say they are sure I have made a conquest; but for my part I declare I never think about him from one hour's end to another."

"Aye, aye, that is very pretty talking—but it won't do—the Doctor is the man, I see."

"No, indeed!" replied her cousin, with affected earnestness, "and I beg you will contradict it, if you ever hear it talked of."

Mrs. Jennings directly gave her the gratifying assurance that she certainly would *not*, and Miss Steele was made completely happy.

"I suppose you will go and stay with your brother and sister, Miss Dashwood, when they come to town," said Lucy.

"No, I do not think we shall."

"What a charming thing it is that Mrs. Dashwood can spare you both for so long a time together!"

"Long a time, indeed!" interposed Mrs. Jennings. "Why, their visit is but just begun!"

"I am sorry we cannot see your sister, Miss Dashwood," said Miss Steele. "I am sorry she is not well."

"You are very good. My sister will be equally sorry to miss the pleasure of seeing you; but she has been very much plagued lately with nervous head-aches, which make her unfit for company or conversation."

"Oh, dear, that is a great pity! But such old friends as Lucy and me! I think she might see *us*."

Elinor, with great civility, declined the proposal.

Chapter 33

After some opposition, Marianne yielded to her sister's entreaties, and consented to go out with her and Mrs. Jennings one morning for half an hour. She expressly conditioned, however, for paying no visits, and would do no more than accompany them to Gray's in Sackville Street, where Elinor was carrying on a negotiation for the exchange of a few old-fashioned jewels of her mother.

When they stopped at the door, Mrs. Jennings recollected that there was a lady at the other end of the street on whom she ought to call; and as she had no business at Gray's, it was resolved, that while her young friends transacted their's, she should pay her visit and return for them.

On ascending the stairs, the Miss Dashwoods found one gentleman only was standing there, and it is probable that Elinor was not without hope of exciting his politeness to a quicker dispatch. He was giving orders for a toothpick-case for himself, and till its size, shape, and ornaments were determined, all of which, after examining and debating for a quarter of an hour over every toothpick-case in the shop, were finally arranged by his own inventive fancy, he had no leisure to bestow any other attention on the two ladies, than what was comprised in three or four very broad stares.

Marianne was spared from the troublesome feelings of contempt and resentment, on this impertinent examination of their features, by remaining unconscious of it all; for she was as well able to collect her thoughts within herself, and be as ignorant of what was passing around her, in Mr. Gray's shop, as in her own bedroom.

At last the affair was decided. The ivory, the gold, and the pearls, all received their appointment, and the gentleman having named the last day on which his existence could be continued without the possession of the toothpick-case, drew on his gloves with leisurely care, and bestowing another glance on the Miss Dashwoods, but such a one as seemed rather to demand than express admiration, walked off with a happy air of real conceit and affected indifference.

Elinor lost no time in bringing her business forward, was on the point of concluding it, when another gentleman presented himself at her side. She turned her eyes towards his face, and found him with some surprise to be her brother.

Their affection and pleasure in meeting was just enough to make a very creditable appearance in Mr. Gray's shop. John Dashwood was really far from being sorry to see his sisters again; it rather gave them satisfaction; and his inquiries after their mother were respectful and attentive.

"I wished very much to call upon you yesterday," said he, "but it was impossible, for we were obliged to take Harry to see the wild beasts at Exeter Exchange; and we spent the rest of the day with Mrs. Ferrars. But tomorrow I think I shall certainly be able to call in Berkeley Street, and be introduced to your friend Mrs. Jennings. And the Middletons too, you must introduce me to *them*. They are excellent neighbours to you in the country, I understand."

"Excellent indeed. Their attention to our comfort, their friendliness in every particular, is more than I can express."

"I am extremely glad to hear it. But so it ought to be; they are people of large fortune, they are related to you and every civility might be reasonably expected. And so you are most comfortably settled in your little cottage and want for nothing! Edward brought us a most charming account of the place, and you all seemed to enjoy it beyond anything."

Elinor did feel a little ashamed of her brother; and was not sorry to be spared the necessity of answering him, by the arrival of Mrs. Jennings's servant, who came to tell her that his mistress waited for them at the door.

Mr. Dashwood attended them down stairs, was introduced to Mrs. Jennings at the door of her carriage.

His visit was duly paid. He came with a pretence at an apology from their sister-in-law, for not coming too; "but she was so much engaged with her mother, that really she had no leisure for going anywhere." Mrs. Jennings, however, assured him directly, that she should not stand upon ceremony, for they were all cousins, and she should certainly wait on Mrs. John Dashwood very soon, and bring her sisters to see her. His manners to *them*, though calm, were perfectly kind; to Mrs. Jennings, most attentively civil; and on Colonel Brandon's coming in soon after himself, he eyed him with a curiosity which seemed to say, that he only wanted to know him to be rich, to be equally civil to *him*.

After staying with them half an hour, he asked Elinor to walk with him to Conduit Street, and introduce him to Sir John and Lady Middleton. The weather was remarkably fine, and she readily consented. As soon as they were out of the house, his enquiries began.

"Who is Colonel Brandon? Is he a man of fortune?"

"Yes; he has very good property in Dorsetshire."

"I am glad of it. He seems a most gentlemanlike man; and I think, Elinor, I may congratulate you on the prospect of a very respectable establishment in life."

"Me, brother! What do you mean?"

"He likes you. I observed him narrowly, and am convinced of it. What is the amount of his fortune?"

"I believe about two thousand a year."

"Two thousand a-year;" and then working himself up to a pitch of enthusiastic generosity, he added, "Elinor, I wish with all my heart it were *twice* as much, for your sake."

"Indeed I believe you," replied Elinor; "but I am very sure that Colonel Brandon has not the smallest wish of marrying *me*."

"You are mistaken, Elinor. Perhaps just at present he may be undecided; the smallness of your fortune may make him hang back; but there can be no reason why you should not try for him. It is not to be supposed that any prior attachment on your side— in short, you know as to an attachment of that kind, it is quite out of the question, the objections are insurmountable—you have too much sense not to see all that. Colonel Brandon must be the man. It is a match that must give universal satisfaction. In short, it is a kind of thing that will be exceedingly welcome to *all parties*."

Elinor would not vouchsafe any answer.

"It would be something remarkable, now," he continued, "something droll, if Fanny should have a brother and I a sister, settling at the same time."

"Is Mr. Edward Ferrars," said Elinor, with resolution, "going to be married?"

"It is not actually settled, but there is such a thing in agitation. He has a most excellent mother. Mrs. Ferrars, with the utmost liberality, will come forward, and settle on him a thousand a year, if the match takes place. The lady is the Hon. Miss Morton, with thirty thousand pounds. A thousand a-year is a great deal for a mother to give away, to make over for ever; but Mrs. Ferrars has a noble spirit. To give you another instance of her liberality: the other day, as soon as we came to town, aware that money could not be very plenty with us just now, she put bank-notes into Fanny's hands to the amount of two hundred pounds. And extremely acceptable it is, for we must live at a great expense while we are here."

He paused for her assent and compassion; and she forced herself to say,

"Your expenses both in town and country must certainly be considerable; but your income is a large one."

"Not so large, I dare say, as many people suppose. I have made a little purchase within this half year; East Kingham Farm, you must remember the place, where old Gibson used to live. The land was so very desirable for me in every respect, so immediately adjoining my own property, that I felt it my duty to buy it. I could not have answered it to my conscience to let it fall into any other hands. A man must pay for his convenience; and it *has* cost me a vast deal of money."

"More than you think it really and intrinsically worth."

"Why, I hope not that. I might have sold it again, the next day, for more than I gave: but, with regard to the purchase-money, I might have been very unfortunate indeed; for the stocks were at that time so low, that if I had not happened to have the necessary sum in my banker's hands, I must have sold out to very great loss."

Elinor could only smile.

"Other great and inevitable expenses too we have had on first coming to Norland. Our respected father, as you well know, bequeathed all the Stanhill effects that remained at Norland to your mother. In consequence of it, we have been obliged to make large purchases of linen, china, &c. to supply the place of what was taken away. You may guess, after all these expenses, how very far we must be from being rich, and how acceptable Mrs. Ferrars's kindness is."

"Certainly," said Elinor; "and assisted by her liberality, I hope you may yet live to be in easy circumstances."

"Another year or two may do much towards it," he gravely replied; "but however there is still a great deal to be done."

Having now said enough to make his poverty clear, his

thoughts took a cheerfuller turn, and he began to congratulate Elinor on having such a friend as Mrs. Jennings.

"She seems a most valuable woman indeed. Her inviting you to town is certainly a vast thing in your favour; and indeed, it speaks altogether so great a regard for you, that in all probability when she dies you will not be forgotten. She must have a great deal to leave."

"Nothing at all, I should rather suppose; for she has only her jointure, which will descend to her children."

"But it is not to be imagined that she lives up to her income, and whatever she saves, she will be able to dispose of."

"And do you not think it more likely that she should leave it to her daughters, than to us?"

"Her daughters are both exceedingly well married, and therefore I cannot perceive the necessity of her remembering them further. By her taking so much notice of you, and she can hardly do all this, without being aware of the expectation it raises."

"But she raises none in those most concerned. Indeed, brother, your anxiety for our welfare and prosperity carries you too far."

"Why, to be sure," said he, seeming to recollect himself, "people have little, have very little in their power. But, my dear Elinor, what is the matter with Marianne? She looks very unwell, has lost her colour, and is grown quite thin."

"She is not well, she has had a nervous complaint on her for several weeks."

"I am sorry for that. At her time of life, anything of an illness destroys the bloom forever! She was as handsome a girl last September, as I ever saw; and as likely to attract the men. I remember Fanny used to say that she would marry sooner and better than you did. I question whether Marianne *now*, will marry a man worth more than five or six hundred a-year, at the utmost, and I am very much deceived if *you* do not do better."

Elinor tried very seriously to convince him that there was no likelihood of her marrying Colonel Brandon; but it was an expectation of too much pleasure to himself to be relinquished. He had just compunction enough for having done nothing for his sisters himself, to be exceedingly anxious that everybody else should do a great deal; and an offer from Colonel Brandon, or a legacy from Mrs. Jennings, was the easiest means of atoning for his own neglect.

They were lucky enough to find Lady Middleton at home, and Sir John came in before their visit ended. Abundance of civilities passed on all sides. Sir John was ready to like anybody, and though Mr. Dashwood did not seem to know much about horses, he soon set him down as a very good-natured fellow: while Lady Middleton saw enough of fashion in his appearance to think his acquaintance worth having; and Mr. Dashwood went away delighted with both.

Chapter 34

Mrs. John Dashwood had so much confidence in her husband's judgment, that she waited the very next day both on Mrs. Jennings and her daughter; and her confidence was rewarded by finding even the former, even the woman with whom her sisters were staying, by no means unworthy her notice; and as for Lady Middleton, she found her one of the most charming women in the world!

Lady Middleton was equally pleased with Mrs. Dashwood. There was a kind of cold hearted selfishness on both sides, which mutually attracted them.

The same manners, however, which recommended Mrs. John Dashwood to the good opinion of Lady Middleton did not suit the fancy of Mrs. Jennings, and to HER she appeared nothing more than a little proud-looking woman of uncordial address, who met her husband's sisters without any affection, and almost without having anything to say to them.

Elinor wanted very much to know, though she did not chuse to ask, whether Edward was then in town; but nothing would have induced Fanny voluntarily to mention his name before her, till able to tell her that his marriage with Miss Morton was resolved on, or till her husband's expectations on Colonel Brandon were answered. The intelligence however, which SHE would not give, soon flowed from another quarter. Lucy came very shortly to claim Elinor's compassion on being unable to see Edward, though he had arrived in town with Mr. and Mrs. Dashwood. He dared not come to Bartlett's Buildings for fear of detection, they could do nothing at present but write.

Edward assured them himself of his being in town, within a very short time, by twice calling in Berkeley Street. Elinor was pleased that he had called; and still more pleased that she had missed him.

The Dashwoods were so prodigiously delighted with the Middletons that they determined to give them a dinner; and soon after their acquaintance began, invited them to dine in Harley Street, where they had taken a very good house for three months. Their sisters and Mrs. Jennings were invited likewise, and John Dashwood was careful to secure Colonel Brandon. They were to meet Mrs. Ferrars; but Elinor could not learn whether her sons were to be of the party. The expectation of seeing her, however, was enough to make her interested in the engagement.

The interest with which she thus anticipated the party, was soon afterwards increased, more powerfully than pleasantly, by her hearing that the Miss Steeles were also to be at it.

So well had they recommended themselves to Lady Middleton that she was as ready as Sir John to ask them to spend a week or two in Conduit Street.

Their claims to the notice of Mrs. John Dashwood, as the nieces of the gentleman who for many years had had the care of her brother, might not have done much, however, towards procuring them seats at her table; and Lucy had seldom been happier in her life, than she was on receiving Mrs. John Dashwood's card.

On Elinor its effect was very different. She began immediately to determine, that Edward who lived with his mother, must be asked as his mother was, to a party given by his sister; and to see him for the first time, after all that passed, in the company of Lucy!—she hardly knew how she could bear it!

These apprehensions, perhaps, were not founded entirely on reason, and certainly not at all on truth. They were relieved however, not by her own recollection, but by the good will of Lucy, who believed herself to be inflicting a severe disappointment when she told her that Edward certainly would not be in Harley Street on Tuesday.

The important Tuesday came that was to introduce the two young ladies to this formidable mother-in-law.

"Pity me, dear Miss Dashwood!" said Lucy, as they walked up the stairs together. I declare I can hardly stand. Good gracious! In a moment I shall see the person that all my happiness depends on—that is to be my mother!"

Mrs. Ferrars was a little, thin woman, upright, even to formality, in her figure, and serious, even to sourness, in her aspect. Her complexion was sallow; and her features small, without beauty, and naturally without expression; but a lucky contraction of the brow had rescued her countenance from the disgrace of insipidity, by giving it the strong characters of pride and ill nature. She was not a woman of many words; for, unlike people in general, she proportioned them to the number of her ideas; and of the few syllables that did escape her, not one fell to the share of Miss Dashwood, whom she eyed with the spirited determination of disliking her at all events.

Elinor could not *now* be made unhappy by this behaviour, and the difference of her manners to the Miss Steeles, a difference which seemed purposely made to humble her more, only amused her. She could not but smile to see the graciousness of both mother and daughter towards the very person, whom of all others, had they known as much as she did, they would have been most anxious to mortify; while she herself, who had comparatively no power to wound them, sat pointedly slighted by both.

Lucy was all exultation on being so honorably distinguished; and Miss Steele wanted only to be teazed about Dr. Davies to be perfectly happy.

The dinner was a grand one, the servants were numerous, and everything bespoke the Mistress's inclination for show, and the Master's ability to support it. In spite of the improvements and additions which were making to the Norland estate, and in spite of its owner having once been within some thousand pounds of being obliged to sell out at a loss, no poverty of any kind, except of conversation, appeared—but there, the deficiency was considerable. John Dashwood had not much to say for himself that was worth hearing, and his wife had still less. But there was no peculiar disgrace in this; for it was very much the case with the chief of their visitors, who almost all laboured under one or other of these disqualifications for being agreeable: want of sense, either natural or improved—want of elegance—want of spirits—or want of temper.

When the ladies withdrew to the drawing-room after dinner, this poverty was particularly evident, for the gentlemen *had* supplied the discourse with some variety—but then it was all over; and one subject only engaged the ladies till coffee came in, which was the comparative heights of Harry Dashwood, and Lady Middleton's second son William.

The parties stood thus:

The two mothers, though each really convinced that her own son was the tallest, politely decided in favour of the other.

The two grandmothers, with not less partiality, but more sincerity, were equally earnest in support of their own descendant.

Lucy, who was hardly less anxious to please one parent than the other, thought the boys were both remarkably tall for their age, and could not conceive that there could be the smallest difference in the world between them.

Elinor, having once delivered her opinion on William's side, by which she offended Mrs. Ferrars and Fanny still more, did not see the necessity of enforcing it by any farther assertion; and Marianne, when called on for hers, offended them all, by declaring that she had no opinion to give, as she had never thought about it.

Before her removing from Norland, Elinor had painted a very pretty pair of screens for her sister-in-law, which being now just mounted and brought home, ornamented her present drawing room; and these screens, catching the eye of John Dashwood on his following the other gentlemen into the room, were officiously handed by him to Colonel Brandon for his admiration.

"These are done by my eldest sister," said he. "I do not know whether you have ever happened to see any of her performances before, but she is in general reckoned to draw extremely well."

The Colonel warmly admired the screens, as he would have done anything painted by Miss Dashwood; and they were handed round for general inspection. Mrs. Ferrars, not aware of their being Elinor's work, particularly requested to look at them; and after they had received gratifying testimony of Lady Middletons's approbation, Fanny presented them to her mother, considerately informing her, at the same time, that they were done by Miss Dashwood.

"Hum," said Mrs. Ferrars, "very pretty," and without regarding them at all, returned them to her daughter.

Perhaps Fanny thought for a moment that her mother had been quite rude enough,—for, colouring a little, she immediately said, "They are very pretty, ma'am—aren't they?" But then again, the dread of having been too civil, too encouraging herself, probably came over her, for she presently added, "Do you not think they are something in Miss Morton's style of painting, Ma'am?—She *does* paint most delightfully!"

"Beautifully indeed! But she does everything well."

Marianne could not bear this. Such ill-timed praise of another, at Elinor's expense, though she had not any notion of what was principally meant by it, provoked her immediately to say with warmth, "This is admiration of a very particular kind! What is Miss Morton to us? Who knows, or who cares, for her? It is Elinor of whom *we* think and speak."

Mrs. Ferrars looked exceedingly angry, and drawing herself up more stiffly than ever, pronounced in retort this bitter philippic, "Miss Morton is Lord Morton's daughter."

Fanny looked very angry too, and her husband was all in a fright at his sister's audacity. Elinor was much more hurt by Marianne's warmth than she had been by what produced it; but Colonel Brandon's eyes, as they were fixed on Marianne, declared that he noticed only what was amiable in it, the affectionate heart which could not bear to see a sister slighted in the smallest point.

Marianne's feelings did not stop here. The cold insolence of Mrs. Ferrars's general behaviour to her sister, seemed, to her, to foretell such difficulties and distresses to Elinor, as her own wounded heart taught her to think of with horror; and urged by a strong impulse of affectionate sensibility, she moved after a moment, to her sister's chair, and putting one arm round her neck, and one cheek close to hers, said in a low, but eager, voice,

"Dear, dear Elinor, don't mind them. Don't let them make *you* unhappy."

She could say no more; her spirits were quite overcome, and hiding her face on Elinor's shoulder, she burst into tears. Colonel Brandon rose up and went to them without knowing what he did. Mrs. Jennings, with a very intelligent "Ah! poor dear," immediately gave her salts; and Sir John felt so desperately enraged against the author of this nervous distress, that he instantly changed his seat to one close by Lucy Steele, and gave her, in a whisper, a brief account of the whole shocking affair.

In a few minutes, however, Marianne was recovered enough to put an end to the bustle, and sit down among the rest; though her spirits retained the impression of what had passed, the whole evening.

"Poor Marianne!" said her brother to Colonel Brandon, in a low voice. "She has not such good health as her sister, she has not Elinor's constitution; and one must allow that there is something very trying to a young woman who *has been* a beauty in the loss of her personal attractions. You would not think it perhaps, but Marianne *was* remarkably handsome a few months ago; quite as handsome as Elinor. Now you see it is all gone."

Chapter 35

Elinor's curiosity to see Mrs. Ferrars was satisfied. She had enough of her pride, her meanness, and her determined prejudice against herself, to comprehend all the difficulties that must have perplexed the engagement, and retarded the marriage, of Edward and herself, had he been otherwise free.

She wondered that Lucy's spirits could be so very much blind her as to make the attention which seemed only paid her because she was *not Elinor*, appear a compliment to herself—or to allow her to derive encouragement from a preference only given her, because her real situation was unknown. But that it was so, had not only been declared by Lucy's eyes at the time, but was declared over again the next morning more openly, for at her particular desire, Lady Middleton set her down in Berkeley Street on the chance of seeing Elinor alone.

The chance proved a lucky one, for a message from Mrs. Palmer soon after she arrived, carried Mrs. Jennings away.

"My dear friend," cried Lucy, as soon as they were by themselves, "I come to talk to you of my happiness. Could anything be so flattering as Mrs. Ferrars's way of treating me yesterday? You know how I dreaded the thoughts of seeing her; but the very moment I was introduced, there was such an affability in her behaviour as really should seem to say, she had quite took a fancy to me."

"She was certainly very civil to you."

"Civil! Did you see nothing but only civility? I saw a vast deal more. No pride, no hauteur, and your sister just the same—all sweetness and affability!"

"Undoubtedly, if they had known your engagement," said she, "nothing could be more flattering than their treatment of you; but as that was not the case—"

"I guessed you would say so," replied Lucy quickly, "but there was no reason in the world why Mrs. Ferrars should seem to like me, if she did not, and her liking me is everything. Mrs. Ferrars is a charming woman, and so is your sister."

To this Elinor had no answer to make, and did not attempt any.

"Are you ill, Miss Dashwood? You seem low."

"I never was in better health."

"I am glad of it with all my heart. I should be sorry to have *you* ill; you, that have been the greatest comfort to me in the world!"

Elinor tried to make a civil answer, though doubting her own success. But it seemed to satisfy Lucy, for she directly replied, "Indeed I am perfectly convinced of your regard for me, and next to Edward's love, it is the greatest comfort I have. Poor Edward! But now there is one good thing, we shall be able to meet, and meet pretty often, for Lady Middleton's delighted with Mrs. Dashwood, so we shall be a good deal in Harley Street, I dare say, and Edward spends half his time with his sister. Besides, Lady Middleton and Mrs. Ferrars will visit now;—and Mrs. Ferrars and your sister were both so good to say more than once, they should always be glad to see me. They are such charming women! I am sure if ever you tell your sister what I think of her, you cannot speak too high."

But Elinor would not give her any encouragement to hope that she *should* tell her sister. Lucy continued, "I am sure I should have seen it in a moment, if Mrs. Ferrars had took a dislike to me. For where she *does* dislike, I know it is most violent."

Elinor was prevented from making any reply to this civil triumph, by the door's being thrown open, the servant's announcing Mr. Ferrars, and Edward's immediately walking in.

It was a very awkward moment; and the countenance of each showed that it was so. Edward seemed to have as great an inclination to walk out of the room again, as to advance further into it. The ladies recovered themselves first. It was not Lucy's business to put herself forward, and the appearance of secrecy must still be kept up. She could therefore only *look* her tenderness, and after slightly addressing him, said no more.

But Elinor had more to do; and so anxious was she, for his sake and her own, to do it well, that she forced herself, after a moment's recollection, to welcome him, with a look and manner that were almost easy. She would not allow the presence of Lucy, nor the consciousness of some injustice towards herself, to deter her from saying that she was happy to see him.

Her manners gave some re-assurance to Edward, and he had courage enough to sit down; but his embarrassment still exceeded that of the ladies.

Lucy, with a demure and settled air, seemed determined to make no contribution to the comfort of the others, and would not say a word; and almost everything that *was* said, proceeded from Elinor, who was obliged to volunteer all the information about her mother's health, their coming to town, &c. which Edward ought to have inquired about, but never did.

Her exertions did not stop here; for she soon afterwards felt herself so heroically disposed as to determine, under pretence of fetching Marianne, to leave the others by themselves; and she really did it, and *that* in the handsomest manner, for she loitered away several minutes on the landing-place, before she went to her sister. When that was once done, however, it was time for the raptures of Edward to cease; for Marianne's joy hurried her into the drawing-room immediately. Her pleasure in seeing him was like every other of her feelings, strong in itself, and strongly spoken.

"Dear Edward!" she cried, "this is a moment of great happiness! This would almost make amends for everything?"

Edward tried to return her kindness as it deserved, but before such witnesses he dared not say half what he really felt. Marianne was looking with the most speaking tenderness, sometimes at Edward and sometimes at Elinor, regretting only that their delight in each other should be checked by Lucy's unwelcome presence. Edward was the first to speak, and it was to notice Marianne's altered looks, and express his fear of her not finding London agree with her.

"Oh, don't think of me!" she replied with spirited earnestness. "Don't think of *my* health. Elinor is well, you see. That must be enough for us both."

This remark was not calculated to make Edward or Elinor more easy, nor to conciliate the good will of Lucy.

"Do you like London?" said Edward, willing to say anything that might introduce another subject.

"Not at all. I expected much pleasure in it, but I have found none. The sight of you, Edward, is the only comfort it has afforded."

She paused; no one spoke.

"I think, Elinor," she presently added, "we must employ Edward to take care of us in our return to Barton."

Poor Edward muttered something, but what it was, nobody knew, not even himself. But Marianne, who saw his agitation, and could easily trace it to whatever cause best pleased herself, was perfectly satisfied, and soon talked of something else.

"We spent such a day, Edward, in Harley Street yesterday! So dull, so wretchedly dull! But I have much to say to you on that head, which cannot be said now. But why were you not there, Edward? Why did you not come?"

"I was engaged elsewhere."

"Engaged! But what was that, when such friends were to be met?"

"Perhaps, Miss Marianne," cried Lucy, eager to take some revenge on her, "you think young men never stand upon engagements, if they have no mind to keep them."

Elinor was very angry, but Marianne seemed entirely insensible of the sting; for she calmly replied, "Not so, indeed; for, seriously speaking, I am very sure that conscience only kept Edward from Harley Street. And I really believe he *has* the most delicate conscience in the world. He is the most fearful of giving pain, of wounding expectation, and the most incapable of being selfish, of anybody I ever saw."

The nature of her commendation, in the present case, however, happened to be particularly ill-suited to the feelings of two thirds of her auditors, and was so very unexhilarating to Edward, that he very soon got up to go away.

"Going so soon!" said Marianne; "my dear Edward, this must not be."

And drawing him a little aside, she whispered her persuasion that Lucy could not stay much longer. But even this encouragement failed, for he would go; and Lucy soon afterwards went away.

"What can bring her here so often?" said Marianne, on her leaving them. "Could not she see that we wanted her gone! How teasing to Edward!"

"Why so? We were all his friends, and Lucy has been the longest known to him of any."

Marianne looked at her steadily, and said, "You know, Elinor, that this is a kind of talking which I cannot bear. If you only hope to have your assertion contradicted, as I must suppose to be the case, you ought to recollect that I am the last person in the world to do it. I cannot descend to be tricked out of assurances, that are not really wanted."

She then left the room; and Elinor dared not follow her to say more, for bound as she was by her promise of secrecy to Lucy, she could give no information that would convince Marianne; and painful as the consequences of her still continuing in an error might be, she was obliged to submit to it.

Chapter 36

Within a few days after this meeting, the newspapers announced to the world, that the lady of Thomas Palmer, Esq. was safely delivered of a son and heir; a very interesting and satisfactory paragraph, at least to all those intimate connections who knew it before.

This event, highly important to Mrs. Jennings's happiness, produced a temporary alteration in the disposal of her time, for as she wished to be as much as possible with Charlotte, she went thither every morning as soon as she was dressed, and did not return till late in the evening; and the Miss Dashwoods, at the particular request of the Middletons, spent the whole of every day in Conduit Street.

Though nothing could be more polite than Lady Middleton's behaviour to Elinor and Marianne, she did not really like them at all. Because they neither flattered herself nor her children, she could not believe them good-natured; and because they were fond of reading, she fancied them satirical.

Their presence was a restraint both on her and on Lucy. It checked the idleness of one, and the business of the other. Lady Middleton was ashamed of doing nothing before them, and the flattery which Lucy was proud to think of and administer at other times, she feared they would despise her for offering. Miss Steele was the least discomposed of the three, by their presence; and it was in their power to reconcile her to it entirely. Would either of them only have given her a full and minute account of the whole affair between Marianne and Mr. Willoughby, she would have thought herself amply rewarded for the sacrifice of the best place by the fire after dinner. But this conciliation was not granted; for though she often threw out expressions of pity for her sister to Elinor, no effect was produced, but a look of indifference from the former, or of disgust in the latter.

All these jealousies and discontents, however, were so totally unsuspected by Mrs. Jennings, that she thought it a delightful thing for the girls to be together. She joined them sometimes at Sir John's, sometimes at her own house; but wherever it was, she always came in excellent spirits, full of delight and importance, attributing Charlotte's well doing to her own care, and ready to give so exact, so minute a detail of her situation, as only Miss Steele had curiosity enough to desire.

I come now to the relation of a misfortune, which about this time befell Mrs. John Dashwood. It so happened that while her two sisters with Mrs. Jennings were first calling on her in Harley Street, another of her acquaintance had dropped in. This last-arrived lady, on merely hearing the name of the Miss Dashwoods, and understanding them to be Mr. Dashwood's sister, immediately concluded them to be staying in Harley Street; and this misconstruction produced within a day or two afterwards, cards of invitation for them as well as for their brother and sister, to a small musical party at her house. The consequence of which was, that Mrs. John Dashwood was obliged to submit not only to the exceedingly great inconvenience of sending her carriage for the Miss Dashwoods, but, what was still worse, must be subject to all the unpleasantness of appearing to treat them with attention.

Marianne had now been brought by degrees, so much into the habit of going out every day, that it was become a matter of indifference to her, whether she went or not: and she prepared quietly and mechanically for every evening's engagement, though without expecting the smallest amusement from any.

To her dress and appearance she was grown so perfectly indifferent, as not to bestow half the consideration on it, during the whole of her toilet, which it received from Miss Steele in the first five minutes of their being together, when it was finished. She saw everything, and asked everything; was never easy till she knew the price of every part of Marianne's dress; and was not without hopes of finding out before they parted, how much her washing cost per week, and how much she had every year to spend upon herself. The impertinence of these kind of scrutinies, moreover, was generally concluded with a compliment which was considered by Marianne as the greatest impertinence of all.

With such encouragement as this, was she dismissed on the present occasion, to her brother's carriage; which they were ready to enter five minutes after it stopped at the door.

The party, like other musical parties, comprehended a great many people who had real taste for the performance, and a great many more who had none at all.

As Elinor was neither musical, nor affecting to be so, she made no scruple of turning her eyes from the grand pianoforte, whenever it suited her, and would fix them at pleasure on any other object in the room. In one of these excursive glances she perceived among a group of young men, the very he, who had given them a lecture on toothpick-cases at Gray's. She perceived him soon afterwards looking at herself, and speaking familiarly to her brother; and had just determined to find out his name from the latter, when they both came towards her, and Mr. Dashwood introduced him to her as Mr. Robert Ferrars.

He addressed her with easy civility, and twisted his head into a bow which assured her as plainly as words could have done, that he was exactly the coxcomb she had heard him described to be by Lucy. While she wondered at the difference of the two young men, she did not find that the emptiness of conceit of the one, put her out of all charity with the modesty and worth of the other. Why they *were* different, Robert exclaimed to her himself, for talking of his brother, and lamenting the extreme *gaucherie* which he really believed kept him from mixing in proper society, he candidly and generously attributed it much less to any natural deficiency, than to the misfortune of a private education; while he himself, though probably without any particular, any material superiority by nature, merely from the advantage of a public school, was as well fitted to mix in the world as any other man.

"Upon my soul," he added, "I believe it is nothing more; and so I often tell my mother, when she is grieving about it. 'My dear Madam,' I always say to her, 'If you had only sent him to Westminster as well as myself, instead of sending him to Mr. Pratt's, all this would have been prevented.'"

Elinor would not oppose his opinion, because, whatever might be her general estimation of the advantage of a public school, she could not think of Edward's abode in Mr. Pratt's family, with any satisfaction.

"You reside in Devonshire, I think," was his next observation, "in a cottage near Dawlish."

"For my own part," said he, "I am excessively fond of a cottage; there is always so much comfort, so much elegance about them. And I protest, if I had any money to spare, I should buy a little land and build one myself, within a short distance of London, where I might drive myself down at any time, and collect a few friends about me, and be happy.

"Some people imagine that there can be no accommodations, no space in a cottage; but this is all a mistake. I was last month at my friend Elliott's, near Dartford. Lady Elliott wished to give a dance. 'But how can it be done?' said she. There is not a room in this cottage that will hold ten couple, and where can the supper be?' I immediately saw that there could be no difficulty in it, so I said, 'My dear Lady Elliott, do not be uneasy. The dining parlour will admit eighteen couple with ease; card-tables may be placed in the drawing-room; the library may be open for tea and other refreshments; and let the supper be set out in the saloon.' So that, in fact, you see, if people do but know how to set about it, every comfort may be as well enjoyed in a cottage as in the most spacious dwelling."

Elinor agreed to it all, for she did not think he deserved the compliment of rational opposition.

As John Dashwood had no more pleasure in music than his eldest sister, his mind was equally at liberty to fix on anything else; and a thought struck him during the evening, which he communicated to his wife, for her approbation, when they got home. The consideration of Mrs. Dennison's mistake, in supposing his sisters their guests, had suggested the propriety of their being really invited to become such, while Mrs. Jennings's engagements kept her from home. It was altogether an attention which the delicacy of his conscience pointed out to be requisite to its complete enfranchisement from his promise to his father. Fanny was startled at the proposal.

"I do not see how it can be done," said she, "without affronting Lady Middleton, for they spend every day with her; otherwise I should be exceedingly glad to do it. You know I am always ready to pay them any attention in my power, as my taking them out this evening shews. But they are Lady Middleton's visitors. How can I ask them away from her?"

Her husband, but with great humility, did not see the force of her objection. "They had already spent a week in this manner in Conduit Street, and Lady Middleton could not be displeased at their giving the same number of days to such near relations."

Fanny paused a moment, and then, with fresh vigour, said, "My love I would ask them with all my heart, if it was in my power. But I had just settled within myself to ask the Miss Steeles to spend a few days with us. They are very well behaved, good kind of girls; and I think the attention is due to them, as their uncle did so very well by Edward. I am sure you will like them; indeed, you *do* like them, you know, very much already, and so does my mother; and they are such favourites with Harry!"

Mr. Dashwood was convinced. He saw the necessity of inviting the Miss Steeles immediately, and his conscience was pacified by the resolution of inviting his sisters another year; at the same time, however, slyly suspecting that another year would make the invitation needless, by bringing Elinor to town as Colonel Brandon's wife, and Marianne as *their* visitor.

Fanny, rejoicing in her escape, and proud of the ready wit that had procured it, wrote the next morning to Lucy, to request her company and her sister's. Such an opportunity of being with Edward and his family was, above all things, the most material to her interest, and such an invitation the most gratifying to her feelings! It was an advantage that could not be too gratefully acknowledged, nor too speedily made use of.

When the note was shown to Elinor, as it was within ten minutes after its arrival, it gave her, for the first time, some share in the expectations of Lucy; for such a mark of uncommon kindness, vouchsafed on so short an acquaintance, seemed to declare that the good-will towards her arose from something more than merely malice against herself; and might be brought, by time and address, to do everything that Lucy wished. Her flattery had already subdued the pride of Lady Middleton, and made an entry into the close heart of Mrs. John Dashwood; and these were effects that laid open the probability of greater.

The Miss Steeles removed to Harley Street, and all that reached Elinor of their influence there, strengthened her expectation of the event. Sir John, who called on them more than once, brought home such accounts of the favour they were in, as must be universally striking. Mrs. Dashwood had never been so much pleased with any young women in her life, as she was with them; had given each of them a needle book made by some emigrant; called Lucy by her Christian name; and did not know whether she should ever be able to part with them.

Chapter 37

Mrs. Palmer was so well at the end of a fortnight, that her mother felt it no longer necessary to give up the whole of her time to her; and, contenting herself with visiting her once or twice a day, returned from that period to her own home.

About the third or fourth morning after their being thus resettled in Berkeley Street, Mrs. Jennings, on returning from her ordinary visit to Mrs. Palmer, entered the drawing-room, where Elinor was sitting by herself, with an air of such hurrying importance as prepared her to hear something wonderful; and giving her time only to form that idea, began directly to justify it, by saying, "Lord! my dear Miss Dashwood! have you heard the news?"

"No, ma'am. What is it?"

"Something so strange! When I got to Mr. Palmer's, I found Charlotte quite in a fuss about the child. She was sure it was very ill—it cried, and fretted, and was all over pimples. So I looked at it directly, and, 'Lord! my dear,' says I, 'it is nothing in the world, but the red gum.' But Charlotte, she would not be satisfied, so Mr. Donavan was sent for; and luckily he happened to just come in from Harley Street, so he stepped over directly, and as soon as ever he saw the child, he said just as we did, that it was nothing in the world but the red gum, and then Charlotte was easy. And so, just as he was going away again, it came into my head, I am sure I do not know how I happened to think of it, but it came into my head to ask him if there was any news. So upon that, he smirked, and simpered, and looked grave, and seemed to know something or other, and at last he said in a whisper, 'For fear any unpleasant report should reach the young ladies under your care as to their sister's indisposition, I think it advisable to say, that I believe there is no great reason for alarm; I hope Mrs. Dashwood will do very well.'"

"What! Is Fanny ill?"

"That is exactly what I said, my dear. So then it all came out: Mr. Edward Ferrars, the very young man I used to joke with you about, Mr. Edward Ferrars, it seems, has been engaged above this twelvemonth to my cousin Lucy! There is no great wonder in their liking one another; but that matters should be brought so forward between them, and nobody suspect it! —*that* is strange! Well, and so this was kept a great secret, for fear of Mrs. Ferrars, and neither she nor your brother or sister suspected a word of the matter—till this very morning, poor Nancy, popped it all out. 'Lord!' thinks she to herself, 'they are all so fond of Lucy, to be sure they will make no difficulty about it;' and so, away she went to your sister, who was sitting all alone at her carpet-work, little suspecting what was to come—for she had just been saying to your brother, only five minutes before, that she thought to make a match between Edward and some Lord's daughter or other, I forget who. She fell into violent hysterics immediately, with such screams as reached your brother's ears, as he was sitting in his own dressing-room down stairs. So up he flew directly, and a terrible scene took place, for Lucy was come to them by that time, little dreaming what was going on. Poor soul! I pity *her*. And I must say, I think she was used very hardly; for your sister scolded like any fury, and soon drove her into a fainting fit. Nancy, she fell upon her knees, and cried bitterly; and your brother, he walked about the room, and said he did not know what to do. Mrs. Dashwood declared they should not stay a minute longer in the house, and your brother was forced to go down upon *his* knees too, to persuade her to let them stay till they had packed up their clothes. Lord! What a taking poor Mr. Edward will be in when he hears of it! To have his love used so scornfully! For they say he is monstrous fond of her, as well he may. I should not wonder, if he was to be in the greatest passion! —and Mr. Donavan thinks just the same. He and I had a great deal of talk about it; and the best of all is, that he is gone back again to Harley Street, that he may be within call when Mrs. Ferrars is told of it. I have no notion of people's making such a to-do about money and greatness. There is no reason on earth why Mr. Edward and Lucy should not marry; for I am sure Mrs. Ferrars may afford to do very well by her son, and though Lucy has next to nothing herself, she knows better than anybody how to make the most of everything; I dare say, if Mrs. Ferrars would only allow him five hundred a-year, she would make as good an appearance with it as anybody else would with eight."

Here Mrs. Jennings ceased, and as Elinor had had time enough to collect her thoughts, she was able to give such an answer, and make such observations, as the subject might naturally be supposed to produce. Happy to find that she was not suspected of any extraordinary interest in it; that Mrs. Jennings had ceased to imagine her at all attached to Edward; she felt very well able to speak of the affair without embarrassment.

She could hardly determine what her own expectation of its event really was; though she earnestly tried to drive away the notion of its being possible to end otherwise at last, than in the marriage of Edward and Lucy.

As Mrs. Jennings could talk on no other subject, Elinor soon saw the necessity of preparing Marianne for its discussion. No time was to be lost in undeceiving her, in making her acquainted with the real truth.

Elinor's office was a painful one. She was going to remove

what she really believed to be her sister's chief consolation, to give such particulars of Edward as she feared would ruin him forever in her good opinion,-and to make Marianne, by a resemblance in their situations, feel all her own disappointment over again.

She was very far from wishing to dwell on her own feelings, or to represent herself as suffering much, any otherwise than as the self-command she had practised since her first knowledge of Edward's engagement, might suggest a hint of what was practicable to Marianne. Her narration was clear and simple; it was not accompanied by violent agitation, nor impetuous grief. *That* belonged rather to the hearer, for Marianne listened with horror, and cried excessively. Edward seemed a second Willoughby; and acknowledging as Elinor did, that she *had* loved him most sincerely, could she feel less than herself! As for Lucy Steele, she considered her so totally unamiable, so absolutely incapable of attaching a sensible man, that she could not be persuaded at first to believe, and afterwards to pardon, any former affection of Edward for her. She would not even admit it to have been natural; and Elinor left her to be convinced that it was so, by that which only could convince her, a better knowledge of mankind.

Her first communication had reached no farther than to state the fact of the engagement, and the length of time it had existed. Marianne's feelings had then broken in, and put an end to all regularity of detail. The first question on her side, which led to further particulars, was, "How long has this been known to you, Elinor?"

"I have known it these four months. When Lucy first came to Barton Park last November, she told me in confidence of her engagement."

At these words, Marianne's eyes expressed the astonishment which her lips could not utter. After a pause of wonder, she exclaimed—

"Four months! Have you known of this four months? So calm! So cheerful! How have you been supported?"

"By feeling that I was doing my duty. My promise to Lucy, obliged me to be secret. I owed to my family and friends, not to create in them a solicitude about me, which it could not be in my power to satisfy."

Marianne seemed much struck.

"Four months! And yet you loved him!"

"Yes. But I did not love only him; and while the comfort of others was dear to me, I was glad to spare them from knowing how much I felt. I have many things to support me. I am not conscious of having provoked the disappointment by any imprudence of my own, I have borne it as much as possible without spreading it further. I acquit Edward of essential misconduct. I wish him very happy. Lucy does not want sense, and that is the foundation on which everything good may be built. And after all, Marianne, after all that is bewitching in the idea of a single and constant attachment, and all that can be said of one's happiness depending entirely on any particular person, it is not meant—it is not fit—it is not possible that it should be so. Edward will marry Lucy; he will marry a woman superior in person and understanding to half her sex; and time and habit will teach him to forget that he ever thought another superior to *her*."

"If such is your way of thinking," said Marianne, "if the loss of what is most valued is so easily to be made up by something else, your resolution, your self-command, are, perhaps, a little less to be wondered at."

"I understand you. You do not suppose that I have ever felt much. For four months, Marianne, I have had all this hanging on my mind, knowing that it would make you and my mother most unhappy whenever it were explained to you, yet unable to prepare you for it in the least. It was told me, it was in a manner forced on me by the very person herself, whose prior engagement ruined all my prospects; and told me, as I thought, with triumph. This person's suspicions, therefore, I have had to oppose, by endeavouring to appear indifferent where I have been most deeply interested. I have known myself to be divided from Edward forever, without hearing one circumstance that could make me less desire the connection. I have had to contend against the unkindness of his sister, and the insolence of his mother; and have suffered the punishment of an attachment, without enjoying its advantages. If you can think me capable of ever feeling—surely you may suppose that I have suffered *now*. If I had not been bound to silence, perhaps nothing could have kept me entirely—not even what I owed to my dearest friends—from openly showing that I was *very* unhappy."

Marianne was quite subdued.

"Oh! Elinor," she cried, "you have made me hate myself forever. How barbarous have I been to you who have borne with me in all my misery!"

In such a frame of mind as she was now in, Elinor had no difficulty in obtaining from her whatever promise she required; and at her request, Marianne engaged never to speak of the affair to any one with the least appearance of bitterness; to meet Lucy without betraying the smallest increase of dislike to her; and even to see Edward himself, if chance should bring them together, without any diminution of her usual cordiality.

She performed her promise of being discreet, to admiration. She attended to all that Mrs. Jennings had to say upon the subject, with an unchanging complexion. She listened to her praise of Lucy with only moving from one chair to another, and when Mrs. Jennings talked of Edward's affection, it cost her only a spasm in her throat. Such advances towards heroism in her sister, made Elinor feel equal to anything herself.

The next morning brought a further trial of it, in a visit from their brother, who came with a most serious aspect to talk over the dreadful affair, and bring them news of his wife.

"You have heard, I suppose," said he with great solemnity, as soon as he was seated, "of the very shocking discovery that took place under our roof yesterday."

They all looked their assent; it seemed too awful a moment for speech.

"Your sister," he continued, "has suffered dreadfully. Poor Fanny! She was in hysterics all yesterday. But I would not alarm you too much. Donavan says there is nothing materially to be apprehended; her constitution is a good one. She says she never shall think well of anybody again; and one cannot wonder at it, after being so deceived! It was quite out of the benevolence of her heart, that she had asked these young women to her house; merely because she thought they deserved some attention, were harmless, well-behaved girls, and would be pleasant companions. And now to be so rewarded! 'I wish, with all my heart,' says poor Fanny in her affectionate way, 'that we had asked your sisters instead of them.'"

Here he stopped to be thanked; which being done, he went on.

"What poor Mrs. Ferrars suffered, when first Fanny broke it to her, is not to be described. While she with the truest affection had been planning a most eligible connection for him, was it to be supposed that he could be all the time secretly engaged to another person! We consulted together, however, as to what should be done, and at last she determined to send for Edward. He came. But I am sorry to relate what ensued. All that Mrs. Ferrars could say to make him put an end to the engagement, assisted too as you may well suppose by my arguments, and Fanny's entreaties, was of no avail. Duty, affection, everything was disregarded. I never thought Edward so stubborn, so unfeeling before. His mother explained to him her liberal designs, in case of his marrying Miss

Morton; told him she would settle on him the Norfolk estate, which, clear of land-tax, brings in a good thousand a-year; offered even, when matters grew desperate, to make it twelve hundred; and in opposition to this, if he still persisted in this low connection, represented to him the certain penury that must attend the match. His own two thousand pounds she protested should be his all; she would never see him again; and so far would she be from affording him the smallest assistance, that if he were to enter into any profession with a view of better support, she would do all in her power to prevent him advancing in it."

Here Marianne, in an ecstasy of indignation, clapped her hands together, and cried, "Gracious God! Can this be possible!"

"Well may you wonder, Marianne," replied her brother, "at the obstinacy which could resist such arguments as these. Your exclamation is very natural."

Marianne was going to retort, but she remembered her promises, and forbore.

"All this, however," he continued, "was urged in vain. Edward said very little; but what he did say, was in the most determined manner. Nothing should prevail on him to give up his engagement."

"Then," cried Mrs. Jennings with blunt sincerity, no longer able to be silent, "he has acted like an honest man! If he had done otherwise, I should have thought him a rascal. I have some little concern in the business, as well as yourself, for Lucy Steele is my cousin, and I believe there is not a better kind of girl in the world, nor one who more deserves a good husband."

John Dashwood was greatly astonished; but his nature was calm, not open to provocation, and he never wished to offend anybody, especially anybody of good fortune. He therefore replied, "I would by no means speak disrespectfully of any relation of yours, madam. Miss Lucy Steele is, I dare say, a very deserving young woman, but in the present case you know, the connection must be impossible. And to have entered into a secret engagement with a young man under her uncle's care, the son of a woman especially of such very large fortune as Mrs. Ferrars, is perhaps, altogether a little extraordinary. In short, I do not mean to reflect upon the behaviour of any person whom you have a regard for, Mrs. Jennings. We all wish her extremely happy; and Mrs. Ferrars's conduct throughout the whole, has been such as every conscientious, good mother, in like circumstances, would adopt. It has been dignified and liberal. Edward has drawn his own lot, and I fear it will be a bad one."

"Well, sir," said Mrs. Jennings, "and how did it end?"

"I am sorry to say, ma'am, in a most unhappy rupture: Edward is dismissed for ever from his mother's notice. He left her house yesterday, but where he is gone, or whether he is still in town, I do not know; for WE of course can make no inquiry."

"Poor young man! —and what is to become of him?"

"What, indeed, ma'am! It is a melancholy consideration. Born to the prospect of such affluence! I cannot conceive a situation more deplorable. The interest of two thousand pounds—how can a man live on it?—and when to that is added the recollection, that he might, but for his own folly, within three months have been in the receipt of two thousand, five hundred a-year (for Miss Morton has thirty thousand pounds,) I cannot picture to myself a more wretched condition. We must all feel for him; and the more so, because it is totally out of our power to assist him."

"Poor young man!" cried Mrs. Jennings, "I am sure he should be very welcome to bed and board at my house; and so I would tell him if I could see him. It is not fit that he should be living about at his own charge now, at lodgings and taverns."

Elinor's heart thanked her for such kindness towards Edward, though she could not forbear smiling at the form of it.

"If he would only have done as well by himself," said John Dashwood, "as all his friends were disposed to do by him, he might now have been in his proper situation, and would have wanted for nothing. But as it is, it must be out of anybody's power to assist him. And there is one thing more preparing against him, which must be worse than all—his mother has determined, with a very natural kind of spirit, to settle *that* estate upon Robert immediately, which might have been Edward's, on proper conditions."

"Well!" said Mrs. Jennings, "that is *her* revenge. Everybody has a way of their own. But I don't think mine would be, to make one son independent, because another had plagued me."

"Can anything be more galling to the spirit of a man," continued John, "than to see his younger brother in possession of an estate which might have been his own? Poor Edward! I feel for him sincerely."

A few minutes more spent in the same kind of effusion, concluded his visit; he went away; leaving the three ladies unanimous in their sentiments on the present occasion, as far at least as it regarded Mrs. Ferrars's conduct, the Dashwoods', and Edward's.

Chapter 38

Mrs. Jennings was very warm in her praise of Edward's conduct, but only Elinor and Marianne understood its true merit. *They* only knew how little he had had to tempt him to be disobedient, and how small was the consolation, beyond the consciousness of doing right, that could remain to him in the loss of friends and fortune. Elinor gloried in his integrity; and Marianne forgave all his offences in compassion for his punishment. But though confidence between them was, by this public discovery, restored to its proper state, it was not a subject on which either of them were fond of dwelling when alone. Elinor avoided it upon principle, as tending to fix still more upon her thoughts, by the too warm, too positive assurances of Marianne, that belief of Edward's continued affection for herself which she rather wished to do away; and Marianne's courage soon failed her, in trying to converse upon a topic which always left her more dissatisfied with herself than ever, by the comparison it necessarily produced between Elinor's conduct and her own.

Nothing new was heard by them, for a day or two afterwards, of affairs in Harley Street, or Bartlett's Buildings. But though so much of the matter was known to them already, that Mrs. Jennings might have had enough to do in spreading that knowledge farther, without seeking after more, she had resolved from the first to pay a visit of comfort and inquiry to her cousins as soon as she could;

and nothing but the hindrance of more visitors than usual, had prevented her going to them within that time.

The third day succeeding their knowledge of the particulars, was so fine, so beautiful a Sunday as to draw many to Kensington Gardens, though it was only the second week in March. Mrs. Jennings and Elinor were of the number; but Marianne, who knew that the Willoughbys were again in town, and had a constant dread of meeting them, chose rather to stay at home, than venture into so public a place.

An intimate acquaintance of Mrs. Jennings joined them soon after they entered the Gardens, and Elinor was not sorry that by her continuing with them, and engaging all Mrs. Jennings's conversation, she was herself left to quiet reflection. She saw nothing of the Willoughbys, nothing of Edward, and for some time nothing of anybody who could by any chance whether grave or gay, be interesting to her. But at last she found herself with some surprise, accosted by Miss Steele, who, though looking rather shy, expressed great satisfaction in meeting them, and on receiving encouragement from the particular kindness of Mrs. Jennings, left her own party for a short time, to join their's. Mrs. Jennings immediately whispered to Elinor, "Get it all out of her, my dear. She will tell you any thing if you ask. You see I cannot leave Mrs. Clarke."

It was lucky, however, for Mrs. Jennings's curiosity and Elinor's too, that she would tell anything WITHOUT being asked; for nothing would otherwise have been learnt.

"I am so glad to meet you;" said Miss Steele, taking her familiarly by the arm—"for I wanted to see you of all things in the world." And then lowering her voice, "I suppose Mrs. Jennings has heard all about it. Is she angry?"

"Not at all, I believe, with you."

"That is a good thing. And Lady Middleton, is *she* angry?"

"I cannot suppose it possible that she should."

"I am monstrous glad of it. Good gracious! I have had such a time of it! I never saw Lucy in such a rage in my life. She vowed at first she would never trim me up a new bonnet, nor do any thing else for me again, so long as she lived; but now she is quite come to, and we are as good friends as ever. Look, she made me this bow to my hat, and put in the feather last night. There now, YOU are going to laugh at me too. But why should not I wear pink ribbons?"

She had wandered away to a subject on which Elinor had nothing to say, and therefore soon judged it expedient to find her way back again to the first.

"Well, but Miss Dashwood," speaking triumphantly, "people may say what they chuse about Mr. Ferrars's declaring he would not have Lucy, for it is no such thing I can tell you; and it is quite a shame for such ill-natured reports to be spread abroad. Whatever Lucy might think about it herself, you know, it was no business of other people to set it down for certain."

"I never heard any thing of the kind hinted at before, I assure you," said Elinor.

"Oh, did not you? But it *was* said, I know, very well, and by more than one; for Miss Godby told Miss Sparks, that nobody in their senses could expect Mr. Ferrars to give up a woman like Miss Morton, with thirty thousand pounds to her fortune, for Lucy Steele that had nothing at all. I believe in my heart Lucy gave it up all for lost; for we came away from your brother's Wednesday, and we saw nothing of him not all Thursday, Friday, and Saturday. However this morning he came just as we came home from church; and then it all came out, how he had been sent for Wednesday to Harley Street, and been talked to by his mother and all of them, and how he had declared before them all that he loved nobody but Lucy, and nobody but Lucy would he have. And how he had been so worried by what passed, that as soon as he had went away from his mother's house, he had got upon his horse, and rid into the country, somewhere or other; and how he had stayed about at an inn all Thursday and Friday, on purpose to get the better of it. And after thinking it all over and over again, he said, it seemed to him as if, now he had no fortune, and no nothing at all, it would be quite unkind to keep her on to the engagement, because it must be for her loss, for he had nothing but two thousand pounds, and no hope of anything else. He could not bear to think of her doing no better, and so he begged, if she had the least mind for it, to put an end to the matter directly, and leave him shift for himself. I will take my oath he never dropped a syllable of being tired of her, or of wishing to marry Miss Morton, or anything like it. But, to be sure, Lucy would not give ear to such kind of talking; so she told him directly—she told him directly, she had not the least mind in the world to be off, for she could live with him upon a trifle, and how little so ever he might have, she should be very glad to have it all, you know, or something of the kind. So then he was monstrous happy, and talked on some time about what they should do, and they agreed he should take orders directly, and they must wait to be married till he got a living. And just then I could not hear any more, for my cousin called from below to tell me Mrs. Richardson was come in her coach, and would take one of us to Kensington Gardens; so I was forced to go into the room and interrupt them, to ask Lucy if she would like to go, but she did not care to leave Edward."

"I do not understand what you mean by interrupting them," said Elinor; "you were all in the same room together, were not you?"

"No, indeed, not us. La! Miss Dashwood, do you think people make love when anybody else is by? No, no; they were shut up in the drawing-room together, and all I heard was only by listening at the door."

"How!" cried Elinor; "have you been repeating to me what

you only learnt yourself by listening at the door? How could you behave so unfairly by your sister?"

"Oh, la! there is nothing in *that*. I only stood at the door, and heard what I could. And I am sure Lucy would have done just the same by me."

Elinor tried to talk of something else; but Miss Steele could not be kept beyond a couple of minutes, from what was uppermost in her mind.

"Edward talks of going to Oxford soon," said she; "but now he is lodging at No.—, Pall Mall. He have got some business at Oxford, he says; so he must go there for a time; and after *that*, as soon as he can light upon a Bishop, he will be ordained. I wonder what curacy he will get! Good gracious! (giggling as she spoke) I'd lay my life I know what my cousins will say, when they hear of it. They will tell me I should write to the Doctor, to get Edward the curacy of his new living. I know they will; but I am sure I would not do such a thing for all the world."

"Well," said Elinor, "it is a comfort to be prepared against the worst. You have got your answer ready."

Miss Steele was going to reply on the same subject, but the approach of her own party made another more necessary.

"Oh, la! here come the Richardsons. I had a vast deal more to say to you, but I must not stay away from them not any longer. Goodbye, I am sorry Miss Marianne was not here. Remember me kindly to her. La! if you have not got your spotted muslin on! I wonder you was not afraid of its being torn."

Such was her parting concern; for after this, she had time only to pay her farewell compliments to Mrs. Jennings, before her company was claimed by Mrs. Richardson; and Elinor was left in possession of knowledge which might feed her powers of reflection some time, though she had learnt very little more than what had been already foreseen and foreplanned in her own mind. Edward's marriage with Lucy was as firmly determined on, and the time of its taking place remained as absolutely uncertain, as she had concluded it would be;—every thing depended, exactly after her expectation, on his getting that preferment, of which, at present, there seemed not the smallest chance.

As soon as they returned to the carriage, Mrs. Jennings was eager for information; but as Elinor wished to spread as little as possible intelligence that had in the first place been so unfairly obtained, she confined herself to the brief repetition of such simple particulars, as she felt assured that Lucy, for the sake of her own consequence, would choose to have known. The continuance of their engagement, and the means that were able to be taken for promoting its end, was all her communication; and this produced from Mrs. Jennings the following natural remark.

"Wait for his having a living! They will wait a twelvemonth, and finding no good comes of it, will set down upon a curacy of fifty pounds a-year. Lord help 'em! How poor they will be! I must see what I can give them towards furnishing their house."

The next morning brought Elinor a letter by the two-penny post from Lucy herself. It was as follows:

Bartlett's Building, March.

I hope my dear Miss Dashwood will excuse the liberty I take of writing to her; but I know your friendship for me will make you pleased to hear such a good account of myself and my dear Edward, after all the troubles we have went through lately. We have had great trials, and great persecutions, but however, at the same time, gratefully acknowledge many friends, yourself not the least among them, whose great kindness I shall always thankfully remember, as will Edward too, who I have told of it. I am sure you will be glad to hear, as likewise dear Mrs. Jennings, I spent two happy hours with him yesterday afternoon, he would not hear of our parting, though earnestly did I, as I thought my duty required, urge him to it for prudence sake, and would have parted for ever on the spot, would he consent to it; but he said it should never be. Our prospects are not very bright, to be sure, but we must wait, and hope for the best; he will be ordained shortly; and should it ever be in your power to recommend him to anybody that has a living to bestow, am very sure you will not forget us, and dear Mrs. Jennings too, trust she will speak a good word for us to Sir John. I hope Mrs. Jennings won't think it too much trouble to give us a call, should she come this way any morning. My paper reminds me to conclude; and begging to be most gratefully and respectfully remembered to her, and to Sir John, and Lady Middleton, and the dear children, when you chance to see them, and love to Miss Marianne,

I am, &c.

As soon as Elinor had finished it, she performed what she concluded to be its writer's real design, by placing it in the hands of Mrs. Jennings, who read it aloud with many comments of satisfaction and praise.

"Very well indeed! How prettily she writes! Aye, that was quite proper to let him be off if he would. That was just like Lucy. Poor soul! I wish I *could* get him a living, with all my heart. She calls me dear Mrs. Jennings, you see. Yes, yes, I will go and see her, sure enough. How attentive she is, to think of everybody! Thank you, my dear, for showing it me. It is as pretty a letter as ever I saw, and does Lucy's head and heart great credit."

Chapter 39

The Miss Dashwoods had now been rather more than two months in town, and Marianne's impatience to be gone increased every day. She sighed for the air, the liberty, the quiet of the country; and fancied that if any place could give her ease, Barton must do it. Elinor was hardly less anxious than herself for their removal, and only so much less bent on its being effected immediately, as that she was conscious of the difficulties of so long a journey, which Marianne could not be brought to acknowledge. She began, however, seriously to turn her thoughts towards its accomplishment, and had already mentioned their wishes to their kind hostess, who resisted them with all the eloquence of her good-will, when a plan was suggested, which, though detaining them from home yet a few weeks longer, appeared to Elinor altogether much more eligible than any other. The Palmers were to remove to Cleveland about the end of March, for the Easter holidays; and Mrs. Jennings, with both her friends, received a very warm invitation from Charlotte to go with them. This would not, in itself, have been sufficient for the delicacy of Miss Dashwood;—but it was inforced with so much real politeness by Mr. Palmer himself, as, joined to the very great amendment of his manners towards them since her sister had been known to be unhappy, induced her to accept it with pleasure.

When she told Marianne what she had done, however, her first reply was not very auspicious.

"Cleveland!" she cried, with great agitation. "No, I cannot go to Cleveland."

"You forget," said Elinor gently, "that its situation is not . . . that it is not in the neighbourhood of . . ."

"But it is in Somersetshire. I cannot go into Somersetshire."

Elinor would not argue upon the propriety of overcoming such feelings; represented it, therefore, as a measure which would fix the time of her returning to that dear mother, whom she so much wished to see, in a more eligible, more comfortable manner, than any other plan could do. From Cleveland, which was within a few miles of Bristol, the distance to Barton was not beyond one day, though a long day's journey; and their mother's servant might easily come there to attend them down.

Mrs. Jennings was so far from being weary of her guests that she pressed them very earnestly to return with her again from Cleveland. Elinor was grateful for the attention, but it could not alter her design; and their mother's concurrence being readily gained, everything relative to their return was arranged as far as it could be.

"Ah! Colonel, I do not know what you and I shall do without the Miss Dashwoods;"—was Mrs. Jennings's address to him when he first called on her, after their leaving her was settled—"for they are quite resolved upon going home from the Palmers;—and how forlorn we shall be, when I come back!—Lord! We shall sit and gape at one another as dull as two cats."

Perhaps Mrs. Jennings was in hopes, by this vigorous sketch of their future ennui, to provoke him to make that offer, which might give himself an escape from it; and if so, she had soon afterwards good reason to think her object gained; for, on Elinor's moving to the window to take more expeditiously the dimensions of a print, which she was going to copy for her friend, he followed her to it with a look of particular meaning, and conversed with her there for several minutes. The effect of his discourse on the lady too, could not escape her observation, for though she was too honorable to listen, and had even changed her seat, on purpose that she might NOT hear, to one close by the piano forte on which Marianne was playing, she could not keep herself from seeing that Elinor changed colour, attended with agitation, and was too intent on what he said to pursue her employment. Some words of the Colonel's inevitably reached her ear, in which he seemed to be apologising for the badness of his house. This set the matter beyond a doubt. She wondered, indeed, at his thinking it necessary to do so; but supposed it to be the proper etiquette. What Elinor said in reply she could not distinguish, but judged from the motion of her lips, that she did not think *that* any material objection. They then talked on for a few minutes longer without her catching a syllable, when another lucky stop in Marianne's performance brought her these words in the Colonel's calm voice,

"I am afraid it cannot take place very soon."

Astonished and shocked at so unlover-like a speech, she was almost ready to cry out, "Lord! What should hinder it?" But checking her desire, confined herself to this silent ejaculation: "This is very strange!—sure he need not wait to be older."

This delay on the Colonel's side, however, did not seem to offend or mortify his fair companion in the least, for on their breaking up the conference soon afterwards, and moving different ways, Mrs. Jennings very plainly heard Elinor say, and with a voice which showed her to feel what she said, "I shall always think myself very much obliged to you."

Mrs. Jennings was delighted with her gratitude, and only wondered that after hearing such a sentence, the Colonel should be able to take leave of them, as he immediately did, with the utmost sang-froid, and go away without making her any reply!

What had really passed between them was to this effect.

"I have heard," said he, with great compassion, "of the injustice your friend Mr. Ferrars has suffered from his family; for if I understand the matter right, he has been entirely cast off by them for persevering in his engagement with a very deserving young woman.— Have I been rightly informed?—Is it so?—"

Elinor told him that it was.

"The cruelty, the impolitic cruelty," he replied, with great feeling, "of dividing, or attempting to divide, two young people long attached to each other, is terrible. I have seen Mr. Ferrars two or three times in Harley Street, and am much pleased with him. I understand that he intends to take orders. Will you be so good as to tell him that the living of Delaford, now just vacant, as I am informed by this day's post, is his, if he think it worth his acceptance. It is a rectory, but a small one; the late incumbent, I believe, did not make more than two hundred pounds per annum, and though it is certainly capable of improvement, I fear, not to such an amount as to afford him a very comfortable income. Such as it is, however, my pleasure in presenting him to it, will be very great."

Elinor's astonishment at this commission could hardly have been greater, had the Colonel been really making her an offer of his hand. Her emotion was such as Mrs. Jennings had attributed to a very different cause; but whatever minor feelings less pure, less pleasing, might have a share in that emotion, and her gratitude for the particular friendship, which together prompted Colonel Brandon to this act, were strongly felt, and warmly expressed. She promised to undertake the commission with pleasure, if it were really his wish to put off so agreeable an office to another. But at the same time, she could not help thinking that no one could so well perform it as himself; but Colonel Brandon, on motives of equal delicacy, still seemed so desirous of its being given through her means. Edward, she believed, was still in town, and fortunately she had heard his address from Miss Steele. She could undertake therefore to inform him of it, in the course of the day. After this had been settled, Colonel Brandon began to talk of his own advantage in securing so respectable and agreeable a neighbour, and *then* it was that he mentioned with regret, that the house was small and indifferent.

"The smallness of the house," said she, "I cannot imagine any inconvenience to them, for it will be in proportion to their family and income."

By which the Colonel was surprised to find that *she* was considering Mr. Ferrars's marriage as the certain consequence of the presentation; for he did not suppose it possible that Delaford living could supply such an income, as anybody in his style of life would venture to settle on, and he said so.

"This little rectory *can* do no more than make Mr. Ferrars comfortable as a bachelor; it cannot enable him to marry. I am sorry to say that my patronage ends with this. What I am now doing indeed, seems nothing at all, since it can advance him so little towards what must be his principal, his only object of happiness. His marriage must still be a distant good;—at least, I am afraid it cannot take place very soon."

Such was the sentence which, when misunderstood, so justly offended the delicate feelings of Mrs. Jennings; but after this narration of what really passed between Colonel Brandon and Elinor, while they stood at the window, the gratitude expressed by the latter on their parting, may perhaps appear in general, not less reasonably excited, nor less properly worded than if it had arisen from an offer of marriage.

Chapter 40

"Well, Miss Dashwood," said Mrs. Jennings, sagaciously smiling, as soon as the gentleman had withdrawn, "I do not ask you what the Colonel has been saying to you; for though, upon my honour, I *tried* to keep out of hearing. I never was better pleased in my life, and I wish you joy of it with all my heart."

"Thank you, ma'am," said Elinor. "It is a matter of great joy to me; and I feel the goodness of Colonel Brandon most sensibly. There are few people who have so compassionate a heart! I never was more astonished in my life."

"Lord, my dear! You are very modest. I have often thought of late, there was nothing more likely to happen."

"You judged from your knowledge of the Colonel's general benevolence; but at least you could not foresee that the opportunity would so very soon occur."

"Opportunity!" repeated Mrs. Jennings—"When a man has once made up his mind to such a thing, somehow or other he will soon find an opportunity. Well, my dear, I wish you joy of it again and again; and if ever there was a happy couple in the world, I think I shall soon know where to look for them."

"You mean to go to Delaford after them I suppose," said Elinor, with a faint smile.

"Aye, my dear, that I do, indeed. And as to the house being a bad one, I do not know what the Colonel would be at, for it is as good a one as ever I saw."

"He spoke of its being out of repair."

"Well, and whose fault is that? Why doesn't he repair it?"

They were interrupted by the servant's coming in to announce the carriage being at the door; and Mrs. Jennings immediately preparing to go, said, "Well, my dear, I must be gone before I have had half my talk out. But, however, we may have it all over in the evening; for we shall be quite alone. I do not ask you to go with me, for I dare say your mind is too full of the matter to care for company; and besides, you must long to tell your sister all about it."

Marianne had left the room before the conversation began.

"Certainly, ma'am, I shall tell Marianne of it; but I shall not mention it at present to anybody else."

"Oh! Very well," said Mrs. Jennings rather disappointed. "Then you would not have me tell it to Lucy."

"No, ma'am, not even Lucy if you please. Till I have written to Mr. Ferrars, I think it ought not to be mentioned to anybody else. I shall do *that* directly. It is of importance that no time should be lost with him, for he will of course have much to do relative to his ordination."

This speech at first puzzled Mrs. Jennings exceedingly. A few moments' reflection, however, produced a very happy idea, and she exclaimed; "Oh, ho! I understand you. Mr. Ferrars is to be the man. Well, so much the better for him. Ay, to be sure, he must be ordained in readiness; and I am very glad to find things are so forward between you. But, my dear, is not this rather out of character? Should not the Colonel write himself?"

Elinor did not quite understand the beginning of Mrs. Jennings's speech, neither did she think it worth inquiring into; and therefore only replied to its conclusion.

"Colonel Brandon is so delicate a man, that he rather wished any one to announce his intentions to Mr. Ferrars than himself."

"And so *you* are forced to do it. Well *that* is an odd kind of delicacy! However, I will not disturb you. You know your own concerns best. So goodby, my dear. I have not heard of any thing to please me so well since Charlotte was brought to bed."

How Elinor should begin—how she should express herself in her note to Edward, was now all her concern. She equally feared to say too much or too little, and sat deliberating over her paper, with the pen in her hand, till broken in on by the entrance of Edward himself.

He had met Mrs. Jennings at the door in her way to the carriage, as he came to leave his farewell card; and she had obliged him to enter, by saying that Miss Dashwood was above, and wanted to speak with him on very particular business.

Elinor had just been congratulating herself, in the midst of her perplexity, that however difficult it might be to express herself properly by letter, it was at least preferable to giving the information by word of mouth, when her visitor entered. Her astonishment and confusion were very great on his so sudden appearance. She had not seen him before since his engagement became public. He too was much distressed; and they sat down together in a most promising state of embarrassment. Whether he had asked her pardon for his intrusion on first coming into the room, he could not recollect; but determining to be on the safe side, he made his apology in form as soon as he could say anything, after taking a chair.

"Mrs. Jennings told me," said he, "that you wished to speak with me, or I certainly should not have intruded on you in such a manner; though at the same time, I should have been extremely sorry to leave London without seeing you and your sister. I go to Oxford tomorrow."

"You would not have gone, however," said Elinor, recovering

herself, "without receiving our good wishes, even if we had not been able to give them in person. I have something of consequence to inform you of, which I was on the point of communicating by paper. I am charged with a most agreeable office. Colonel Brandon has desired me to say, that understanding you mean to take orders, he has great pleasure in offering you the living of Delaford now just vacant, and only wishes it were more valuable. Allow me to congratulate you on having so respectable and well-judging a friend, and to join in his wish that the living—it is about two hundred a-year—were much more considerable, and such as might better enable you to—as might establish all your views of happiness."

What Edward felt, as he could not say it himself, it cannot be expected that anyone else should say for him. He *looked* all the astonishment which such unexpected, such unthought-of information could not fail of exciting; but he said only these two words: "Colonel Brandon!"

"Yes," continued Elinor, gathering more resolution, as some of the worst was over, "Colonel Brandon means it as a testimony of his concern for what has lately passed."

"Colonel Brandon give *me* a living! Can it be possible?"

"The unkindness of your own relations has made you astonished to find friendship anywhere."

"No," replied he, with sudden consciousness, "not to find it in *you*; for I cannot be ignorant that to you, to your goodness, I owe it all."

"You are very much mistaken. I do assure you that you owe it entirely, at least almost entirely, to your own merit, and Colonel Brandon's discernment of it. I have had no hand in it."

For a short time he sat deep in thought, after Elinor had ceased to speak;—at last, and as if it were rather an effort, he said, "Colonel Brandon seems a man of great worth and respectability. I have always heard him spoken of as such, and your brother I know esteems him highly. He is undoubtedly a sensible man, and in his manners perfectly the gentleman."

"Indeed," replied Elinor, "I believe that you will find him, on farther acquaintance, all that you have heard him to be, and as you will be such very near neighbours it is particularly important that he *should* be all this."

Edward made no answer; but when she had turned away her head, gave her a look so serious, so earnest, so uncheerful, as seemed to say, that he might hereafter wish the distance between the parsonage and the mansion-house much greater.

"Colonel Brandon, I think, lodges in St. James Street," said he, soon afterwards, rising from his chair.

Elinor told him the number of the house.

"I must hurry away then, to give him those thanks which you will not allow me to give *you*."

Elinor did not offer to detain him; and they parted, with a very earnest assurance on *her* side of her unceasing good wishes for his happiness in every change of situation that might befall him; on *his*, with rather an attempt to return the same good will, than the power of expressing it.

"When I see him again," said Elinor to herself, as the door shut him out, "I shall see him the husband of Lucy."

When Mrs. Jennings came home, her mind was so much more occupied by the important secret in her possession, than by anything else, that she reverted to it again as soon as Elinor appeared.

"Well, my dear," she cried, "I sent you up the young man. You did not find him very unwilling to accept your proposal?"

"No, ma'am; *that* was not very likely."

"Well, and how soon will he be ready?"

"Really," said Elinor, "I know so little of these kind of forms, that I can hardly even conjecture as to the time, or the preparation necessary; but I suppose two or three months will complete his ordination."

"Two or three months!" cried Mrs. Jennings; "Can the Colonel wait two or three months! And though one would be very glad to do a kindness by poor Mr. Ferrars, I do think it is not worthwhile to wait two or three months for him. Sure somebody else might be found that would do as well."

"My dear ma'am," said Elinor, "what can you be thinking of? Why, Colonel Brandon's only object is to be of use to Mr. Ferrars."

"Lord bless you, my dear! Sure you do not mean to persuade me that the Colonel only marries you for the sake of giving ten guineas to Mr. Ferrars!"

The deception could not continue after this; and an explanation immediately took place, by which both gained considerable amusement for the moment, without any material loss of happiness to either, for Mrs. Jennings only exchanged one form of delight for another, and still without forfeiting her expectation of the first.

"Aye, aye, the parsonage is but a small one," said she, "and very likely *may* be out of repair; but to hear a man apologising, as I thought, for a house that to my knowledge has five sitting rooms on the ground-floor! It seems quite ridiculous. But, my dear, we must touch up the Colonel to do something to the parsonage, and make it comfortable for them, before Lucy goes to it."

"But Colonel Brandon does not seem to have any idea of the living's being enough to allow them to marry."

"The Colonel is a ninny, my dear; because he has two thousand a-year himself, he thinks that nobody else can marry on less. Take my word for it, that, if I am alive, I shall be paying a visit at Delaford Parsonage before Michaelmas; and I am sure I shan't go if Lucy isn't there."

Elinor was quite of her opinion, as to the probability of their not waiting for anything more.

Chapter 41

Edward, having carried his thanks to Colonel Brandon, proceeded with his happiness to Lucy; and such was the excess of it by the time he reached Bartlett's Buildings, that she was able to assure Mrs. Jennings, who called on her again the next day with her congratulations, that she had never seen him in such spirits before in her life.

Her own happiness, and her own spirits, were at least very certain; and she joined Mrs. Jennings most heartily in her expectation of their being all comfortably together in Delaford Parsonage before Michaelmas. So far was she, at the same time, from any backwardness to give Elinor that credit which Edward *would* give her, that she spoke of her friendship for them both with the most grateful warmth, was ready to own all their obligation to her. As for Colonel Brandon, she was not only ready to worship him as a saint, but was moreover truly anxious that he should be treated as one in all worldly concerns; anxious that his tithes should be raised to the utmost; and scarcely resolved to avail herself, at Delaford, as far as she possibly could, of his servants, his carriage, his cows, and his poultry.

It was now above a week since John Dashwood had called in Berkeley Street, and as since that time no notice had been taken by them of his wife's indisposition, beyond one verbal enquiry, Elinor began to feel it necessary to pay her a visit. Marianne, not contented with absolutely refusing to go herself, was very urgent to prevent her sister's going at all; and Mrs. Jennings, though her carriage was always at Elinor's service, so very much disliked Mrs. John Dashwood, that not even her curiosity to see how she looked after the late discovery, nor her strong desire to affront her by taking Edward's part, could overcome her unwillingness to be in her company again. The consequence was that Elinor set out by herself.

Mrs. Dashwood was denied; but before the carriage could turn from the house, her husband accidentally came out. He expressed great pleasure in meeting Elinor, and assuring her that Fanny would be very glad to see her, invited her to come in.

They walked up stairs in to the drawing-room. Nobody was there.

"Fanny is in her own room, I suppose," said he. "I will go to her presently, for I am sure she will not have the least objection in the world to seeing *you*. Why would not Marianne come?"

Elinor made what excuse she could for her.

"I am not sorry to see you alone," he replied, "for I have a good deal to say to you. This living of Colonel Brandon's, has he really given it to Edward? I heard it yesterday by chance, and was coming to you on purpose to enquire farther about it."

"It is perfectly true."

"Really! Well, this is very astonishing! And now that livings fetch such a price! What was the value of this?"

"About two hundred a year."

"Very well—and for the next presentation to a living of that value—supposing the late incumbent to have been old and sickly, and likely to vacate it soon, he might have got I dare say, fourteen hundred pounds. And how came he not to have settled that matter before this person's death? *Now* indeed it would be too late to sell it, but a man of Colonel Brandon's sense! I suppose; however, on recollection, that the case may probably be *this*. Edward is only to hold the living till the person to whom the Colonel has really sold the presentation, is old enough to take it."

Elinor contradicted it, however, very positively; and by relating that she had herself been employed in conveying the offer from Colonel Brandon to Edward, and, therefore, must understand the terms on which it was given, obliged him to submit to her authority.

"It is truly astonishing!" he cried, after hearing what she said, "what could be the Colonel's motive?"

"A very simple one—to be of use to Mr. Ferrars."

"Well, well; whatever Colonel Brandon may be, Edward is a very lucky man.—You will not mention the matter to Fanny however, she will not like to hear it much talked of."

Elinor had some difficulty here to refrain from observing, that she thought Fanny might have borne with composure, an acquisition of wealth to her brother, by which neither she nor her child could be possibly impoverished.

"Mrs. Ferrars," added he, lowering his voice to the tone becoming so important a subject, "knows nothing about it at present, and I believe it will be best to keep it entirely concealed from her as long as may be."

"But why should such precaution be used? Though it is not to be supposed that Mrs. Ferrars can have the smallest satisfaction in knowing that her son has money enough to live upon, yet why, upon her late behaviour, is she supposed to feel at all? She has done with her son, she cast him off for ever. She would not be so weak as to throw away the comfort of a child, and yet retain the anxiety of a parent!"

"Ah! Elinor," said John, "your reasoning is very good, but it is founded on ignorance of human nature. When Edward's unhappy match takes place, depend upon it his mother will feel as much as if she had never discarded him. Mrs. Ferrars can never forget that Edward is her son."

"You surprise me; I should think it must nearly have escaped her memory by *this* time."

"You wrong her exceedingly. Mrs. Ferrars is one of the most affectionate mothers in the world."

Elinor was silent.

"We think *now*," said Mr. Dashwood, after a short pause, "of *Robert's* marrying Miss Morton."

Elinor, smiling at the grave and decisive importance of her brother's tone, calmly replied, "The lady, I suppose, has no choice in the affair."

"Choice! How do you mean?"

"I only mean that I suppose, from your manner of speaking, it must be the same to Miss Morton whether she marry Edward or Robert."

"Certainly, there can be no difference; for Robert will now to all intents and purposes be considered as the eldest son; and as to anything else, they are both very agreeable young men: I do not know that one is superior to the other."

"Of *one* thing, my dear sister," kindly taking her hand, and speaking in an awful whisper, —"I may assure you. I have good reason to think—indeed I have it from the best authority; whatever objections there might be against a certain—a certain connection—you understand me—it would have been far preferable to her, it would not have given her half the vexation that *this* does. I was exceedingly pleased to hear that Mrs. Ferrars considered it in that light. 'It would have been beyond comparison,' she said, 'the least evil of the two.' But however, all that is quite out of the question—not to be thought of or mentioned—as to any attachment you know—it never could be—all that is gone by. But I thought I would just tell you of this, because I knew how much it must please you. Not that you have any reason to regret, my dear Elinor. There is no doubt of your doing exceedingly well—quite as well, or better, perhaps, all things considered. Has Colonel Brandon been with you lately?"

Elinor had heard enough, if not to gratify her vanity, and raise her self-importance, to agitate her nerves and fill her mind;—and she was therefore glad to be spared from the necessity of saying much in reply herself, and from the danger of hearing any thing more from her brother, by the entrance of Mr. Robert Ferrars. After a few moments' chat, John Dashwood, recollecting that Fanny was yet uninformed of her sister's being there, quitted the room in quest of her; and Elinor was left to improve her acquaintance with Robert, who, by the gay unconcern, the happy self-complacency of his manner while enjoying so unfair a division of his mother's love and liberality, to the prejudice of his banished brother, earned only by his own dissipated course of life, and that brother's integrity, was confirming her most unfavourable opinion of his head and heart.

They had scarcely been two minutes by themselves, before he began to speak of Edward; for he, too, had heard of the living, and was very inquisitive on the subject. Elinor repeated the particulars of it, as she had given them to John; and their effect on Robert, though very different, was not less striking than it had been on *him*. He laughed most immoderately. The idea of Edward's being a clergyman, and living in a small parsonage-house, diverted him beyond measure;—and when to that was added the fanciful imagery of Edward reading prayers in a white surplice, and publishing the banns of marriage between John Smith and Mary Brown, he could conceive nothing more ridiculous.

"We may treat it as a joke," said he, "but, upon my soul, it is a most serious business. Poor Edward! He is ruined forever. You must not judge of him, Miss Dashwood, from *your* slight acquaintance. His manners are certainly not the happiest in nature. But we are not all born, you know, with the same powers, the same address. I declare and protest to you I never was so shocked in my life, as when it all burst forth. I could not believe it. My mother was the first person who told me of it; and I, immediately said to her, 'My dear madam, I do not know what you may intend to do on the occasion, but as for myself, I must say, that if Edward does marry this young woman, I never will see him again.' Poor Edward! He has done for himself completely; but, as I directly said to my mother, I am not in the least surprised at it; from his style of education, it was always to be expected."

"Have you ever seen the lady?"

"Yes; once, while she was staying in this house. The merest awkward country girl without style, or elegance, and almost without beauty. Just the kind of girl I should suppose likely to captivate poor Edward. I offered immediately, as soon as my mother related the affair to me, to talk to him myself, and dissuade him from the match; but it was too late *then*, I found, to do anything. But had I been informed of it a few hours earlier, I certainly should have represented it to Edward in a very strong light. 'My dear fellow,' I should have said; 'You are making a most disgraceful connection, and such a one as your family are unanimous in disapproving.' He must be starved, you know;— that is certain; absolutely starved."

He had just settled this point with great composure, when the entrance of Mrs. John Dashwood put an end to the subject. But though *she* never spoke of it out of her own family, Elinor could see its influence on her mind, in the something like confusion of countenance with which she entered, and an attempt at cordiality in her behaviour to herself. She even proceeded so far as to be concerned to find that Elinor and her sister were so soon to leave town, as she had hoped to see more of them; an exertion in which her husband, seemed to distinguish every \thing that was most affectionate and graceful.

Chapter 42

One other short call in Harley Street, in which Elinor received her brother's congratulations on their travelling so far towards Barton without any expense, and on Colonel Brandon's being to follow them to Cleveland in a day or two, completed the intercourse of the brother and sisters in town; and a faint invitation from Fanny, to come to Norland whenever it should happen to be in their way, which of all things was the most unlikely to occur, with a more warm, though less public, assurance, from John to Elinor, of the promptitude with which he should come to see her at Delaford, was all that foretold any meeting in the country.

Very early in April, and tolerably early in the day, the two parties from Hanover Square and Berkeley Street set out from their respective homes, to meet, by appointment, on the road. For the convenience of Charlotte and her child, they were to be more than two days on their journey, and Mr. Palmer, travelling more expeditiously with Colonel Brandon, was to join them at Cleveland soon after their arrival.

Marianne could not bid adieu to the house in which she had for the last time enjoyed those hopes, and that confidence, in Willoughby, which were now extinguished forever, without great pain. Nor could she leave the place in which Willoughby remained, without shedding many tears.

Elinor was more positive. She had no such object for her lingering thoughts to fix on, she was pleased to be free herself from the persecution of Lucy's friendship, she was grateful for bringing her sister away unseen by Willoughby since his marriage, and she looked forward with hope to what a few months of tranquility at Barton might do towards restoring Marianne's peace of mind, and confirming her own.

Their journey was safely performed. The second day brought them into the cherished, or the prohibited, county of Somerset, for as such was it dwelt on by turns in Marianne's imagination; and in the forenoon of the third they drove up to Cleveland.

Cleveland was a spacious, modern-built house, situated on a sloping lawn. It had its open shrubbery, and closer wood walk, a road of smooth gravel winding round a plantation, led to the front.

Marianne entered the house with a heart swelling with emotion from the consciousness of being only eighty miles from Barton, and not thirty from Combe Magna; and before she had been five minutes within its walls, she quitted it again, stealing away through the winding shrubberies, now just beginning to be in beauty, to gain a distant eminence; where, from its Grecian temple, her eye, wandering over a wide tract of country to the south-east, could fondly rest on the farthest ridge of hills in the horizon, and fancy that from their summits Combe Magna might be seen.

She returned just in time to join the others as they quitted the house, on an excursion through its more immediate premises; and the rest of the morning was easily whiled away, in lounging round the kitchen garden, examining the bloom upon its walls, and listening to the gardener's lamentations upon blights, in dawdling through the green-house, where the loss of her favourite plants, unwarily exposed, and nipped by the lingering frost, raised the laughter of Charlotte.

The morning was fine and dry, and Marianne, in her plan of employment abroad, had not calculated for any change of weather during their stay at Cleveland. With great surprise therefore, did she find herself prevented by a settled rain from going out again after dinner. She had depended on a twilight walk to the Grecian temple, and perhaps all over the grounds, and an evening merely cold or damp would not have deterred her from it; but a heavy and settled rain even *she* could not fancy dry or pleasant weather for walking.

Their party was small, and the hours passed quietly away. Mrs. Palmer had her child, and Mrs. Jennings her carpet-work; they talked of the friends they had left behind, arranged Lady Middleton's engagements, and wondered whether Mr. Palmer and Colonel Brandon would get farther than Reading that night. Elinor, however little concerned in it, joined in their discourse; and Marianne, who had the knack of finding her way in every house to the library, however it might be avoided by the family in general, soon procured herself a book.

Nothing was wanting on Mrs. Palmer's side that constant and friendly good humour could do, to make them feel themselves welcome. The openness and heartiness of her manner was engaging; her folly, though evident was not disgusting, because it was not conceited; and Elinor could have forgiven everything but her laugh.

The two gentlemen arrived the next day to a very late dinner. Elinor had seen so little of Mr. Palmer, and in that little had seen so much variety in his address to her sister and herself, that she knew not what to expect to find him in his own family. She found him, however, perfectly the gentleman in his behaviour to all his visitors, and only occasionally rude to his wife and her mother; she found him very capable of being a pleasant companion, and only prevented from being so always, by too great an aptitude to fancy himself as much superior to people in general, as he must feel himself to be to Mrs. Jennings and Charlotte. She liked him, however, upon the whole, much better than she had expected, and in her heart was not sorry that she could like him no more.

Of Edward, or at least of some of his concerns, she now received intelligence from Colonel Brandon, who treating her at once as the disinterested friend of Mr. Ferrars, and the kind of confidant of himself, talked to her a great deal of the parsonage at Delaford, described its deficiencies, and told her what he meant to do himself towards removing them. His behaviour to her after an absence of only ten days, might very well justify Mrs. Jennings's persuasion of his attachment, and would have been enough, perhaps, had not Elinor still, as from the first, believed Marianne his real favourite, to make her suspect it herself. But as it was, such a notion had scarcely ever entered her head, except by Mrs. Jennings's suggestion; and she could not help believing herself the nicest observer of the two; and while his looks of anxious solicitude on Marianne's feeling, in her head and throat, the beginning of a heavy cold, because unexpressed by words, entirely escaped the latter lady's observation; *she* could discover in them the quick feelings, and needless alarm of a lover.

Two delightful twilight walks on the third and fourth evenings of her being there, assisted by the still greater imprudence of sitting in her wet shoes and stocking, had given Marianne a cold so violent as, though for a day or two trifled with or denied, would force itself by increasing ailments on the concern of everybody, and the notice of herself. Though heavy and feverish, with a pain in her limbs, and a cough, and a sore throat, a good night's rest was to cure her entirely; and it was with difficulty that Elinor prevailed on her, when she went to bed, to try one or two of the simplest of the remedies.

Chapter 43

Marianne got up the next morning at her usual time; to every inquiry replied that she was better, and tried to prove herself so, by engaging in her accustomary employments. But a day spent in sitting shivering over the fire with a book in her hand, which she was unable to read, or in lying, weary and languid, on a sofa, did not speak much in favour of her amendment; and when, at last, she went early to bed, more and more indisposed, Colonel Brandon was only astonished at her sister's composure, who trusted, like Marianne, to the certainty and efficacy of sleep, and felt no real alarm.

A very restless and feverish night, however, disappointed the expectation of both; and when Marianne, after persisting in rising, confessed herself unable to sit up, and returned voluntarily to her bed, Elinor was very ready to adopt Mrs. Jennings's advice, of sending for the Palmers' apothecary.

He came, examined his patient, and though encouraging Miss Dashwood to expect that a very few days would restore her sister to health, yet, by pronouncing her disorder to have a putrid tendency, and allowing the word "infection" to pass his lips, gave instant alarm to Mrs. Palmer, on her baby's account. Mrs. Jennings, who had been inclined from the first to think Marianne's complaint more serious than Elinor, now looked very grave on Mr. Harris's report, and confirming Charlotte's fears and caution, urged the necessity of her immediate removal with her infant. Her departure, therefore, was fixed on; and within an hour after Mr. Harris's arrival, she set off, with her little boy and his nurse, for the house of a near relation of Mr. Palmer's, who lived a few miles on the other side of Bath; whither her husband promised, at her earnest entreaty, to join her in a day or two. Mrs. Jennings, however, with a kindness of heart which made Elinor really love her, declared her resolution of not stirring from Cleveland as long as Marianne remained ill, and Elinor found her on every occasion a most willing and active helpmate, desirous to share in all her fatigues, and often by her better experience in nursing, of material use.

Poor Marianne, languid and low from the nature of her malady, and feeling herself universally ill, could no longer hope that tomorrow would find her recovered; and the idea of what tomorrow would have produced, but for this unlucky illness, made every ailment severe; for on that day they were to have begun their journey home; and, attended the whole way by a servant of Mrs. Jennings, were to have taken their mother by surprise on the following forenoon. The little she said was all in lamentation of this inevitable delay; though Elinor tried to raise her spirits, and make her believe, as she *then* really believed herself, that it would be a very short one.

The next day produced little or no alteration in the state of the patient. Their party was now farther reduced; for Mr. Palmer, was persuaded at last by Colonel Brandon to perform his promise of following her; and while he was preparing to go, Colonel Brandon himself, began to talk of going likewise. Here, however, the kindness of Mrs. Jennings interposed most acceptably; for to send the Colonel away while his love was in so much uneasiness on her sister's account, would be to deprive them both, she thought, of every comfort; and therefore telling him at once that his stay at Cleveland was necessary to herself, that she should want him to play at piquet of an evening, while Miss Dashwood was above with her sister, &c. she urged him so strongly to remain, that he could not long even affect to demur.

Marianne was, of course, kept in ignorance of all these arrangements. She knew not that she had been the means of sending the owners of Cleveland away, in about seven days from the time of their arrival. It gave her no surprise that she saw nothing of Mrs. Palmer; and as it gave her likewise no concern, she never mentioned her name.

Two days passed away from the time of Mr. Palmer's departure, and her situation continued, with little variation, the same. Mr. Harris, who attended her every day, still talked boldly of a speedy recovery, and Miss Dashwood was equally sanguine. Mrs. Jennings had determined very early in the seizure that Marianne would never get over it, and Colonel Brandon, tried to reason himself out of fears, which the different judgment of the apothecary seemed to render absurd. He could not expel from his mind the persuasion that he should see Marianne no more.

On the morning of the third day however, the gloomy anticipations of both were almost done away; for when Mr. Harris arrived, he declared his patient materially better. Her pulse was much stronger, and every symptom more favourable than on the preceding visit.

But the day did not close so auspiciously as it began. Towards the evening Marianne became ill again, growing more heavy, restless, and uncomfortable than before. Her sister, however, still sanguine, was willing to attribute the change to nothing more than the fatigue of having sat up to have her bed made; and carefully administering the cordials prescribed, saw her, with satisfaction, sink at last into a slumber, from which she expected the most beneficial effects. Her sleep, though not so quiet as Elinor wished to see it, lasted a considerable time; and anxious to observe the result of it herself, she resolved to sit with her during the whole of it. Mrs. Jennings, knowing nothing of any change in the patient, went unusually early to bed; and Elinor remained alone with Marianne.

The repose of the latter became more and more disturbed; and her sister, who watched, with unremitting attention her continual change of posture, and heard the frequent but inarticulate sounds of complaint which passed her lips, was almost wishing to rouse her from so painful a slumber, when Marianne, suddenly awakened by some accidental noise in the house, started hastily up, and, with feverish wildness, cried out, "Is mama coming —"

"Not yet," cried the other, concealing her terror, and assisting Marianne to lie down again, "but she will be here, I hope, before it is long."

"But she must not go round by London," cried Marianne, in the same hurried manner. "I shall never see her, if she goes by London."

Elinor perceived with alarm that she was not quite herself, and eagerly felt her pulse. It was lower and quicker than ever, and Marianne, still talking wildly of mama; Elinor's alarm increased so rapidly, as to determine her on sending instantly for Mr. Harris, and despatching a messenger to Barton for her mother. To consult with Colonel Brandon on the best means of effecting the latter, was a thought which immediately followed the resolution of its performance; and as soon she had rung up the maid to take her place by her sister, she hastened down to the drawing-room, where she knew he was generally to be found.

It was no time for hesitation. Her fears and her difficulties were immediately before him. Her fears, he had no courage, no confidence to attempt the removal of:—he listened to them in silent despondence;—but her difficulties were instantly obviated, for with a readiness that seemed to speak the occasion, and the service pre-arranged in his mind, he offered himself as the messenger who should fetch Mrs. Dashwood. Elinor made no resistance that was not easily overcome. She thanked him with brief, though fervent gratitude, and while he went to hurry off his servant with a message to Mr. Harris, and an order for post-horses directly, she wrote a few lines to her mother.

The comfort of such a friend at that moment as Colonel Brandon—or such a companion for her mother, how gratefully was it felt! As far as the shock of such a summons *could* be lessened to her, his presence, his manners, his assistance, would lessen it.

Not a moment was lost in delay of any kind. The horses arrived, even before they were expected, and Colonel Brandon only pressing her hand with a look of solemnity, hurried into the carriage. It was then about twelve o'clock, and she returned to her sister's apartment to wait for the arrival of the apothecary, and to watch by her the rest of the night. Hour after hour passed away in sleepless pain and delirium on Marianne's side, and in the most cruel anxiety on Elinor's, before Mr. Harris appeared.

Marianne's ideas were still, at intervals, fixed incoherently on her mother, and whenever she mentioned her name, it gave a pang to the heart of poor Elinor, who fancied that all relief might soon be in vain, that everything had been delayed too long, and pictured to herself her suffering mother arriving too late to see this darling child, or to see her rational.

She was on the point of sending again for Mr. Harris when he arrived. His opinion, however, made some little amends for his delay, for though acknowledging a very unexpected and unpleasant alteration in his patient, he would not allow the danger to be material, and talked of the relief which a fresh mode of treatment must procure, with a confidence which, in a lesser degree, was communicated to Elinor. He promised to call again in the course of three or four hours, and left both the patient and her anxious attendant more composed than he had found them.

With strong concern, and with many reproaches for not being called to their aid, did Mrs. Jennings hear in the morning of what had passed. Her former apprehensions left her no doubt of the event; and though trying to speak comfort to Elinor, her conviction of her sister's danger would not allow her to offer the comfort of hope. The rapid decay, the early death of a girl so young, so lovely as Marianne, must have struck a less interested person with concern. On Mrs. Jennings's compassion she had other claims. She had been for three months her companion, was still under her care, and she was known to have been greatly injured, and long unhappy.

Mr. Harris was punctual in his second visit;—but he came to be disappointed in his hopes of what the last would produce. His medicines had failed;—the fever was unabated; and Marianne only more quiet—not more herself—remained in a heavy stupor. Elinor, catching all, and more than all, his fears in a moment, proposed to call in further advice. But he judged it unnecessary: he had still something more to try, some more fresh application, of whose success he was as confident as the last, and his visit concluded with encouraging assurances which reached the ear, but could not enter the heart of Miss Dashwood.

About noon, however, she began—but with a caution—a dread of disappointment which for some time kept her silent, even to her friend—to fancy, to hope she could perceive a slight amendment in her sister's pulse; she waited, watched, and examined it again and again; and at last, with an agitation more difficult to bury under exterior calmness, than all her foregoing distress, ventured to communicate her hopes. Mrs. Jennings, though forced, on examination, to acknowledge a temporary revival, tried to keep her young friend from indulging a thought of its continuance; and Elinor, conning over every injunction of distrust, told herself likewise not to hope. But it was too late. Hope had already entered; and feeling all its anxious flutter, she bent over her sister to watch she hardly knew for what. Half an hour passed away, and the favourable symptom yet blessed her.

Others even arose to confirm it. Her breath, her skin, her lips, all flattered Elinor with signs of amendment; and Marianne fixed her eyes on her with a rational, though languid, gaze. Anxiety and hope now oppressed her in equal degrees, and left her no moment of tranquillity till the arrival of Mr. Harris at four o'clock; when his assurances, his felicitations on a recovery in her sister even surpassing his expectation, gave her confidence, comfort, and tears of joy.

Marianne was in every respect materially better, and he declared her entirely out of danger. Mrs. Jennings, perhaps satisfied with the partial justification of her forebodings which had been found in their late alarm, allowed herself to trust in his judgment, and admitted, with unfeigned joy, and soon with unequivocal cheerfulness, the probability of an entire recovery.

Elinor could not be cheerful. Her joy was of a different kind, and led to anything rather than to gaiety. Marianne restored to life, health, friends, and to her doting mother, was an idea to fill her heart with sensations of exquisite comfort, and expand it in fervent gratitude; but it led to no outward demonstrations of joy, no words, no smiles. All within Elinor's breast was satisfaction, silent and strong.

She continued by the side of her sister, with little intermission the whole afternoon, calming every fear, satisfying every inquiry of her enfeebled spirits, supplying every succour, and watching almost every look and every breath. The possibility of a relapse would of course, in some moments, occur to remind her of what anxiety was—but when she saw, on her frequent and minute examination, that every symptom of recovery continued, and saw Marianne at six o'clock sink into a quiet, steady, and to all appearance comfortable, sleep, she silenced every doubt.

The time was now drawing on, when Colonel Brandon might be expected back. At ten o'clock, she trusted, or at least not much later her mother would be relieved from the dreadful suspense in which she must now be travelling towards them. The Colonel, too! Perhaps scarcely less an object of pity!—Oh!—how slow was the progress of time which yet kept them in ignorance!

At seven o'clock, leaving Marianne still sweetly asleep, she joined Mrs. Jennings in the drawing-room to tea. Of breakfast she had been kept by her fears, and of dinner by their sudden reverse, from eating much;—and the present refreshment, therefore, with such feelings of content as she brought to it, was particularly welcome. Mrs. Jennings would have persuaded her, at its conclusion, to take some rest before her mother's arrival, and allow *her* to take her place by Marianne; but Elinor had no sense of fatigue, no capability of sleep at that moment about her, and she was not to be kept away from her sister an unnecessary instant.

The night was cold and stormy. The wind roared round the house, and the rain beat against the windows; but Elinor, all happiness within, regarded it not. Marianne slept through every blast; and the travellers—they had a rich reward in store, for every present inconvenience.

The clock struck eight. Had it been ten, Elinor would have been convinced that at that moment she heard a carriage driving up to the house; and so strong was the persuasion that she *did*, in spite of the *almost* impossibility of their being already come, that she opened a window shutter, to be satisfied of the truth. The flaring lamps of a carriage were immediately in view. By their uncertain light she thought she could discern it to be drawn by four horses; and this, while it told the excess of her poor mother's alarm, gave some explanation to such unexpected rapidity.

Never in her life had Elinor found it so difficult to be calm, as at that moment. The knowledge of what her mother must be feeling as the carriage stopt at the door—of her doubt—her dread—perhaps her despair! —and of what *she* had to tell! With such knowledge it was impossible to be calm. All that remained to be done was to be speedy; and, therefore staying only till she could leave Mrs. Jennings's maid with her sister, she hurried down stairs.

She rushed to the drawing-room, she entered it, and saw only Willoughby.

Chapter 44

Elinor obeyed the first impulse of her heart in turning instantly to quit the room, and her hand was already on the lock, when its action was suspended by his hastily advancing, and saying, in a voice rather of command than supplication, "Miss Dashwood, for half an hour—for ten minutes—I entreat you to stay."

"No, sir," she replied with firmness, "I shall *not* stay. The servants, I suppose, forgot to tell you that Mr. Palmer was not in the house."

"Had they told me," he cried with vehemence, "that Mr. Palmer and all his relations were at the devil, it would not have turned me from the door. My business is with you, and only you."

"With me!"—in the utmost amazement. "Well, sir, be quick—and if you can, less violent."

"Sit down, and I will be both."

She hesitated; she knew not what to do. The possibility of Colonel Brandon's arriving and finding her there, came across her. But she had promised to hear him, and her curiosity no less than her honor was engaged. After a moment's recollection, therefore, concluding that prudence required dispatch, and that her acquiescence would best promote it, she walked silently towards the table, and sat down.

"Pray be quick, sir," said Elinor, impatiently; "I have no time to spare."

He was sitting in an attitude of deep meditation, and seemed not to hear her.

"Your sister," said he, with abruptness, a moment afterwards, "is out of danger. But is it true? Is it really true?"

Elinor would not speak. He repeated the inquiry with yet greater eagerness.

"For God's sake tell me, is she out of danger, or is she not?"

"We hope she is."

"Had I known as much half an hour ago—But since I *am* here," speaking with a forced vivacity as he returned to his seat? Miss Dashwood, tell me honestly"—a deeper glow overspreading his cheeks—"do you think me most a knave or a fool?"

Elinor looked at him with greater astonishment than ever. She began to think that he must be in liquor;—the strangeness of such a visit, and of such manners, seemed no otherwise intelligible; and with this impression she immediately rose, saying, "Mr. Willoughby, I advise you at present to return to Combe—I am not at leisure to remain with you longer. Whatever your business may be with me, will it be better recollected and explained to-morrow."

"I understand you," he replied, with an expressive smile, and a voice perfectly calm; "yes, I am very drunk. A pint of porter with my cold beef at Marlborough was enough to over-set me."

"At Marlborough!"

"Yes, I left London this morning at eight o'clock, and the only ten minutes I have spent out of my chaise since that time procured me a nuncheon at Marlborough."

The steadiness of his manner, and the intelligence of his eye as he spoke, convincing Elinor, that he was not brought there by intoxication, she said, "Mr. Willoughby, you *ought* to feel, and I certainly *do*—that after what has passed—your coming here in this manner, and forcing yourself upon my notice, requires a very particular excuse. What is it, that you mean by it?"

"I mean," aid he, with serious energy—"if I can, to make you hate me one degree less than you do NOW. I mean to offer some kind of explanation, some kind of apology, for the past; to open my whole heart to you, and by convincing you, that though I have been always a blockhead, I have not been always a rascal."

"Is this the real reason of your coming?"

"Upon my soul it is," was his answer, with a warmth, which brought all the former Willoughby to her remembrance, and in spite of herself made her think him sincere.

"If that is all, you may be satisfied already, for Marianne *does*—she has *long* forgiven you."

"Has she?" he cried, in the same eager tone. "Then she has forgiven me before she ought to have done it. But she shall forgive me again, and on more reasonable grounds. *Now* will you listen to me?"

Elinor bowed her assent.

"I do not know," said he, after a pause of expectation on her side, and thoughtfulness on his own,—"how *you* may have accounted for my behaviour to your sister. When I first became intimate in your family, I had no other intention, no other view in the acquaintance than to pass my time pleasantly while I was obliged to remain in Devonshire. Your sister's lovely person and interesting manners could not but please me; and her behaviour to me almost from the first, was of a kind—It is astonishing, when I reflect on what it was, and what she was, that my heart should have been so insensible! But at first I must confess, my vanity only was elevated by it. Careless of her happiness, thinking only of my own amusement, giving way to feelings which I had always been too much in the habit of indulging, I endeavoured, by every means in my power, to make myself pleasing to her, without any design of returning her affection."

Miss Dashwood, at this point, turning her eyes on him with the most angry contempt, stopped him, by saying, "It is hardly worth while, Mr. Willoughby, for you to relate, or for me to listen any longer."

"I insist on you hearing the whole of it," he replied, "My fortune was never large, and I had always been expensive. Every year since my coming of age, or even before, I believe, had added to my debts; and though the death of my old cousin, Mrs. Smith, was to set me free; yet that event being uncertain, it had been for some time my intention to re-establish my circumstances by marrying a woman of fortune. To attach myself to your sister, therefore, was not a thing to be thought of; and with a meanness, selfishness, cruelty—I was acting in this manner, trying to engage her regard, without a thought of returning it. But one thing may be said for me: even in that horrid state of selfish vanity, I did not know the extent of the injury I meditated, because I did not *then* know what it was to love. But have I ever known it? Well may it be doubted; for, had I really loved, could I have sacrificed my feelings to vanity, to avarice? But I have done it. To avoid a comparative poverty, which her affection and her society would have deprived of all its horrors, I have, by raising myself to affluence, lost everything that could make it a blessing."

"You did then," said Elinor, a little softened, "believe yourself at one time attached to her?"

"Yes, I found myself, by insensible degrees, sincerely fond of her; and the happiest hours of my life were what I spent with her. Even *then*, however, when fully determined on paying my addresses to her, I allowed myself most improperly to put off, from day to day, the moment of doing it, from an unwillingness to enter into an engagement while my circumstances were so greatly embarrassed. At last, however, my resolution was taken, and I had determined, as soon as I could engage her alone, to justify the attentions I had so invariably paid her, and openly assure her of an affection which I had already taken such pains to display. But in the interim— before I could have an opportunity

249

of speaking with her in private—a circumstance occurred—an unlucky circumstance, to ruin all my resolution, and with it all my comfort. A discovery took place,"—here he hesitated and looked down. "Mrs. Smith had somehow or other been informed, I imagine by some distant relation, of an affair, a connection—but I need not explain myself further," he added, looking at her with an heightened colour and an enquiring eye—"You have probably heard the whole story long ago."

"I have," returned Elinor, colouring likewise, and hardening her heart anew against any compassion for him, "I have heard it all. And how you will explain away any part of your guilt in that dreadful business, I confess is beyond my comprehension."

"Remember," cried Willoughby, "from whom you received the account. I acknowledge that her situation and her character ought to have been respected by me. I do not mean to justify myself, but at the same time cannot leave you to suppose that because she was injured she was irreproachable, and because I was a libertine, *she* must be a saint. If the violence of her passions, the weakness of her understanding—I do not mean, however, to defend myself. Her affection for me deserved better treatment, and I often, with great self-reproach, recall the tenderness which, for a very short time, had the power of creating any return. I wish—I heartily wish it had never been. But I have injured more than herself; and I have injured one, whose affection for me—was scarcely less warm than hers."

"Your indifference, however, towards that unfortunate girl is no apology for your cruel neglect of her. You must have known, that while you were enjoying yourself in Devonshire pursuing fresh schemes, always gay, always happy, she was reduced to the extremest indigence."

"But, upon my soul, I did *not* know it," he warmly replied; "I did not recollect that I had omitted to give her my direction; and common sense might have told her how to find it out."

"Well, sir, and what said Mrs. Smith?"

"She taxed me with the offence at once, and my confusion may be guessed. The purity of her life, the formality of her notions, her ignorance of the world—everything was against me. My visit ended in a total breach. By one measure I might have saved myself. In the height of her morality, she offered to forgive the past, if I would marry Eliza. That could not be—and I was formally dismissed from her favour and her house. The night following this affair was spent by me in deliberating on what my future conduct should be. My affection for Marianne, my thorough conviction of her attachment to me—it was all insufficient to outweigh that dread of poverty, which I was naturally inclined to feel, and expensive society had increased. I had reason to believe myself secure of my present wife, if I chose to address her, and I persuaded myself to think that nothing else in common prudence remained for me to do. I was engaged to dine with you on that very day; some apology was therefore necessary for my breaking this engagement. But whether I should write this apology, or deliver it in person, was a point of long debate. To see Marianne, I felt, would be dreadful, and I even doubted whether I could see her again."

"Why did you call, Mr. Willoughby?" said Elinor, reproachfully; "a note would have answered every purpose."

"It was necessary to my own pride. I could not bear to leave the country in a manner that might lead you, or the rest of the neighbourhood, to suspect any part of what had really passed between Mrs. Smith and myself. The sight of your dear sister, however, was really dreadful; and, to heighten the matter, I found her alone. I had left her only the evening before, so fully, so firmly resolved within myself on doing right! A few hours were to have engaged her to me forever. Her sorrow, her disappointment, her deep regret, when I told her that I was obliged to leave Devonshire so immediately—I never shall forget it—united too with such reliance, such confidence in me!—Oh, God!—what a hard-hearted rascal I was!"

They were both silent for a few moments. Elinor first spoke.

"Did you tell her that you should soon return?"

"I do not know what I told her," he replied, impatiently. "Less than was due to the past, beyond a doubt, and in all likelihood much more than was justified by the future. Then came your dear mother to torture me farther, with all her kindness and confidence. I was miserable. Miss Dashwood, you cannot have an idea of the comfort it gives me to look back on my own misery. I owe such a grudge to myself for the stupid, rascally folly of my own heart, that all my past sufferings under it are only triumph and exultation to me now. Well, I went, left all that I loved, and went to those to whom, at best, I was only indifferent."

He stopped.

"Well, sir," said Elinor, "and this is all?"

"Ah!—no—have you forgot what passed in town? That infamous letter. Did she show it you?"

"Yes, I saw every note that passed."

"When the first of hers reached me my feelings were very, very painful. Every line, every word was a dagger to my heart. To know that Marianne was in town was a thunderbolt."

Elinor's heart, which had undergone many changes in the course of this extraordinary conversation, was now softened again; yet she felt it her duty to check such ideas in her companion as the last.

"This is not right, Mr. Willoughby. Remember that you are married. Relate only what in your conscience you think necessary for me to hear."

"Marianne's note, by assuring me that she was as constant in her own feelings, and as full of faith in the constancy of mine as ever, awakened all my remorse. I say awakened, because time and London, business and dissipation, had in some measure quieted it, and I had been growing a fine hardened villain, fancying myself indifferent to her. But this note made me know myself better. I felt that she was infinitely dearer to me than any other woman in the world, and that I was using her infamously. But everything was then just settled between Miss Grey and me. To retreat was impossible. All that I had to do was to avoid you both. I sent no answer to Marianne, and for some time I was even determined not to call in Berkeley Street; but at last, judging it wiser to affect the air of a cool, common acquaintance than anything else, I watched you all safely out of the house one morning, and left my name."

"Watched us out of the house!"

"Even so. You would be surprised to hear how often I watched you, how often I was on the point of falling in with you. I avoided the Middletons as much as possible, as well as everybody else who was likely to prove an acquaintance in common. Not aware of their being in town, however, I blundered on Sir John, I believe, the first day of his coming, and the day after I had called at Mrs. Jennings's. He asked me to a party, a dance at his house in the evening. Had he *not* told me as an inducement that you and your sister were to be there, I should have felt it too certain a thing, to trust myself near him. The next morning brought another short note from Marianne—still affectionate, open, artless, confiding—everything that could make *my* conduct most hateful. I could not answer it. I tried, but could not frame a sentence. Well, at last, as I need not tell you, you were forced on me; and what a sweet figure I cut! What an evening of agony it was! Marianne, beautiful as an angel on one side, calling me Willoughby in such a tone! Oh, God! And Sophia, jealous as the devil on the other hand, looking all that was. Well, I ran away from you all as soon as I could; but not before I had seen Marianne's sweet face as white as death. *That* was the last, last look I ever had of her. Yet when I thought of her to-day as really dying, it was a kind of comfort to me to imagine that I knew exactly how she would appear to those, who saw her last in this world."

A short pause of mutual thoughtfulness succeeded. Willoughby first rousing himself, broke it thus: "Well, let me make haste and be gone. Your sister is certainly better, certainly out of danger?"

"We are assured of it."

"Your poor mother, too!—doting on Marianne."

"But the letter, Mr. Willoughby, your own letter; have you anything to say about that?"

"Yes, yes, *that* in particular. Your sister wrote to me again, you know, the very next morning. You saw what she said. I was breakfasting at the Ellisons, and her letter, with some others, was brought to me there from my lodgings. It happened to catch Sophia's eye before it caught mine. She opened the letter directly, and read its contents. She was well paid for her impudence. She read what made her wretched. Her wretchedness I could have borne, but her passion—her malice. At all events it must be appeased. And, in short—what do you think of my wife's style of letter-writing? Delicate—tender—truly feminine—was it not?"

"Your wife! The letter was in your own hand-writing."

"Yes, but I had only the credit of servilely copying such sentences as I was ashamed to put my name to. The original was all her own. But what could I do! We were engaged, everything in preparation, the day almost fixed. But I am talking like a fool. Preparation!—Day!—In honest words, her money was necessary to me, and in a situation like mine, any thing was to be done to prevent a rupture. And after all, what did it signify to my character in the opinion of Marianne and her friends, in what language my answer was couched? My business was to declare myself a scoundrel, and whether I did it with a bow or a bluster was of little importance. Such were my reasonings, as, in a sort of desperate carelessness, I copied my wife's words, and parted with the last relics of Marianne. Her three notes, and the lock of hair—that too I had always carried about me in the same pocket-book, which was now searched by Madam with the most ingratiating virulence, the dear lock—all, every memento was torn from me."

"You are very wrong, Mr. Willoughby, very blamable," said Elinor. "You ought not to speak in this way, either of Mrs. Willoughby or my sister. You had made your own choice. It was not forced on you. Your wife has a claim to your politeness, to your respect, at least. She must be attached to you, or she would not have married you. To treat her with unkindness, to speak of her slightingly is no atonement to Marianne."

"Do not talk to me of my wife," said he with a heavy sigh. "She does not deserve your compassion. She knew I had no regard for her when we married. And now do you pity me, Miss Dashwood? Have I explained away any part of my guilt?"

"Yes, you have certainly removed something—a little. You have proved yourself, on the whole, less faulty than I had believed you. You have proved your heart less wicked, much less wicked. But I hardly know—the misery that you have inflicted—I hardly know what could have made it worse."

"Will you repeat to your sister when she is recovered, what I have been telling you? You tell me that she has forgiven me already. Tell her of my misery and my penitence—tell her that my heart was never inconstant to her, and if you will, that at this moment she is dearer to me than ever."

"I will tell her all that is necessary to what may comparatively be called, your justification. But you have not explained to me the particular reason of your coming now, nor how you heard of her illness."

"Last night, in Drury Lane lobby, I ran against Sir John Middleton, and when he saw who I was—he spoke to me. That he had cut me ever since my marriage, I had seen without surprise or resentment. Now, however, his good-natured, honest, stupid soul, full of indignation against me, and concern for your sister, could not resist the temptation of telling me what he knew ought to vex me horridly. As bluntly as he could speak it, therefore, he told me that Marianne Dashwood was dying of a putrid fever at Cleveland. I was too much shocked to be able to pass myself off as insensible even to the undiscerning Sir John. His heart was softened in seeing mine suffer; and when we parted, he almost shook me by the hand while he reminded me of an old promise about a pointer puppy. What I felt on hearing that your sister was dying—and dying too, believing me the greatest villain upon earth, scorning, hating me in her latest moments—what I felt was dreadful! My resolution was soon made, and at eight o'clock this morning I was in my carriage. Now you know all."

Elinor made no answer. Her thoughts were silently fixed on the irreparable injury which too early an independence and its consequent habits of idleness, dissipation, and luxury, had made in the mind, the character, the happiness, of a man who, to every advantage of person and talents, united a disposition naturally open and honest, and a feeling, affectionate temper. The attachment, from which against honour, against feeling, against every better interest he had outwardly torn himself, now, when no longer allowable, governed every thought; and the connection, for the sake of which he had, with little scruple, left her sister to misery, was likely to prove a source of unhappiness to himself of a far more incurable nature. From a reverie of this kind she was recalled at the end of some minutes by Willoughby, who, rousing himself from a reverie at least equally painful, started up in preparation for going, and said: "There is no use in staying here; I must be off."

He held out his hand. She could not refuse to give him hers;—he pressed it with affection.

"As to that," said he, "I must rub through the world as well as I can. Domestic happiness is out of the question. If, however,

I am allowed to think that you and yours feel an interest in my fate and actions, it may be the means—it may put me on my guard—at least, it may be something to live for. Marianne to be sure is lost to me forever. Were I even by any blessed chance at liberty again—"

Elinor stopped him with a reproof.

"Well,"—he replied—"once more good bye. I shall now go away and live in dread of one event."

"What do you mean?"

"Your sister's marriage."

"You are very wrong. She can never be more lost to you than she is now."

"But she will be gained by someone else. And if that someone should be the very he whom, of all others, I could least bear—but I will not stay to rob myself of all your compassionate goodwill, by shewing that where I have most injured I can least forgive. Good bye,—God bless you!"

And with these words, he almost ran out of the room.

Chapter 45

Elinor, for some time after he left her, for some time even after the sound of his carriage had died away, remained too much oppressed by a crowd of ideas, widely differing in themselves, but of which sadness was the general result, to think even of her sister.

Willoughby, he, whom only half an hour ago she had abhorred as the most worthless of men, Willoughby, in spite of all his faults, excited a degree of commiseration for the sufferings produced by them, which made her think of him as now separated for ever from her family, with a tenderness, a regret, rather in proportion, as she soon acknowledged within herself—to his wishes than to his merits. She felt that his influence over her mind was heightened by circumstances which ought not in reason to have weight; by that person of uncommon attraction, that open, affectionate, and lively manner which it was no merit to possess; and by that still ardent love for Marianne, which it was not even innocent to indulge.

When at last she returned to the unconscious Marianne, she found her just awaking, refreshed by so long and sweet a sleep to the extent of her hopes. Elinor's heart was full. The past, the present, the future, Willoughby's visit, Marianne's safety, and her mother's expected arrival, threw her altogether into an agitation of spirits which kept off every indication of fatigue, and made her only fearful of betraying herself to her sister. Within half an hour after Willoughby's leaving the house, she was again called down stairs by the sound of another carriage.—Eager to save her mother from every unnecessary moment's horrible suspense, she ran immediately into the hall, and reached the outward door just in time to receive and support her as she entered it.

Mrs. Dashwood, whose terror as they drew near the house had produced almost the conviction of Marianne's being no more, had no voice to inquire after her, no voice even for Elinor; but SHE, waiting neither for salutation nor inquiry, instantly gave the joyful relief;—and her mother, catching it with all her usual warmth, was in a moment as much overcome by her happiness, as she had been before by her fears.

As soon as Mrs. Dashwood had recovered herself, to see Marianne was her first desire; and in two minutes she was with her beloved child, rendered dearer to her than ever by absence, unhappiness, and danger. Elinor's delight, as she saw what each felt in the meeting, was only checked by an apprehension of its robbing Marianne of farther sleep;—but Mrs. Dashwood could be calm, when the life of a child was at stake, and Marianne, satisfied in knowing her mother was near her, and conscious of being too weak for conversation, submitted readily to the silence and quiet prescribed by every nurse around her. Mrs. Dashwood *would* sit up with her all night; and Elinor, in compliance with her mother's entreaty, went to bed. But the rest was kept off by irritation of spirits. Willoughby, "poor Willoughby," as she now allowed herself to call him, was constantly in her thoughts; she would not but have heard his vindication for the world, and now blamed, now acquitted herself for having judged him so harshly before. But her promise of relating it to her sister was invariably painful. She dreaded the performance of it, dreaded what its effect on Marianne might be; doubted whether after such an explanation she could ever be happy with another; and for a moment wished Willoughby a widower. Then, remembering Colonel Brandon, reproved herself, felt that to HIS sufferings and his constancy far more than to his rival's, the reward of her sister was due.

Marianne continued to mend every day, and the brilliant cheerfulness of Mrs. Dashwood's looks and spirits proved her to be, as she repeatedly declared herself, one of the happiest women in the world. Marianne was restored to her from a danger in which, as she now began to feel, her own mistaken judgment in encouraging the unfortunate attachment to Willoughby, had contributed to place her;—and in her recovery she had yet another source of joy unthought of by Elinor. It was thus imparted to her, as soon as any opportunity of private conference between them occurred.

"At last we are alone. My Elinor, you do not yet know all my happiness. Colonel Brandon loves Marianne. He has told me so himself."

Her daughter, feeling by turns both pleased and pained, surprised and not surprised, was all silent attention.

"You are never like me, dear Elinor, or I should wonder at your composure now. Had I sat down to wish for any possible good to my family, I should have fixed on Colonel Brandon's marrying one of you as the object most desirable. And I believe Marianne will be the most happy with him of the two. I, you may well believe, could talk of nothing but my child; he could not conceal his distress; I saw that it equalled my own, and he perhaps, thinking that mere friendship, as the world now goes, would not justify so warm a sympathy—or rather, not thinking at all, I suppose—giving way to irresistible feelings, made me acquainted with his earnest, tender, constant, affection for Marianne. He has loved her, my Elinor, ever since the first moment of seeing her. His regard for her, infinitely surpassing anything that Willoughby ever felt or feigned, as much more warm, as more sincere or constant—which ever we are to call it—has subsisted through all the knowledge of dear Marianne's unhappy prepossession for that worthless young man! And without selfishness—without encouraging a hope!—could he have seen her happy with another—Such a noble mind!—such openness, such sincerity!—no one can be deceived in *him*."

"Colonel Brandon's character," said Elinor, "as an excellent man, is well established."

"I know it is,"—replied her mother seriously, "or after such a warning, I should be the last to encourage such affection, or even to be pleased by it. But his coming for me as he did, with such active, such ready friendship, is enough to prove him one of the worthiest of men."

"His character, however," answered Elinor, "does not rest on *one* act of kindness, to which his affection for Marianne, were humanity out of the case, would have prompted him. To Mrs. Jennings, to the Middletons, he has been long and intimately known; they equally love and respect him; and even my own knowledge of him, I shall be as ready as yourself to think our connection the greatest blessing to us in the world. What answer did you give him?—Did you allow him to hope?"

"Oh! my love, I could not then talk of hope to him or to myself. Marianne might at that moment be dying. Yet after a time I *did* say, for at first I was quite overcome—that if she lived, as I trusted she might, my greatest happiness would lie in promoting their marriage. Time, a very little time, I tell him, will do everything; Marianne's heart is not to be wasted for ever on such a man as Willoughby. His own merits must soon secure it."

"To judge from the Colonel's spirits, however, you have not yet made him equally sanguine."

"No. He thinks Marianne's affection too deeply rooted for any change in it under a great length of time, and even supposing her heart again free, is too diffident of himself to believe, that with such a difference of age and disposition he could ever attach her. There, however, he is quite mistaken. His age is only so much beyond hers as to be an advantage, as to make his character and principles fixed; and his disposition, I am well convinced, is exactly the very one to make your sister happy. And his person, his manners too, are all in his favour. My partiality does not blind me; he certainly is not so handsome as Willoughby turned out as really amiable, as he has proved himself the contrary, Marianne would yet never have been so happy with *him*, as she will be with Colonel Brandon."

She paused. Her daughter could not quite agree with her, but her dissent was not heard, and therefore gave no offence.

"At Delaford, she will be within an easy distance of me," added Mrs. Dashwood, "even if I remain at Barton; and in all probability,—for I hear it is a large village, indeed there certainly MUST be some small house or cottage close by, that would suit us quite as well as our present situation."

Poor Elinor! Here was a new scheme for getting her to Delaford!—but her spirit was stubborn.

"His fortune too!—for at my time of life you know, everybody cares about THAT;—and though I neither know nor desire to know, what it really is, I am sure it must be a good one."

Chapter 46

Marianne's illness, though weakening in its kind, had not been long enough to make her recovery slow; and with youth, natural strength, and her mother's presence in aid, it proceeded so smoothly as to enable her to remove, within four days after the arrival of the latter, into Mrs. Palmer's dressing-room. When there, at her own particular request, for she was impatient to pour forth her thanks to him for fetching her mother, Colonel Brandon was invited to visit her.

His emotion on entering the room, in seeing her altered looks, was such as, in Elinor's conjecture, must arise from something more than his affection for Marianne, or the consciousness of its being known to others; and she soon discovered in his melancholy eye and varying complexion as he looked at her sister, the probable recurrence of many past scenes of misery to his mind, brought back by that resemblance between Marianne and Eliza already acknowledged, and now strengthened by the hollow eye, the sickly skin.

Mrs. Dashwood, not less watchful of what passed than her daughter, but with a mind very differently influenced, and therefore watching to very different effect, saw nothing in the Colonel's behaviour but what arose from the most simple and self-evident sensations, while in the actions and words of

Marianne she persuaded herself to think that something more than gratitude already dawned.

At the end of another day or two, Mrs. Dashwood, began to talk of removing to Barton. At Colonel Brandon's and Mrs. Jennings's united request in return, Mrs. Dashwood was prevailed on to accept the use of his carriage on her journey back, for the better accommodation of her sick child; and the Colonel, at the joint invitation of Mrs. Dashwood and Mrs. Jennings, whose active good-nature made her friendly and hospitable for other people as well as herself, engaged with pleasure to redeem it by a visit at the cottage, in the course of a few weeks.

The day of separation and departure arrived; and Marianne, after taking so particular and lengthened a leave of Mrs. Jennings, and bidding Colonel Brandon farewell with a cordiality of a friend, was carefully assisted by him into the carriage. Mrs. Dashwood and Elinor then followed, and the others were left by themselves, to talk of the travellers, and feel their own dullness, till Mrs. Jennings was summoned to her chaise to take comfort in the gossip of her maid for the loss of her two young companions; and Colonel Brandon immediately afterwards took his solitary way to Delaford.

The Dashwoods were two days on the road, and Marianne bore her journey on both, without essential fatigue. Everything that the most zealous affection, the most solicitous care could do to render her comfortable, was the office of each watchful companion, and each found their reward in her bodily ease, and her calmness of spirits. To Elinor, the observation of the latter was particularly grateful. She, who had seen her week after week so constantly suffering, oppressed by anguish of heart which she had neither courage to speak of, nor fortitude to conceal, now saw with a joy, which no other could equally share, an apparent composure of mind, which, in being the result as she trusted of serious reflection, must eventually lead her to contentment and cheerfulness.

As they approached Barton, she grew silent and thoughtful, and turning away her face from their notice, sat earnestly gazing through the window. But here, Elinor could neither wonder nor blame; and when she saw, as she assisted Marianne from the carriage, that she had been crying, she saw only an emotion too natural in itself to raise anything less tender than pity, and in its unobtrusiveness entitled to praise. In the whole of her subsequent manner, she traced the direction of a mind awakened to reasonable exertion; for no sooner had they entered their common sitting-room, than Marianne turned her eyes around it with a look of resolute firmness, as if determined at once to accustom herself to the sight of every object with which the remembrance of Willoughby could be connected.—She said little, but every sentence aimed at cheerfulness, and though a sigh sometimes escaped her, it never passed away without the atonement of a smile.

The next morning produced no abatement in these happy symptoms.

"When the weather is settled, and I have recovered my strength," said she, "we will take long walks together every day. We will walk to the farm at the edge of the down, and see how the children go on. I mean never to be later in rising than six, and from that time till dinner I shall divide every moment between music and reading. There are many works well worth reading at the Park; and there are others of more modern production which I know I can borrow of Colonel Brandon. By reading only six hours a-day, I shall gain in the course of a twelve-month a great deal of instruction which I now feel myself to want."

Elinor honoured her for a plan which originated so nobly as this; though smiling to see the same eager fancy which had been leading her to the extreme of languid indolence and selfish repining, now at work in introducing excess into a scheme of such rational employment and virtuous self-control. Her smile however changed to a sigh when she remembered that promise to Willoughby was yet unfulfilled, and feared she had that to communicate which might again unsettle the mind of Marianne, and ruin at least for a time this fair prospect of busy tranquillity. Willing therefore to delay the evil hour, she resolved to wait till her sister's health were more secure, before she appointed it. But the resolution was made only to be broken.

Marianne had been two or three days at home, before the weather was fine enough for an invalid like herself to venture out. But at last a soft, genial morning appeared; such as might tempt the daughter's wishes and the mother's confidence; and Marianne, leaning on Elinor's arm, was authorised to walk as long as she could without fatigue, in the lane before the house.

They had advanced only so far beyond the house as to admit a full view of the hill, the important hill behind, when pausing with her eyes turned towards it, Marianne calmly said: "There, exactly there," pointing with one hand, "on that projecting mound, there I fell; and there I first saw Willoughby."

Her voice sunk with the word, but presently reviving she added, "I am thankful to find that I can look with so little pain on the spot! Shall we ever talk on that subject, Elinor?" hesitatingly it was said. "Or will it be wrong? I can talk of it now, I hope, as I ought to do."

Elinor tenderly invited her to be open.

"As for regret," said Marianne, "I have done with that, as far as *he* is concerned. At present, if I could be satisfied on one point, if I could be allowed to think that he was not *always* acting a part, not *always* deceiving me; but above all, if I could be assured that he never was so *very* wicked as my fears have sometimes fancied him, since the story of that unfortunate girl"—

She stopped. Elinor joyfully treasured her words as she answered, "If you could be assured of that, you think you should be easy?"

"Yes. My peace of mind is doubly involved in it; for not only is it horrible to suspect a person, who has been what *he* has been to *me*, of such designs, but what must it make me appear to myself?"

"How then," asked her sister, "would you account for his behaviour?"

"I would suppose him, Oh, how gladly would I suppose him, only fickle, very, very fickle."

Elinor said no more. She was debating within herself on the eligibility of beginning her story directly, or postponing it till Marianne were in stronger health;—and they crept on for a few minutes in silence.

"I am not wishing him too much good," said Marianne at last with a sigh, "when I wish his secret reflections may be no more unpleasant than my own."

"Do you compare your conduct with his?"

"No. I compare it with what it ought to have been; I compare it with yours."

"Our situations have borne little resemblance."

"They have borne more than our conduct. My illness has given me leisure and calmness for serious recollection. I considered the past: I saw in my own behaviour, since the beginning of our acquaintance with him last autumn, nothing but a series of imprudence towards myself, and want of fortitude under them had almost led me to the grave. My illness, I well knew, had been entirely brought on by myself by such negligence of my own health, as I had felt even at the time to be wrong. Had I died, in what peculiar misery should I have left you, my nurse, my friend, my sister! How should I have lived in *your* remembrance! My mother too! How could you have consoled her! Everybody seemed injured by me. The kindness, the unceasing kindness of Mrs. Jennings, I had repaid with ungrateful contempt. To the Middletons, to the Palmers, the Steeles, to every common acquaintance even, I had been insolent and unjust. To John, to Fanny—yes, even to them, little as they deserve, I had given less than their due. But you,—you above all, above my mother, had been wronged by me. I, and only I, knew your heart and its sorrows; yet to what did it influence me?—not to any compassion that could benefit you or myself."

Here ceased the rapid flow of her self-reproving spirit; and Elinor, impatient to soothe, though too honest to flatter, gave her instantly that praise and support which her frankness and her contrition so well deserved. Marianne pressed her hand and replied, "You are very good. The future must be my proof. I have laid down my plan, and if I am capable of adhering to it—my feelings shall be governed and my temper improved. I shall now live solely for my family. You, my mother, and Margaret, must henceforth be all the world to me; you will share my affections entirely between you. As for Willoughby—to say that I shall soon or that I shall ever forget him, would be idle. His remembrance can be overcome by no change of circumstances or opinions. But it shall be regulated, it shall be checked by religion, by reason, by constant employment."

She paused—and added in a low voice, "If I could but know *his* heart, everything would become easy."

Elinor, who had now been for some time reflecting on the propriety or impropriety of speedily hazarding her narration, without feeling at all nearer decision than at first, heard this; and perceiving that as reflection did nothing, resolution must do all, soon found herself leading to the fact.

She managed the recital, as she hoped, with address; prepared her anxious listener with caution; related simply and honestly the chief points on which Willoughby grounded his apology. Marianne said not a word. She trembled, her eyes were fixed on the ground, and her lips became whiter than even sickness had left them. She caught every syllable with panting eagerness; her hand, unknowingly to herself, closely pressed her sister's, and tears covered her cheeks.

Elinor, dreading her being tired, led her towards home; and till they reached the door of the cottage, easily conjecturing what her curiosity must be though no question was suffered to speak it, talked of nothing but Willoughby, and their conversation together. As soon as they entered the house, Marianne with a kiss of gratitude and these two words just articulate through her tears, "Tell mama," withdrew from her sister and walked slowly up stairs. Elinor would not attempt to disturb a solitude so reasonable as what she now sought; and she turned into the parlour to fulfill her parting injunction.

Chapter 47

Mrs. Dashwood did not hear unmoved the vindication of her former favourite. She rejoiced in his being cleared from some part of his imputed guilt;—she was sorry for him;—she wished him happy. But the feelings of the past could not be recalled. Nothing could restore him with a faith unbroken, a character unblemished, to Marianne. Nothing could replace him, therefore, in her former esteem, nor injure the interests of Colonel Brandon.

In the evening, when they were all three together, Marianne began voluntarily to speak of him again;—but that it was not without an effort, the restless, unquiet thoughtfulness in which she had been for some time previously sitting—her rising colour, as she spoke,—and her unsteady voice, plainly showed.

"I wish to assure you both," said she, "that I see everything—as you can desire me to do. It is a great relief to me—I have now heard exactly what I wished to hear. I am now perfectly satisfied, I wish for no change. I never could have been happy with him, after knowing, as sooner or later I must have known, all this."

"I know it—I know it," cried her mother. "Happy with a man of libertine practices! No—my Marianne has not a heart to be made happy with such a man!"

Marianne sighed, and repeated, "I wish for no change."

"You consider the matter," said Elinor, "exactly as a good mind and a sound understanding must consider it; and I dare say you perceive, as well as myself, not only in this, but in many other circumstances, reason enough to be convinced that your marriage must have involved you in many certain troubles and disappointments, in which you would have been poorly supported by an affection, on his side, much less certain. Had you married, you must have been always poor. His demands and your inexperience together, on a small, very small income, must have brought on distresses which would not be the *less* grievous to you, from having been entirely unknown and unthought of before. *Your* sense of honour and honesty would have led you, I know, when aware of your situation, to attempt all the economy that would appear to you possible: and, perhaps, as long as your frugality retrenched only on your own comfort, you might have been suffered to practice it, but beyond that, had you endeavoured, however reasonably, to abridge *his* enjoyments, is it not to be feared, that instead of prevailing on feelings so selfish to consent to it, you would have lessened your own influence on his heart, and made him regret the connection which had involved him in such difficulties?"

Marianne's lips quivered, and she repeated the word "Selfish?" in a tone that implied—"do you really think him selfish?"

"The whole of his behaviour," replied Elinor, "from the beginning to the end of the affair, has been grounded on selfishness. His own enjoyment, or his own ease, was, in every particular, his ruling principle."

"It is very true. *My* happiness never was his object."

"At present," continued Elinor, "he regrets what he has done. And why does he regret it?—Because it has not made him happy. He thinks only that he has married a woman of a less amiable temper than yourself. But does it follow that had he married you, he would have been happy? He would have had a wife of whose temper he could make no complaint, but he would have been always necessitous—always poor; and probably would soon have learned to rank the innumerable comforts of a clear estate and good income as of far more importance, even to domestic happiness, than the mere temper of a wife."

"I have not a doubt of it," said Marianne; "and I have nothing to regret—nothing but my own folly."

"Rather say your mother's imprudence, my child," said Mrs. Dashwood; "*She* must be answerable."

Marianne would not let her proceed; and Elinor, satisfied that each felt their own error, wished to avoid any survey of the past that might weaken her sister's spirits; she, therefore, pursuing the first subject, immediately continued, "One observation may, I think, be fairly drawn from the whole of the story—that all Willoughby's difficulties have arisen from the first offence against virtue, in his behaviour to Eliza Williams."

Marianne assented most feelingly to the remark; and her mother was led by it to an enumeration of Colonel Brandon's injuries and merits, warm as friendship and design could unitedly dictate. Her daughter did not look, however, as if much of it were heard by her.

Elinor grew impatient for some tidings of Edward. Some letters had passed between her and her brother, in consequence of Marianne's illness; and in the first of John's, there had been this sentence: "We know nothing of our unfortunate Edward, and can make no enquiries on so prohibited a subject, but conclude him to be still at Oxford;" which was all the intelligence of Edward afforded her by the correspondence, for his name was not even mentioned in any of the succeeding letters. She was not doomed, however, to be long in ignorance of his measures.

Their man-servant had been sent one morning to Exeter on business; and when, as he waited at table, he had satisfied the inquiries of his mistress as to the event of his errand, this was his voluntary communication—

"I suppose you know, ma'am, that Mr. Ferrars is married."

Marianne gave a violent start, fixed her eyes upon Elinor, saw her turning pale, and fell back in her chair in hysterics. Mrs. Dashwood, had intuitively taken the same direction, was shocked to perceive by Elinor's countenance how much she really suffered, and a moment afterwards, alike distressed by Marianne's situation, knew not on which child to bestow her principal attention.

The servant, had sense enough to call one of the maids, who, with Mrs. Dashwood's assistance, supported her into the other room. By that time, Marianne was rather better, and her mother leaving her to the care of Margaret and the maid, returned to Elinor, who, though still much disordered, had so far recovered the use of her reason and voice as to be just beginning an inquiry of Thomas, as to the source of his intelligence. Mrs. Dashwood immediately took all that trouble on herself.

"Who told you that Mr. Ferrars was married, Thomas?"

"I see Mr. Ferrars myself, ma'am, this morning in Exeter, and his lady too, Miss Steele as was. They was stopping in a chaise at the door of the New London Inn, as I went there with a message from Sally at the Park to her brother, who is one of the post-boys. I happened to look up as I went by the chaise, and so I see directly it was the youngest Miss Steele; so I took off my hat, and she knew me and called to me, and inquired after you, ma'am, and the young ladies, especially Miss Marianne, and bid me I should give her compliments and Mr. Ferrars's, their best compliments and service, and how sorry they was they had not time to come on and see you, but they was in a great hurry to go forwards."

"But did she tell you she was married, Thomas?"

"Yes, ma'am. She smiled, and said how she had changed her name since she was in these parts."

No, ma'am, only they two."

"Do you know where they came from?"

"They come straight from town, as Miss Lucy—Mrs. Ferrars told me."

"And are they going farther westward?"

"Yes, ma'am—but not to bide long. They will soon be back again, and then they'd be sure and call here."

Mrs. Dashwood now looked at her daughter; but Elinor knew better than to expect them. She recognised the whole of Lucy in the message, and was very confident that Edward would never come near them. She observed in a low voice, to her mother, that they were probably going down to Mr. Pratt's, near Plymouth.

Thomas's intelligence seemed over. Elinor looked as if she wished to hear more.

"Did you see them off, before you came away?"

"No, ma'am—the horses were just coming out, but I could not bide any longer; I was afraid of being late."

"Did Mrs. Ferrars look well?"

"Yes, ma'am, she said how she was very well; and to my mind she was always a very handsome young lady—and she seemed vastly contented."

Mrs. Dashwood could think of no other question, and Thomas and the tablecloth, now alike needless, were soon afterwards dismissed. Marianne had already sent to say, that she should eat nothing more. Mrs. Dashwood's and Elinor's appetites were equally lost, and Margaret might think herself very well off, that with so much uneasiness as both her sisters had lately experienced, so much reason as they had often had to be careless of their meals, she had never been obliged to go without her dinner before.

When the dessert and the wine were arranged, and Mrs. Dashwood and Elinor were left by themselves, they remained long together in a similarity of thoughtfulness and silence. Mrs. Dashwood feared to hazard any remark, and ventured not to offer consolation. She now found that she had erred in relying on Elinor's representation of herself; and justly concluded that every thing had been expressly softened at the time, to spare her from an increase of unhappiness, suffering as she then had suffered for Marianne. She found that she had been misled by the careful, the considerate attention of her daughter, to think the attachment, which once she had so well understood, much slighter in reality, than she had been wont to believe, or than it was now proved to be. She feared that under this persuasion she had been unjust, inattentive, nay, almost unkind, to her Elinor;—that Marianne's affliction, because more acknowledged, more immediately before her, had too much engrossed her tenderness, and led her away to forget that in Elinor she might have a daughter suffering almost as much, certainly with less self-provocation, and greater fortitude.

Chapter 48

Elinor now found that in spite of herself, she had always admitted a hope, while Edward remained single, that something would occur to prevent his marrying Lucy. But he was now married; and she condemned her heart for the lurking flattery, which so much heightened the pain of the intelligence.

That he should be married soon, before he could be in orders, and consequently before he could be in possession of the living, surprised her a little at first. But she soon saw how likely it was that Lucy, in her self-provident care, in her haste to secure him, should overlook everything but the risk of delay. They were married, married in town, and now hastening down to her uncle's. What had Edward felt on being within four miles from Barton, on seeing her mother's servant, on hearing Lucy's message?

They would soon, she supposed, be settled at Delaford. She saw them in an instant in their parsonage-house; saw in Lucy, the active, contriving manager, uniting at once a desire of smart appearance with the utmost frugality; pursuing her own interest in every thought, courting the favour of Colonel Brandon, of Mrs. Jennings, and of every wealthy friend. In Edward—she knew not what she saw, nor what she wished to see; happy or unhappy, nothing pleased her. She turned away her head from every sketch of him.

Elinor flattered herself that some one of their connections in London would write to them to announce the event, and give farther particulars, but day after day passed off, and brought no letter, no tidings.

"When do you write to Colonel Brandon, ma'am?" was an inquiry which sprung from the impatience of her mind to have something going on.

"I wrote to him, my love, last week, and rather expect to see, than to hear from him again. I earnestly pressed his coming to us, and should not be surprised to see him walk in today or tomorrow, or any day."

This was gaining something, something to look forward to. Colonel Brandon must have some information to give.

Scarcely had she so determined it, when the figure of a man on horseback drew her eyes to the window. He stopped at their gate. It was a gentleman, it was Colonel Brandon himself. But—it was *not* Colonel Brandon—neither his air—nor his height. Were it possible, she must say it must be Edward. She looked again. It *was* Edward. She moved away and sat down. "He comes from Mr. Pratt's purposely to see us. I *will* be calm; I *will* be mistress of myself."

She saw her mother and Marianne change colour; saw them look at herself, and whisper a few sentences to each other. She would have given the world to be able to speak—and to make them understand that she hoped no coolness, no slight, would appear in their behaviour to him; but she had no utterance, and was obliged to leave all to their own discretion.

They all waited in silence for the appearance of their visitor. His footsteps were heard along the gravel path; in a moment he was in the passage, and in another he was before them.

His countenance, as he entered the room, was not too happy, even for Elinor. His complexion was white with agitation, and he looked as if fearful of his reception, and conscious that he merited no kind one. Mrs. Dashwood, however, conforming, as she trusted, to the wishes of that daughter, by whom she then meant in the warmth of her heart to be guided in everything, met with a look of forced complacency, gave him her hand, and wished him joy.

He coloured, and stammered out an unintelligible reply. Elinor's lips had moved with her mother's, and, when the moment of action was over, she wished that she had shaken hands with him too. But it was then too late, and with a countenance meaning to be open, she sat down again and talked of the weather.

When Elinor had ceased to rejoice in the dryness of the season, a very awful pause took place. It was put an end to by Mrs. Dashwood, who felt obliged to hope that he had left Mrs. Ferrars very well. In a hurried manner, he replied in the affirmative.

Another pause.

Elinor resolving to exert herself, though fearing the sound of her own voice, now said, "Is Mrs. Ferrars at Longstaple?"

"At Longstaple!" he replied, with an air of surprise. "No, my mother is in town."

"I meant," said Elinor, taking up some work from the table, "to inquire for Mrs. *Edward* Ferrars."

She dared not look up; but her mother and Marianne both turned their eyes on him. He coloured, seemed perplexed, looked doubtingly, and, after some hesitation, said, "Perhaps you mean— my brother—you mean Mrs.—Mrs. *Robert* Ferrars."

"Mrs. Robert Ferrars!" was repeated by Marianne and her mother in an accent of the utmost amazement; and though Elinor could not speak, even *her* eyes were fixed on him with the same impatient wonder.

"Perhaps you do not know—you may not have heard that my brother is lately married to—to the youngest—to Miss Lucy Steele."

His words were echoed with unspeakable astonishment by

all but Elinor, who sat with her head leaning over her work, in a state of such agitation as made her hardly know where she was.

"Yes," said he, "they were married last week, and are now at Dawlish."

Elinor could sit it no longer. She almost ran out of the room, and as soon as the door was closed, burst into tears of joy, which at first she thought would never cease. Edward, who had till then looked anywhere, rather than at her, saw her hurry away, and perhaps saw—or even heard, her emotion; for immediately afterwards he fell into a reverie, and at last, without saying a word, quitted the room, and walked out towards the village—leaving the others in the greatest astonishment and perplexity on a change in his situation, so wonderful and so sudden;—a perplexity which they had no means of lessening but by their own conjectures.

Chapter 49

Unaccountable, however, as the circumstances of his release might appear to the whole family, it was certain that Edward was free. His errand at Barton, in fact, was a simple one. It was only to ask Elinor to marry him; and considering that he was not altogether inexperienced in such a question, it might be strange that he should feel so uncomfortable in the present case as he really did, so much in need of encouragement and fresh air.

How soon he had walked himself into the proper resolution, however, how soon an opportunity of exercising it occurred, in what manner he expressed himself, and how he was received, need not be particularly told. This only need be said;—that when they all sat down to table at four o'clock, about three hours after his arrival, he had secured his lady, engaged her mother's consent, and was the happiest of men. He was released without any reproach to himself, from an entanglement which had long formed his misery, from a woman whom he had long ceased to love; and elevated at once to that security with another, which he must have thought of almost with despair, as soon as he had learnt to consider it with desire.

His heart was now open to Elinor, all its weaknesses, all its errors confessed, and his first boyish attachment to Lucy treated with all the philosophic dignity of twenty-four.

"It was a foolish, idle inclination on my side," said he. Had my brother given me some active profession when I was removed at eighteen from the care of Mr. Pratt, I think—nay, I am sure, it would never have happened; for though I left Longstaple with what I thought, at the time, a most unconquerable preference for his niece, yet had I then had any pursuit, any object to engage my time and keep me at a distance from her for a few months, I should very soon have outgrown the fancied attachment. I returned home to be completely idle; for I was not entered at Oxford till I was nineteen. I had therefore nothing in the world to do, but to fancy myself in love; as I had no friend, no companion in my brother, and disliked new acquaintance, it was not unnatural for me to be very often at Longstaple, where I always felt myself at home. Considering everything, therefore, I hope, foolish as our engagement was, foolish as it has since in every way been proved, it was not at the time an unnatural or an inexcusable piece of folly."

The change which a few hours had wrought in the minds and the happiness of the Dashwoods, was such—so great—as promised them all, the satisfaction of a sleepless night. Mrs. Dashwood, too happy to be comfortable, knew not how to love Edward, nor praise Elinor.

Marianne could speak *her* happiness only by tears. Comparisons would occur—regrets would arise; and her joy, though sincere as her love for her sister, was of a kind to give her neither spirits nor language.

But Elinor—how are *her* feelings to be described?—From the moment of learning that Lucy was married to another, that Edward was free, to the moment of his justifying the hopes which had so instantly followed, she was everything by turns but tranquil. But when the second moment had passed, when she found every doubt, every solicitude removed, compared her situation with what so lately it had been,—saw him honourably released from his former engagement, saw him instantly profiting by the release, to address herself and declare an affection as tender, as constant as she had ever supposed it to be,—she was oppressed, she was overcome by her own felicity.

Edward was now fixed at the cottage at least for a week;—for whatever other claims might be made on him, it was impossible that less than a week should be given up to the enjoyment of Elinor's company, or suffice to say half that was to be said of the past, the present, and the future.

Lucy's marriage, and Elinor's particular knowledge of each party made it appear to her in every view, as one of the most extraordinary and unaccountable circumstances she had ever heard. How they could be thrown together, and by what attraction Robert could be drawn on to marry a girl, of whose beauty she had herself heard him speak without any admiration,—a girl too already engaged to his brother, and on whose account that brother had been thrown off by his family—it was beyond her comprehension to make out.

Edward could only attempt an explanation by supposing, that, perhaps, at first accidentally meeting, the vanity of the one had been so worked on by the flattery of the other, as to lead by degrees to all the rest. Elinor remembered what Robert had told her in Harley Street, of his opinion of what his own mediation in his brother's affairs might have done, if applied to in time. She repeated it to Edward.

"*That* was exactly like Robert," was his immediate observation. "And *that*," he presently added, "might perhaps be in *his* head when the acquaintance between them first began."

How long it had been carrying on between them, however, he was equally at a loss with herself to make out; for at Oxford, where he had remained for choice ever since his quitting London, he had had no means of hearing of her but from herself, and her letters to the very last were neither less frequent, nor less affectionate than usual. When at last it burst on him in a letter from Lucy herself, he had been for some time, he believed, half stupified between the wonder, the horror, and the joy of such a deliverance. He put the letter into Elinor's hands.

DEAR SIR,

Being very sure I have long lost your affections, I have thought myself at liberty to bestow my own on another, and have no doubt of being as happy with him as I once used to think I might be with you; but I scorn to accept a hand while the heart was another's. I can safely say I owe you no ill-will, and am sure you will be too generous to do us any ill offices. Your brother has gained my affections entirely, and as we could not live without one another, we are just returned from the altar, and are now on our way to Dawlish for a few weeks.

"Your sincere well-wisher, friend, and sister,

LUCY FERRARS.

Elinor read and returned it without any comment.

"I will not ask your opinion of it as a composition," said Edward. In a sister it is bad enough, but in a wife! How I have blushed over the pages of her writing!—and I believe I may say that since the first half year of our foolish business, this is the only letter I ever received from her, of which the substance made me any amends for the defect of the style."

"However it may have come about," said Elinor, after a pause, "they are certainly married. And your mother has brought on herself a most appropriate punishment. The independence she settled on Robert, through resentment against you, has put it in his power to make his own choice; and she has actually been bribing one son with a thousand a-year, to do the very deed which she disinherited the other for intending to do. She will hardly be less hurt, I suppose, by Robert's marrying Lucy, than she would have been by your marrying her."

"She will be more hurt by it, for Robert always was her favourite. She will be more hurt by it, and on the same principle will forgive him much sooner."

Edward had quitted Oxford within four and twenty hours after Lucy's letter arrived, and with only one object before him, the nearest road to Barton, had had no leisure to form any scheme of conduct, with which that road did not hold the most intimate connection. He could do nothing till he were assured of his fate with Miss Dashwood.

That Lucy had certainly meant to deceive, to go off with a flourish of malice against him in her message by Thomas, was perfectly clear to Elinor; and Edward himself, now thoroughly enlightened on her character, had no scruple in believing her capable of the utmost meanness of wanton ill-nature. Till her last letter reached him, he had always believed her to be a well-disposed, good-hearted girl, and thoroughly attached to himself. Nothing but such a persuasion could have prevented his putting an end to an engagement, which, long before the discovery of it laid him open to his mother's anger, had been a continual source of disquiet and regret to him.

"I thought it my duty," said he, "independent of my feelings, to give her the option of continuing the engagement or not, when I was renounced by my mother, and stood to all appearance without a friend in the world to assist me. In such a situation as that, how could I suppose, when she so earnestly, so warmly insisted on sharing my fate, whatever it might be, that any thing but the most disinterested affection was her inducement? And even now, I cannot comprehend on what motive she acted, to be fettered to a man for whom she had not the smallest regard, and who had only two thousand pounds in the world. She could not foresee that Colonel Brandon would give me a living."

"No; but she might suppose that something would occur in your favour; that your own family might in time relent. And at any rate, she lost nothing by continuing the engagement. The connection was certainly a respectable one, and probably gained her consideration among her friends; and, if nothing more advantageous occurred, it would be better for her to marry you than be single."

Edward was, of course, immediately convinced that nothing could have been more natural than Lucy's conduct, nor more self-evident than the motive of it.

Elinor scolded him for having spent so much time with them at Norland, when he must have felt his own inconstancy. He could only plead an ignorance of his own heart, and a mistaken confidence in the force of his engagement.

"I was simple enough to think, that because my *faith* was plighted to another, there could be no danger in my being with you; and that the consciousness of my engagement was to keep my heart as safe and sacred as my honour. I felt that I admired you, but I told myself it was only friendship; and till I began to make comparisons between yourself and Lucy, I did not know how far I was got. After that, I suppose, I *was* wrong in remaining so much in Sussex, and the arguments with which I reconciled myself to the expediency of it, were no better than these: The danger is my own; I am doing no injury to anybody but myself."

Elinor smiled, and shook her head.

Edward heard with pleasure of Colonel Brandon's being expected at the Cottage, as he really wished not only to be better acquainted with him, but to have an opportunity of convincing him that he no longer resented his giving him the living of Delaford."

Now he felt astonished himself that he had never yet been to the place. But so little interest had he taken in the matter, to Elinor herself, who had heard so much of it from Colonel Brandon, and heard it with so much attention, as to be entirely mistress of the subject.

One question after this only remained undecided, between them, one difficulty only was to be overcome. They were brought together by mutual affection, with the warmest approbation of their real friends; their intimate knowledge of each other seemed to make their happiness certain—and they only wanted something to live upon. Edward had two thousand pounds, and Elinor one, which, with Delaford living, was all that they could call their own; for it was impossible that Mrs. Dashwood should advance anything; and they were neither of them quite enough in love to think that three hundred and fifty pounds a-year would supply them with the comforts of life.

Edward was not entirely without hopes of some favourable change in his mother towards him; and on *that* he rested for the residue of their income. But Elinor had no such dependence; for since Edward would still be unable to marry Miss Morton, and his chusing herself had been spoken of in Mrs. Ferrars's flattering language as only a lesser evil than his chusing Lucy Steele, she feared that Robert's offence would serve no other purpose than to enrich Fanny.

About four days after Edward's arrival Colonel Brandon appeared, to complete Mrs. Dashwood's satisfaction, and to give her the dignity of having, for the first time since her living at Barton, more company with her than her house would hold. Edward was allowed to retain the privilege of first comer, and Colonel Brandon therefore walked every night to his old quarters at the Park; from whence he usually returned in the morning.

A three weeks' residence at Delaford, where, in his evening hours at least, he had little to do but to calculate the disproportion between thirty-six and seventeen, brought him to Barton in a temper of mind which needed all the improvement in Marianne's looks, all the kindness of her welcome, and all the encouragement of her mother's language, to make it cheerful. Among such friends, however, and such flattery, he did revive. No rumour of Lucy's marriage had yet reached him:—he knew nothing of what had passed; and the first hours of his visit were consequently spent in hearing and in wondering.

It would be needless to say, that the gentlemen advanced in the good opinion of each other, as they advanced in each other's acquaintance, for it could not be otherwise. Their resemblance in good principles and good sense, in disposition and manner of thinking, would probably have been sufficient to unite them in friendship, without any other attraction; but their being in love with two sisters, and two sisters fond of each other, made that mutual regard inevitable and immediate.

The letters from town, which a few days before would have made every nerve in Elinor's body thrill with transport, now arrived to be read with less emotion that mirth. Mrs. Jennings wrote to tell the wonderful tale, to vent her honest indignation against the jilting girl, and pour forth her compassion towards poor Mr. Edward, who, she was sure, had quite doted upon the worthless hussy, and was now, by all accounts, almost broken-hearted, at Oxford."

Mr. Dashwood's strains were more solemn. Mrs. Ferrars was the most unfortunate of women—poor Fanny had suffered agonies of sensibility—and he considered the existence of each, under such a blow, with grateful wonder. Robert's offence was unpardonable, but Lucy's was infinitely worse. Neither of them were ever again to be mentioned to Mrs. Ferrars; and even, if she might hereafter be induced to forgive her son, his wife should never be acknowledged as her daughter, nor be permitted to appear in her presence. He called on Elinor to join with him in regretting that Lucy's engagement with Edward had not rather been fulfilled, than that she should thus be the means of spreading misery farther in the family.

He thus continued: "Mrs. Ferrars has never yet mentioned Edward's name, which does not surprise us; but, to our great astonishment, not a line has been received from him on the occasion. Perhaps, however, he is kept silent by his fear of offending, and I shall, therefore, give him a hint, by a line to Oxford, that his sister and I both think a letter of proper submission from him, addressed perhaps to Fanny, and by her shewn to her mother, might not be taken amiss; for we all know the tenderness of Mrs. Ferrars's heart."

This paragraph was of some importance to the prospects and conduct of Edward. It determined him to attempt a reconciliation, though not exactly in the manner pointed out by their brother and sister.

"A letter of proper submission!" repeated he; "would they have me beg my mother's pardon for Robert's ingratitude to *her*, and breach of honour to *me*? I know of no submission that *is* proper for me to make."

"You may certainly ask to be forgiven," said Elinor, "because you have offended;—and I should think you might *now* venture so far as to profess some concern for having ever formed the engagement which drew on you your mother's anger."

He agreed that he might.

"And when she has forgiven you, perhaps a little humility may be convenient while acknowledging a second engagement, almost as imprudent in *her* eyes as the first."

He had nothing to urge against it, but still resisted the idea of a letter of proper submission; and therefore, to make it easier to him, it was resolved that, instead of writing to Fanny, he should go to London, and personally intreat her good offices in his favour."

After a visit on Colonel Brandon's side of only three or four days, the two gentlemen quitted Barton together. They were to go immediately to Delaford, that Edward might have some personal knowledge of his future home; and from thence, after staying there a couple of nights, he was to proceed on his journey to town.

Chapter 50

After a proper resistance on the part of Mrs. Ferrars, just so violent and so steady as to preserve her from that reproach which she always seemed fearful of incurring, the reproach of being too amiable, Edward was admitted to her presence, and pronounced to be again her son.

In spite of his being allowed once more to live, however, he did not feel the continuance of his existence secure, till he had revealed his present engagement. With apprehensive caution therefore it was revealed, and he was listened to with unexpected calmness. Mrs. Ferrars, by every argument in her power, told him, that in Miss Morton he would have a woman of higher rank and larger fortune; but when she found that, though perfectly admitting the truth of her representation, he was by no means inclined to be guided by it, she judged it wisest, from the experience of the past, to submit—and therefore, she issued her decree of consent to the marriage of Edward and Elinor.

What she would engage to do towards augmenting their income was next to be considered; and here it plainly appeared, that though Edward was now her only son, he was by no means her eldest; for while Robert was inevitably endowed with a thousand pounds a-year, nor was anything promised either for the present or in future, beyond the ten thousand pounds, which had been given with Fanny.

It was as much, however, as was desired, and more than was expected, by Edward and Elinor; and Mrs. Ferrars herself, by her shuffling excuses, seemed the only person surprised at her not giving more.

With an income quite sufficient to their wants thus secured to them, they had nothing to wait for after Edward was in possession of the living, but the readiness of the house, to which Colonel Brandon, with an eager desire for the accommodation of Elinor, was making considerable improvements; and after waiting some time for their completion, Elinor, as usual, broke through the first positive resolution of not marrying till everything was ready, and the ceremony took place in Barton church early in the autumn.

The first month after their marriage was spent with their friend at the Mansion-house; from whence they could superintend the progress of the Parsonage, and direct everything as they liked on the spot. Mrs. Jennings's prophecies, though rather jumbled together, were chiefly fulfilled; for she was able to visit Edward and his wife in their Parsonage by Michaelmas, and she found in Elinor and her husband, one of the happiest couples in the world.

They were visited on their first settling by almost all their relations and friends. Mrs. Ferrars came to inspect the happiness which she was almost ashamed of having authorised; and even the Dashwoods were at the expense of a journey from Sussex to do them honour.

"I will not say that I am disappointed, my dear sister," said John, as they were walking together one morning before the gates of Delaford House, "but I confess, it would give me great pleasure to call Colonel Brandon brother. His property here, his place, his house, everything is in such respectable and excellent condition! And though, perhaps, Marianne may not seem exactly the person to attract him—yet I think it would altogether be advisable for you to have them now frequently staying with you, for as Colonel Brandon seems a great deal at home, nobody can tell what may happen."

But though Mrs. Ferrars *did* come to see them, they were never insulted by her real favour and preference. *That* was due to the folly of Robert, and the cunning of his wife; and it was earned by them before many months had passed away. The selfish sagacity of the latter, which had at first drawn Robert into the scrape, was the principal instrument of his deliverance from it; for her respectful humility, assiduous attentions, and endless flatteries, as soon as the smallest opening was given for their exercise, reconciled Mrs. Ferrars to his choice, and re-established him completely in her favour.

The whole of Lucy's behaviour in the affair, and the prosperity which crowned it, therefore, may be held forth as a most encouraging instance of what an earnest, an unceasing attention to self-interest, will do in securing every advantage of fortune, with no other sacrifice than that of time and conscience. When Robert first sought her acquaintance, and privately visited her in Bartlett's Buildings, it was only to persuade her to give up the engagement; and as there could be nothing to overcome but the affection of both, he naturally expected that one or two interviews would settle the matter. In that point, however, and that only, he erred; for though Lucy soon gave him hopes that his eloquence would convince her in *time*, another visit, another conversation, was always wanted to produce this conviction. His attendance was by this means secured, and the rest followed in course. Instead of talking of Edward, they came gradually to talk only of Robert, and in short, it became speedily evident to both, that he had entirely supplanted his brother. They passed some months in great happiness at Dawlish; and from thence returning to town, procured the forgiveness of Mrs. Ferrars, by the simple expedient of asking it, which, at Lucy's instigation, was adopted. The forgiveness, at first, indeed, as was reasonable, comprehended only Robert; and Lucy, still remained some weeks longer unpardoned. But perseverance in humility of conduct and messages, in self-condemnation for Robert's offence, and gratitude for the unkindness she was treated with, procured her in time the haughty notice which overcame her by its graciousness, and led soon afterwards, by rapid degrees, to the highest state of affection and influence. Lucy became as necessary to Mrs. Ferrars, as either Robert or Fanny; and while Edward was never cordially forgiven for having once intended to marry her, and Elinor, though superior to her in fortune and birth, was spoken of as an intruder, *She* was in everything considered, and always openly acknowledged, to be a favourite child.

Elinor's marriage divided her as little from her family as could well be contrived, without rendering the cottage at Barton entirely useless, for her mother and sisters spent much more than half their time with her. Mrs. Dashwood was acting on motives of policy as well as pleasure in the frequency of her visits at Delaford; for her wish of bringing Marianne and Colonel Brandon together was hardly less earnest, though rather more liberal than what John had expressed. It was now her darling object. Precious as was the company of her daughter to her, she desired nothing so much as to give up its constant enjoyment to her valued friend; and to see Marianne settled at the mansion-house was equally the wish of Edward and Elinor.

With such a confederacy against her—with a knowledge so intimate of his goodness, what could she do?

Marianne Dashwood was born to an extraordinary fate. She was born to discover the falsehood of her own opinions, and to counteract, by her conduct, her most favourite maxims. She was born to overcome an affection formed so late in life as at seventeen, and with no sentiment superior to strong esteem and lively friendship, voluntarily to give her hand to another!—and *that* other, a man who had suffered no less than herself under the event of a former attachment, whom, two years before, she had considered too old to be married!

But so it was. Instead of falling a sacrifice to an irresistible passion, as once she had fondly flattered herself with expecting, she found herself at nineteen, submitting to new attachments, entering on new duties, placed in a new home, a wife, the mistress of a family, and the patroness of a village.

Colonel Brandon was now as happy, as all those who best loved him, believed he deserved to be; and that Marianne found her own happiness in forming his, was equally the persuasion and delight of each observing friend. Marianne could never love by halves; and her whole heart became, in time, as much devoted to her husband, as it had once been to Willoughby.

Willoughby could not hear of her marriage without a pang; and his punishment was soon afterwards complete in the voluntary forgiveness of Mrs. Smith, who, by stating his marriage with a woman of character, as the source of her clemency, gave him reason for believing that had he behaved with honour towards Marianne, he might at once have been happy and rich. That his repentance of misconduct, which thus brought its own punishment, was sincere, need not be doubted; nor that he long thought of Colonel Brandon with envy, and of Marianne with regret. But that he was forever inconsolable, that he fled from society, or contracted an habitual gloom of temper, or died of a broken heart, must not be depended on—for he did neither. He lived to exert, and frequently to enjoy himself. His wife was not always out of humour, nor his home always uncomfortable; and in his breed of horses and dogs, and in sporting of every kind, he found no inconsiderable degree of domestic felicity.

For Marianne, however—in spite of his incivility in surviving her loss—he always retained that decided regard which interested him in everything that befell her, and made her his secret standard of perfection in woman.

Mrs. Dashwood was prudent enough to remain at the cottage, without attempting a removal to Delaford; and fortunately for Sir John and Mrs. Jennings, when Marianne was taken from them, Margaret had reached an age highly suitable for dancing, and not very ineligible for being supposed to have a lover.

Between Barton and Delaford, there was that constant communication which strong family affection would naturally dictate;— and among the merits and the happiness of Elinor and Marianne, let it not be ranked as the least considerable, that though sisters, and living almost within sight of each other, they could live without disagreement between themselves, or producing coolness between their husbands.

THE END